I0823911

ROBERT B. PARKER'S

BIG SHOT

THE JESSE STONE NOVELS

Robert B. Parker's Big Shot
(by Christopher Farnsworth)

Robert B. Parker's Buried Secrets
(by Christopher Farnsworth)

Robert B. Parker's Fallout
(by Mike Lupica)

Robert B. Parker's Stone's Throw
(by Mike Lupica)

Robert B. Parker's Fool's Paradise
(by Mike Lupica)

Robert B. Parker's The Bitterest Pill
(by Reed Farrel Coleman)

Robert B. Parker's Colorblind
(by Reed Farrel Coleman)

Robert B. Parker's The Hangman's Sonnet
(by Reed Farrel Coleman)

Robert B. Parker's Debt to Pay
(by Reed Farrel Coleman)

Robert B. Parker's The Devil Wins
(by Reed Farrel Coleman)

Robert B. Parker's Blind Spot
(by Reed Farrel Coleman)

Robert B. Parker's Damned If You Do
(by Michael Brandman)

Robert B. Parker's Fool Me Twice
(by Michael Brandman)

Robert B. Parker's Killing the Blues
(by Michael Brandman)

Split Image
Night and Day
Stranger in Paradise
High Profile
Sea Change
Stone Cold
Death in Paradise
Trouble in Paradise
Night Passage

For a comprehensive title list and a preview of upcoming books, visit PRH.com/RobertBParker or Facebook.com/RobertBParkerAuthor.

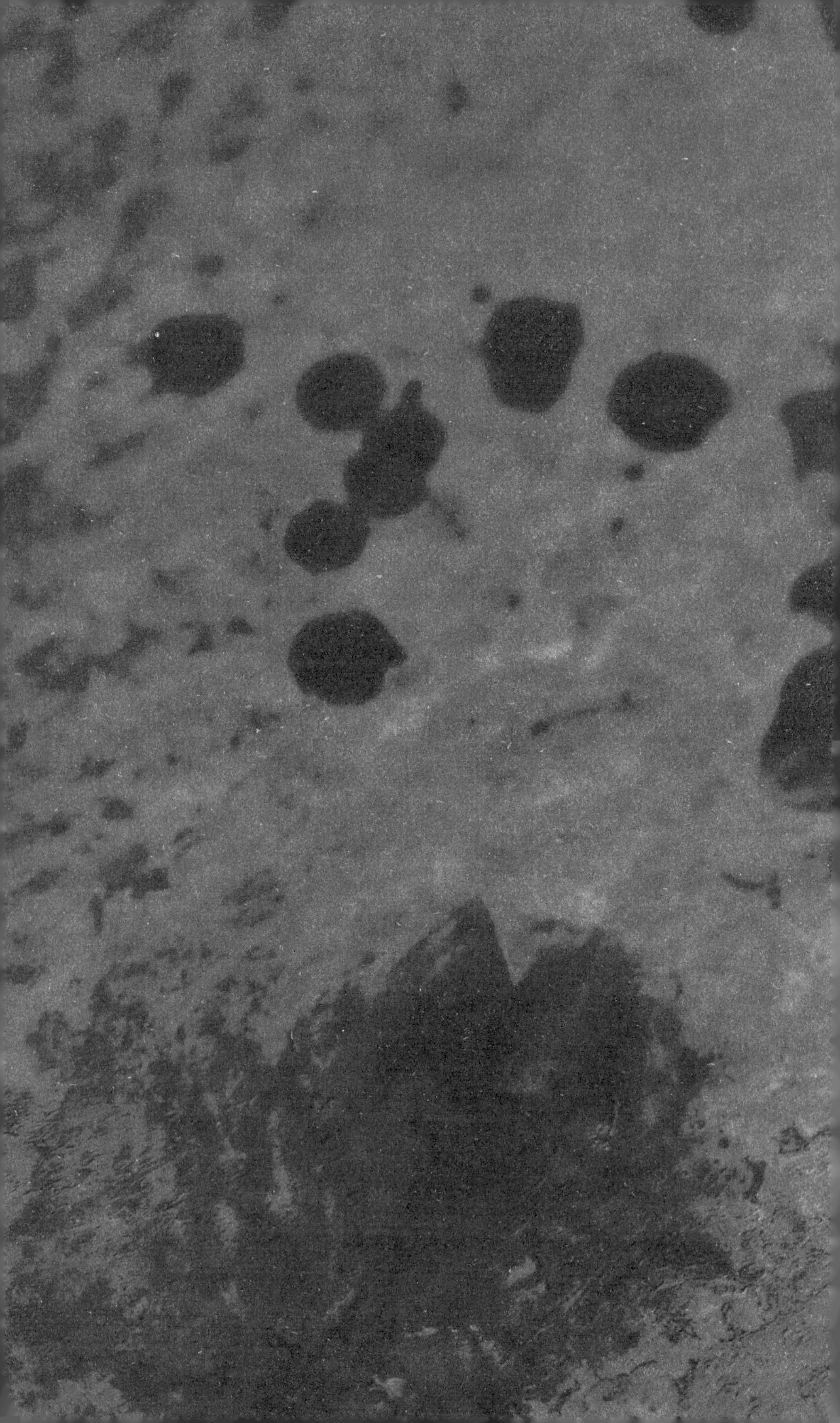

ROBERT B. PARKER'S

BIG SHOT

A JESSE STONE NOVEL

CHRISTOPHER FARNSWORTH

G. P. PUTNAM'S SONS
New York

PUTNAM
— EST. 1838 —

G. P. PUTNAM'S SONS
Publishers Since 1838
An imprint of Penguin Random House LLC
1745 Broadway, New York, NY 10019
penguinrandomhouse.com

Title page photo by Pongchart B/Shutterstock

Hardcover ISBN: 9780593854372
Ebook ISBN: 9780593854396

Printed in the United States of America
1st Printing

The authorized representative in the EU for product safety and compliance is Penguin Random House Ireland, Morrison Chambers, 32 Nassau Street, Dublin D02 YH68, Ireland, https://eu-contact.penguin.ie.

To John Rember,
who set me on the path

ROBERT B. PARKER'S

BIG SHOT

ONE

The car parked on the side of the road was worth more than Jesse Stone had once paid for a house.

There was a lot of money in Paradise, Massachusetts, the seaside town where he'd been chief of police for years now. On a per capita basis, Paradise was probably richer than some European nations.

But for the most part, the longtime residents here still tended to shy away from big displays of wealth.

Jesse was on night traffic patrol. In an eleven-person department, everyone had to take a shift sooner or later, even the chief. Jesse actually appreciated working nights when his turn came around. Most of the time, it was quiet.

The car was a McLaren. Jesse wasn't sure of the exact model number. All he knew about them was that they were expensive and they went fast. It looked like a spaceship that had come in for a landing.

He was a little surprised to see something that expensive this late in the season. Summer was over, and the tourists and the summer people had mostly left. The air was getting cooler at night, and the big parties had all ended. It had been a peaceful few months, for a change. There were the usual drunken idiots (Jesse knew about being a drunken idiot), some bar fights, a couple overdoses, and one high-dollar burglary at a summer rental, but nothing too violent or unusual. Jesse appreciated that. He'd learned to take the quiet moments when he could.

He pulled his department-issued Explorer behind the sports car.

As he stepped out of the Explorer, he saw someone in the driver's seat, head resting against the window. He reached back into the SUV and pressed his siren to give a little whoop.

The man woke up with a start.

Jesse felt relief. He'd found too many bodies in his career. He didn't need another one.

Jesse grabbed the mike of the Explorer's PA system. "Sir, I need you to stay in your seat and put your hands on the wheel where I can see them."

Instead, the man turned around and stared into the glare of Jesse's headlights. White guy. Forties or so. His hair was mussed, and his face looked red and creased. He hadn't shaved in some time.

"Sir . . ." Jesse began again.

But the man either didn't hear or didn't care. He scrabbled at the latch for a moment and then the gull-wing door came up and he half stepped, half fell out of the McLaren.

He popped up quickly, brushing gravel from his palms, and stared back at Jesse and the Explorer.

"The hell do you want?" he said.

Once the man was standing, Jesse could see he was big,

with a barrel chest and thick arms. Could probably bench-press a lot in the gym. He wore a crumpled Oxford shirt unbuttoned to his belly and shorts. No shoes. Not even sandals.

On his bare chest, just below his throat, there was a tattoo. In an Old English font, the words CUI BONO.

"Sir," Jesse said. "Sit back down in the car. Please."

The man spat. Then fixed his bleary gaze on Jesse.

"Look. I'm just trying to get home. Why don't you just get back in your little Tonka truck and leave me alone, okay?"

Jesse walked forward.

"Have you been drinking tonight, sir?"

Jesse stood about an arm's length away from the man. The man frowned. He took a step closer, swaying.

The man gave Jesse a big grin. "I have the right to remain silent. So listen to this."

He closed his mouth with a solid click.

"So that would be a yes on the drinking, then," Jesse said.

Even from a couple feet, Jesse could smell the alcohol on the man. It was on his breath, in his sweat, in his clothing.

Jesse knew that stink better than he'd like. He'd been a drunk for a long time. Now every day was another step away from being that guy again.

Fortunately, sometimes there were people like this man to remind him what he'd looked like.

Jesse tried for reasonable one more time. "Sir," he said. "I'm going to need you to take a Breathalyzer test, but I think we both know what it's going to show. Come with me. I'll get you a place to sleep for the night, and we can deal with the rest in the morning."

That was probably the best possible offer this man would get from any cop.

But he didn't take it that way.

"You think I'm going to jail?" he said, as if he found that hilarious. "No. Absolutely not."

"It's not really up to you at this point, sir."

The man's grin grew even wider. "Nah. See, I don't do jail. Believe me, bigger guys than you have tried."

He laughed suddenly, nearly doubling himself over with his own wit.

Jesse let him. The world was a pretty grim place. Someone might as well find it funny.

"Okay," Jesse said, after he was done. "Time to go. Turn around and put your hands behind your back."

The man spat again, then took another step closer to Jesse. "Make me."

Jesse sighed and waited.

The punch came like a fat, slow softball thrown at a church picnic. Jesse, who'd been on track for the majors until a career-ending injury, caught it easily in one hand. There was a loud *thwack* that echoed through the night.

The man looked stung. He probably thought he'd been pretty clever. Drunks usually thought they were pretty clever.

He tried to pull his hand away. Jesse didn't let him.

The man frowned. Then scowled. He yanked harder, pulling back with both feet.

Jesse applied a little more pressure, squeezing the bones of the man's hand together.

He yowled, his face crumpling like a toddler's after dropping a cookie. "Son of a bitch!" he screamed. "That really hurts!"

Jesse spun him around and put him against the McLaren, then got out his cuffs.

"You have the right to remain silent," Jesse said, beginning the drill.

The Miranda warning was drowned out by the man's sudden string of obscenities. "You think I'm going to jail? I am not going to any goddamn jail!"

"Well," Jesse said. "You say that . . ."

Jesse rifled through the man's pockets. No wallet. No license.

"Any chance you want to tell me your name? It generally makes things easier. You know, paperwork."

Throughout the whole confrontation, Jesse had never raised his voice once.

"Fuck off," the man snapped.

"Funny, I run into a lot of people with that same name," Jesse said.

Jesse got him into the back of the Explorer, where he thrashed around a little more but quickly gave up struggling. Breathing heavily, he settled back into the seat.

Jesse picked up the radio again. "Don't worry. I'm going to call someone to tow your car. They'll be careful."

The man sneered at Jesse in the rearview mirror. "Like I give a shit," he said. "Leave it. I'll just buy another one."

Jesse shrugged, then pulled away from the side of the road, heading toward the station.

The man spoke up again from the backseat. "You just made a huge mistake, buddy. Huge."

"Wouldn't be the first time," Jesse said.

The man glared and his voice grew low and mean.

"I promise you," he said. "You're going to regret this."

"That's exactly what the last guy named Fuckoff told me," Jesse said. "You sure you're not related?"

TWO

Jesse got to the station a little after ten-thirty. One of the few perks of being chief, after being on the night shift. He got almost five whole hours of sleep that way.

Molly Crane, his deputy chief, was already at her desk. "Hey, look who brought in a celebrity last night."

Jesse went straight for the coffeemaker. "I did what now?"

"Of course you don't know. Don't you ever pay attention to the news?"

"I read the sports section."

Molly rolled her eyes at him. "The guy you brought in for drunk and disorderly. Last night."

"I do remember that much. Jesus."

"You're so grumpy before your coffee."

"I've had two cups already."

"Have another. You'll need it. The guy? The one still cooling his heels in cell three?"

Jesse drank more coffee. It did not make him more patient. "Yes. We've established that."

"You really don't know who he is?"

"Our conversation didn't get that far. He took a swing. Didn't give me his name, didn't have any ID. I printed him and put him in the cell. He was passed out when Gabe came by to relieve me at four."

"It's Ramsey Devlin."

Jesse took another sip of coffee.

Molly shook her head. "I'm going to spare you the embarrassment of admitting you have no idea who that is."

"I'm not embarrassed."

"You should be," Molly said. "The hedge fund manager? The federal fraud case? In New York?"

Now it rang a bell. Jesse remembered Molly being outraged about that. But then, Molly was outraged by a lot of things. They blended together.

"The Feds brought him up on wire fraud, right? He got off?"

"You *were* listening," she said. "Yes, the jury acquitted him. And the Feds let him go, and he moved out of Manhattan and came straight to—"

"Let me guess: Paradise's newest citizen."

"Correct."

Now Jesse remembered. For the last six months, the biggest point of controversy in town had been the new house built on Seaside Drive. Someone had snuck in and bought two of the old classic Cape Cods that stood on the high point above the ocean. Then the construction crews knocked them down and dug a new foundation before anyone could object.

Jesse had gotten a lot of calls, and he'd patiently explained to the older residents of Paradise that construction permits were not part of his job. As far as he knew, everything was in order.

Although he agreed the house was a massive eyesore. It rose like a concrete shoebox over the Atlantic, sitting atop a fake lawn and alongside an Olympic-size pool.

The whole thing had gone up incredibly fast. Many people said someone had greased the process along, which Jesse did not think was an outlandish theory.

In the past week or two, Jesse knew there were moving vans at the big, ugly house. It was hard to do anything without people noticing in Paradise. It was still a small town in that way.

"So that's the guy who built the house. Huh," Jesse said. "Well, it matches his car."

"Yeah, where is the car?"

"Still on the road, as far as I know."

"What?" Molly looked at the paperwork on her desk again. "Jesse, that's a McLaren 720S."

"Yup."

"And you left it there? Even in Paradise, you can't just leave a car like that out there."

Jesse shrugged. "He said he didn't want it towed."

"So you chose to listen to a drunk who told you to abandon a car worth a half-million dollars?"

"I figured he didn't want to get it scratched."

Molly gave him a look. Jesse was used to that look. It didn't scare him anymore. Much.

"Yeah, I bet that's what you figured," she said.

"It's his car," Jesse said. "He made his decision."

"Well, you can explain it to the lawyer."

"He's already got a lawyer?"

"Devlin's lawyer was here when I got in. Wanted to see you, wanted his client released immediately. They won't stand for this kind of harassment. He said some shitty things to me."

Jesse raised his eyebrows. "He did?"

"Nothing I couldn't handle. He's going to have my job for this, I'm going to rue the day, I'm just a stupid bitch who shouldn't be a cop. You know. The whole routine."

"I could sing it by heart," Jesse said. "Where is he now?"

"Bothering Ellis, I believe," Molly said, referring to Ellis Munroe, the district attorney. "I told him we don't handle bail here. I made him Ellis's problem."

"Way to delegate," Jesse said.

"It's one of my many gifts. But he'll be back soon."

"Did he really say 'rue the day'?"

"That was the nicest thing he said," Molly said. She took out her phone. "Look, I found this on YouTube about Devlin. To give you an idea of who we're dealing with here."

She pulled up the video and turned the phone toward Jesse. It was an interview on one of the financial channels. Jesse didn't really follow business news. His 401(k) went up and down, and that's as much as he knew about the market.

Devlin, looking a little more polished and smooth onscreen, sat in a chair facing a brunette anchorwoman. He didn't wear a tie with his power suit, and his blinding white shirt was open at the neck, exposing his tattoo.

"Oh, you like that," he said to the anchorwoman, opening the shirt a little more to reveal his bare chest. "That's my firm's motto. It's Latin. *Cui Bono*," he said, pronouncing it "qwee bo-no." "It means 'Who Benefits.' That's our mantra, our guiding philosophy at the Devlin Fund."

"And who benefits?" the anchorwoman asked.

Devlin grinned, showing sharp white teeth. "*Me*," he said. "I always benefit. And that's how our clients benefit, too. I always make sure I make a profit. All I do is win. They get to come along for the ride."

Molly turned off the phone. "Well," Jesse said. "He seems like a real addition to the town."

"I thought we were full up on assholes, but he decided we could use one more," Molly said.

Jesse looked at the bottom of his coffee cup and sighed. "Is there any chance he's going to just take the lesson and move on?"

Molly looked at Jesse for a moment. And then laughed out loud.

"Yeah," Jesse said. "Didn't think so."

THREE

"Look, Sheriff Stone, this small-town intimidation bullshit might work on the yokels, but I assure you we are not impressed."

Jesse thought, *Sheriff?*

And then he thought, *yokels?*

But Devlin's lawyer, Gordon Wilkes, a man with a Satanic goatee and dark curly hair, was only getting started.

He'd walked into the station smiling and laughing with Ellis. Jesse didn't trust anyone who warmed up to people that quickly, especially not a lawyer. But he'd hoped it meant they could process Devlin's bail quickly.

He was wrong. He'd invited both Ellis and Wilkes into his office and closed the door, and Wilkes began lecturing before Jesse could even take his seat.

"Frankly, I would expect this sort of penny-ante corruption from someone in the middle of nowhere, not a police department within minutes of Boston. Did you really think we'd just roll over and let you do this?"

Jesse sat back and put his feet up on the desk. He thought he'd get comfortable until the lawyer wound himself down.

Wilkes saw this and frowned.

"Are you done?" Jesse asked.

The lawyer smirked. "I'm just getting warmed up, Sheriff."

"Sure," Jesse said. He took his feet off the desk and sat up. Then he said, "First of all, it's Chief Stone, not Sheriff Stone."

"Sorry," Wilkes said. "It's just such a nasty little trick, pulling someone in on a phony drunk-driving charge. I figured you for a small-town sheriff."

Jesse ignored that and continued. "Second, it's Jesse. To most people. And third, I found your client passed out on the side of the road. He was clearly inebriated. For his safety and the safety of the general public, we let him sleep it off here."

Wilkes snorted. "You expect me to believe that?"

"I don't really know what you might believe, since we've just met. But that's what happened."

"So you deny that the Feds are giving you orders?"

"I suppose I'd deny it if I knew what you were talking about," Jesse said.

Ellis laughed, a short bark like a seal's. Both Wilkes and Jesse looked at him.

"Sorry," Ellis said. "I was just trying to imagine a federal agent giving you orders, Jesse."

Wilkes looked a little more annoyed. "I'm glad you find this funny, Mr. Munroe. You know your whole town is on the hook for this man's actions."

Jesse turned to Ellis. "Do you know what he means? Because I am lost."

"Don't you ignore me—"

Ellis rubbed his eyes. "Jesse, what I think Mr. Wilkes is trying to say is—"

"You are doing the Feds' dirty work for them," Wilkes interrupted. "You're harassing Ramsey Devlin because they're embarrassed they lost their case, and now you're trying to make his life miserable as payback."

"Oh," Jesse said. "Is that what you think is going on?"

"I know exactly what's going on here."

"Because I thought we were here to bail your client out of jail."

"He shouldn't have been arrested at all!"

"No, he definitely should have," Jesse said. "You are lucky I didn't include assaulting an officer to the charges."

Ellis looked concerned. "He took a swing at you?"

"If you could call it that."

"And he's not in the hospital?"

"Very funny, Ellis," Jesse said. "I barely touched him. I put the cuffs on him. He was passed out by the time I left the cells."

"You see," Wilkes said, as if Jesse had just agreed with him. "You were trying to bait my client into a physical altercation. You admit it."

"Wow," Jesse said, after a moment. "I would love to get a translation program for whatever it is that's coming out of your mouth."

Wilkes's face turned red. He opened his mouth to speak, but Ellis cut him off.

"Okay, hold on," Ellis said. "Let's just lower the temperature here. Okay? Mr. Wilkes here was explaining to me that Mr. Devlin might feel a little persecuted after his run-in with the federal government."

"Yeah, I got that much."

"So he and I were talking about this. We were wondering if you might agree to dropping the charges. Seeing as how Mr. Devlin is new in town."

Now it was Jesse's turn to laugh. "Because he'd never heard of drunk driving laws in New York?"

Ellis managed a tight smile. "Because you've let people sleep it off without charging them before."

"True," Jesse said. "But they didn't throw a punch at me."

"I'm pretty sure some of them did."

"Fair point," Jesse said. "But then they didn't get a lawyer to come and insult my deputy chief first thing in the morning."

Ellis looked at Wilkes. "You insulted Molly?"

"Who the hell is Molly?"

"I wouldn't say he insulted me," Molly called from outside the office. She was always listening. "More like harassed."

"That was a mistake," Ellis said.

Wilkes pursed his lips. "I may have said some things."

"Was one of those things the word *bitch*?" Jesse said, staring right into the man's eyes.

"I don't recall," Wilkes said, but looked away.

"How about 'rue the day'? You remember that?"

"What?"

"Never mind," Jesse said. "You want to apologize?"

Wilkes sat up straight in his chair. "I will not apologize for being passionate on behalf of my client. I'm sorry if that upsets your backwater customs."

Jesse looked at Wilkes. "Seriously," he said. "Where the hell do you think you are?"

Wilkes flinched again, but only got louder. "I am still a lawyer in the United States of America—"

"Oh-kay," Jesse said, standing up. "Ellis, you can do what you want with the charges. I am willing to call no harm, no foul on the punch. But he was drunk behind the wheel. We're sticking with the OUI."

Ellis shrugged and looked at Wilkes as if to say he'd tried. "Well. That's it, then."

Wilkes smirked again. "Oh, I don't think so," he said. Jesse was really beginning to dislike this guy.

He opened his briefcase and withdrew a thick manila file folder, then tossed it onto Jesse's desk. It landed with a heavy thud.

"This is a short record of all the violence you've been involved in," Wilkes said to Jesse. "It only took my office a couple hours to gather all that. Think how much we could find if we really started digging."

Jesse looked at the folder without touching it. "I'm not sure what point you're trying to make."

"You're a dangerous man, Chief Stone. And I'm not going to let you intimidate my client on behalf of the federal government. If you insist on this witch hunt, we'll file suit for wrongful arrest and malicious prosecution. All your dirty secrets will come out in open court. I am prepared to file *today* if you do not drop all charges against my client and apologize to him immediately."

Jesse yawned. He didn't mean to, but he couldn't deny it was great timing.

"Well, you do what you have to do," Jesse said. "I believe you can discuss bail with Ellis here. I'll go get your client."

Wilkes looked nettled. He slid the papers back into his

briefcase. It clearly didn't have the terrifying effect he'd hoped it would.

"Just one more thing," Wilkes said. "Where is my client's car? That is a high-value luxury sports car. I don't want your cops joyriding around in it."

Jesse smiled at the man for the first time since he'd entered the station. "I have some good news for you, Counselor," he said. "I can promise you that not a single one of my people has touched that car."

FOUR

Devlin was snoring heavily when Jesse went back into the cells to get him. Jesse opened the door and shook the man awake.

He blinked and looked around, bleary-eyed, before his eyes snapped into focus on Jesse.

"Oh," he said. "I guess my lawyer finally got here?"

"He's waiting for you outside. He and the DA have arranged bail."

Devlin rolled over and put his feet on the floor. He paused for a moment, head hanging.

"Whoa," he said.

"Head spinning?" Jesse asked.

Devlin looked up, eyes red. "Bite me."

Jesse counted to ten for patience while Devlin squeezed his head and tried to gather the strength to stand up.

"Look. Everyone makes mistakes," Jesse said. "You had too much to drink last night. You said some stupid stuff. A lot of people who live here have done the same thing. This can be your last time in a cell here in Paradise."

Now Devlin laughed. "Oh, you think you can call a truce now? Too late for that, I'm afraid. You had your chance to walk away last night. Now I'm gonna destroy you."

Jesse sighed. He'd tried to reason with the guy. He could tell his therapist, Dix, that he'd tried. He could tell himself he'd kept his temper in check.

"All right," Jesse said. "That's the way you want it. Let's go."

Devlin shot to his feet and then wobbled in place, his face pale. "I'm ready," he said, despite all appearances. "I'll kick your ass right here."

"No," Jesse said, finding his last ounce of patience. "I mean let's go outside and see your lawyer. Then you'll get a summons for a court date."

Devlin belched out a cloud of sulfurous fumes. "You scared?"

Jesse winced. "Only of your breath." He waved Devlin forward. "After you."

Devlin took a few uncertain steps, then began walking toward the door.

"I'm going to end you," he said.

"Yeah, you mentioned that," Jesse said, closing the cell behind him.

Devlin turned around. "I don't think you're taking me seriously," he said. "I am not threatening you. I am telling you a fact. I am reporting what is going to happen. You might think you're untouchable. You're not. And you're going to look back on this moment and know—absolutely know—that this is where it all went wrong for you. Right here."

Jesse checked his reserves of patience once again and discovered he was fresh out. He took another step closer to Devlin, despite the smell of booze and flop sweat. He'd been a drunk long enough himself. He figured he could endure it.

"I know you think you're a pretty clever guy, Mr. Devlin," he said. "You made a lot of money in some kind of scheme and you got away with it, so who knows, maybe you are. But if you were smart, you'd realize you're standing in a jail cell alone with me right now. Which doesn't seem like the smartest move in the world to me."

Devlin went pale again and swallowed. Jesse didn't know if he was sick or scared. He didn't really care, either.

"I suppose you're lucky that I'm not that kind of cop. And I'll tell you again: This can be the last time we ever see each other under these circumstances. But you keep talking like that, sooner or later I'm going to take you seriously. If that happens, you're right: That's going to be the end of this. Only it's not going to happen remotely like you think."

Devlin took a step back from Jesse. Which was a good thing, because Jesse really didn't like being reminded of those times when he'd woken up looking and smelling like Devlin did now.

Then Devlin smiled at Jesse. "Oh, boy," he said. "I think you might even be a challenge. Thanks, Chief. This is going to be fun."

Jesse grabbed Devlin by the shoulder and spun him toward the door.

"You've got a weird idea of a good time," he said, and marched him out of the cells.

FIVE

Salazar didn't like coming north. Even in Florida, the sea was the wrong color, the air tasted bad, and the food was terrible. As soon as he and his five companions stepped off their private jet at the small, private airport outside Fort Lauderdale, he was surrounded by pale, fat North Americans who carried themselves with unearned confidence.

If his employers didn't sell 90 percent of their product in this country, he would never set foot inside the United States again.

But they did, so problems came up from time to time. Salazar fixed those problems. Even as a boy in Colombia, he'd had a knack for cutting through the extraneous details and finding the heart of the solution.

For instance: On his father's estate, he once came across a calf stuck in a fence. There were several of his father's employees trying desperately to get the calf out of the fence, but it was tangled in the wire, which only grew tighter the more it struggled. And the tighter the wire grew, the more it cut the calf, which was already bleeding freely and growing more panicked, and struggling even harder.

The farmworkers tried to approach the animal with their wire cutters and tools, but it kicked and thrashed whenever they got close, which only made things worse.

Salazar was perhaps ten years old, but big for his age already. He asked one of the workers for his knife, and the man gave it to him. Nobody refused the owner's son anything.

Salazar walked slowly toward the calf, taking five minutes or more just to get near, barely seeming to move at all. The calf regarded him with one big, brown eye as Salazar finally got within arm's reach. He placed one hand on the calf's head to calm it.

Then he slashed the calf's throat wide open and stepped back to avoid the blood.

The workers were upset, he remembered, but he didn't know why. With the calf dead, they could easily cut it free and get to work repairing the fence. He'd solved the problem.

When the story got back to his father, he made arrangements for Salazar to begin his apprenticeship with the cartel. Salazar's father, who was a lieutenant in the cartel himself, was asked if perhaps it was too soon, if his boy might be too young. He said, famously, that Salazar would be running the entire operation one day.

That hadn't come to pass just yet. But Salazar had risen very high because of his ability. (Higher even than his father. Shame what happened to him.) And because of that, he was given important jobs like this one.

He had to do one small, annoying chore before he got to work, however.

Ideally, Salazar and his people would have gone farther north without stopping. But they had no trustworthy connections in Boston. The organizations there were too unreliable, too chaotic. As soon as he arrived in the city, Salazar had no doubt every thug and criminal would know it. Which meant the police and DEA would know it before long, too. Salazar also suspected his employers were embarrassed. They didn't want anyone to know they'd made such an enormous mistake.

So he'd been forced to fly to Florida, where most of the cartel's affiliates and customers maintained their operations.

Salazar and his men were traveling as ordinary businessmen. The private Gulfstream was rented through a fractional-share company. The papers in Salazar's briefcase said he was Alberto Suarez, a consultant from Bogotá who worked in the medical supply field. As far as anyone knew, he and his associates were on a sales trip. After they were cleared by customs, they picked up their rental cars and drove out onto the highway.

Salazar had heard tales from the older men in the cartel about the glory days of the business, when they could fly into Miami and walk through the airport with a suitcase full of guns and drugs and no one would stop them. Today it took a little more planning and effort.

Even on a private jet, it would be stupid to try to bring guns into the U.S. *And pointless,* Salazar thought. *Why bring guns to a country that had so many of them?*

They drove up the coastline to a small rest area off the highway, the prearranged meeting point. They pulled their rental cars into an empty parking lot just before seven p.m. The sun was already gone. They sat and waited.

A half hour after the scheduled time, three identical black BMWs moved into the lot as well, stereos thumping louder than their engines.

Salazar put their lateness aside. They were showing him who was in charge. He didn't care.

Six young men piled out of the cars, wearing leather jackets, thick with muscle and attitude. Again, Salazar could choose to take this as an insult if he wanted to. These were clearly junior enforcers, while a man of Salazar's stature should have earned a personal visit from someone higher in the organization.

But again Salazar chose to ignore it.

One of the young men took the lead and walked up to Salazar. He stood six inches below Salazar's chin, a patchy goatee on his face that did nothing to distract from the fast retreat his hairline was making from his forehead.

A white guy looking at the two of them might have said they were both Hispanic or Latino. Salazar would have found that an insult. He was Colombian. The gangs that sold his product were a mix of everything. They barely spoke the same Spanish. The color of their skin meant nothing.

"Enrique," he said, pointing at his own chest. "You Salazar?" he said.

Salazar said, "You know who I am. Otherwise you wouldn't be here."

Enrique scowled. "You know we're doing you a favor here. Might want to show a little more gratitude."

"You're not doing me any favors. Your employer is. And I'm showing you fifty thousand dollars' worth of gratitude already. Show me the guns."

Enrique looked like he was about to say something else,

but then thought better of it. He was a delivery boy, nothing more.

He waved to another pair who looked just like him, only with different-colored hair. They might have been hatched from the same egg. "Diego. Eddie. Open the trunks."

They both pressed buttons on their key fobs and the backs of two of the cars popped open. Salazar and his men walked around to look.

He was pleased. Inside one car's trunk were five Benelli shotguns, boxes of shells, and three H&K MP7s. In the next were a variety of handguns, both revolvers and automatics, and a duffel bag full of boxes of ammunition.

Salazar took a Ruger .357 revolver out of the trunk at random. He checked the rounds already in the cylinder. It opened and closed smoothly.

"All of the other guns are loaded as well?"

"Hey, man, of course. We are full-service."

Salazar nodded. His men took out the weapons and the bags and boxes.

Enrique didn't approve. "Jesus, you have to do that out in the open here?"

Salazar made a show of looking up and down the empty parking lot and the deserted coastline. It was already full dark. No one was within miles of them.

"I think we can risk it."

"Whatever, man," Enrique said and snorted. "I just want you to know: You need to be careful while you're here. Consider it a warning."

Salazar's men stopped in their tracks on their way back to their rental cars. Salazar himself tilted his head slightly and looked at Enrique as if seeing him from a new angle.

"I am sorry. My English is not as good as yours. Sometimes I misunderstand," he said with flawless pronunciation. "What exactly do you mean?"

"I think you know exactly what I mean," Enrique said, and Salazar caught the grins on the faces of the other members of his crew. "We don't need you guys making a buncha noise while you're here. It reflects on us. Those guns come up in any police reports, we'll know you fucked up. And then you better hope the cops already have you, because you do not want to see what we'll do. I'll cut you into pieces and send them home to your mother."

Everything went very still then. Salazar looked at the young man—a boy, really—with his ridiculous little mustache and beard, his greasy skin and hair, his adolescent bravado.

"You're telling us you'll punish us if we don't behave in the way you find acceptable?"

"That's right."

"And I'm to assume your employer is behind this ultimatum as well?"

"You can assume whatever you want, *ese*," Enrique said. "I'm the one telling you how it is. You become a problem, I guarantee I'll solve it."

Salazar nodded. "You know, I want to offer you a gift," he said.

Enrique snorted. "Yeah? Is it my birthday?"

His crew all laughed at that. They thought this was a game.

"A gift of my hard-earned experience. You see, when you make a threat against another man, you're already admitting weakness."

Enrique's smile vanished, and his eyes went cold. But he didn't say anything.

"You're promising to do something if the man offends you in the future. But you've already told him you are powerless to stop him from doing that thing. A strong man doesn't need to threaten. Because there is no possibility that he will be disobeyed. He doesn't warn. He doesn't wait for someone else to do something. He removes the problem."

"Yeah?" Enrique said. "So what? Am I supposed to—"

Whatever Enrique was about to say was lost in the sound of the gunshot Salazar fired, along with most of his face.

Salazar's men had already chosen their targets, and the shotguns and the H&Ks took out the rest of the crew.

"Imagine threatening men with guns in their hands," Salazar said. He was doing his Miami connection a favor, removing idiots like this from their payroll.

It took only a few minutes to pack the six bodies into the trunk and backseat of one of the BMWs. Salazar's men took the other two for themselves.

They formed an orderly convoy behind Salazar's rented cars as they began heading north. They had a long drive ahead, up 95 for more than a thousand miles, toward the little town with the beautiful name: Paradise.

SIX

Do you really not know who Ramsey Devlin is?" Rachel Lowenthal asked Jesse as they got ready for bed.

"I do now," Jesse said.

Rachel was the on-call ER doctor at Bayside Medical Center, which served Paradise and the surrounding area. She and Jesse had met when he'd been badly burned and then hit with debris from a bullet. Jesse had asked her out twice. The second time, she said yes.

He thought it was going pretty well. They'd survived the summer together, despite both of their schedules and the demands of their jobs.

Rachel threw back the covers on her side of the bed as she spoke. She stayed over only a couple nights every couple weeks, but Jesse already thought of it as her side of the bed. He was on his side, mostly ignoring the book in his hands as he waited for her.

He hadn't stayed over at her place, but that was because Rachel had a son, Jacob, who'd just turned seven. Jacob had handled the divorce pretty well, but Rachel didn't want another man waking up in her house just yet. Not until she was sure he'd be around for a while.

Tonight, Jacob was with his father, Mark.

Jesse liked the kid. He actually liked Rachel's ex-husband, too. They'd done the usual sizing-up when they met the first time, each taking a look at the other during a drop-off for one of Mark's custody weekends. A lot of Jesse's girlfriends had exes. People accumulated history. Some of these men were less than thrilled that the women in their lives had moved on, and even unhappier that Jesse was a cop. But Jesse had stared down serial killers; he could handle ugly looks from a divorced dad.

Mark, after a moment's hesitation, smiled and said, "Jacob says he really likes you." He was a lawyer in Boston and a Dodgers fan, a rarity in Red Sox territory. Once he found out Jesse had played in the minors for the organization, they always had a safe subject to discuss. He and Rachel appeared to have the only truly amicable split Jesse had ever seen.

"He's been in town for months. He built that hideous monstrosity on Seaside. Don't tell me you don't know about that."

"I know about that."

"Good," she said. "Otherwise I'd have to check your eyes."

"How do you know so much about him?"

"Well," she said as she shimmied out of her jeans. Jesse loved the shimmy. "I could tell you that I pay attention to the world around me, which you should probably do as well. But there's another reason."

"What's that?"

"You remember I told you Jacob is having trouble at school with that kid who's bullying him?"

"Right. What was his name again?"

"Race."

"Race? Like Race Bannon? Like the Indy 500?"

"More like Master Race," Rachel said. "He's made some comments about Jacob being Jewish."

"Jesus Christ."

Rachel's mouth quirked up in a half-smile. "What, you didn't know I was Jewish?"

"A Jewish doctor? Never heard of that before."

She rolled her eyes. She also peeled off her T-shirt, which admittedly sidelined Jesse's attention for a moment. She put on her nightdress, which mostly helped him concentrate again.

"He's made some antisemitic jokes. Loudly. Near Jacob. He's pushed. He's shoved. He's tripped Jacob on the field during PE and recess."

"A second-grader? And he's making antisemitic comments?"

"They start young, Jesse."

"And the teachers aren't doing anything?"

Rachel had moved into the bathroom to brush her teeth. "No," she said around her toothbrush, then spat. "Well. Not exactly. We had a meeting with the principal, Diane."

Diane Hawley was new to the school as of last year. Jesse had met her but had yet to spend any time with her.

"Diane? In my day, we called our teachers by their last names."

"You also rode a horse to school."

"Uphill. In the snow. Both ways."

"Diane—Ms. Hawley—believes that the boys can manage this conflict more effectively without direct intervention."

"You're kidding."

"Nope." She spat again. "She says that she hasn't witnessed any overt bullying or violence. The school has a zero-tolerance policy, she says. So if she did, Race would be expelled."

"And he hasn't been."

"Therefore, it hasn't happened."

"What did you say?"

Rachel wiped her mouth with one of Jesse's towels. He hated that. She left toothpaste on the towel every time. But he'd learned enough to let stuff like that go.

"I told her that was horseshit."

Jesse laughed.

"Yeah, well, she didn't think it was funny. She said that some parents are overprotective. That kids have to learn resilience. A lot of reasons why she's not doing her job. Didn't really explain the selective blindness."

"Maybe she needs a refresher course on her duties as a responsible adult in a school full of kids?"

"Yeah, that would go over well. You go in there, wearing your badge and gun, threatening the principal—"

"Threatening? I am anything but threatening."

She laughed in Jesse's face. "Oh my God, do you really believe that? Who has told you that?"

"Molly."

"Molly wouldn't find a drone strike threatening."

Jesse thought about it. "Yeah, you're right."

"You're a cop, Jesse. There's no way you go into the school without carrying that weight. It just doesn't work."

She was right. Jesse didn't like it, but she was right. "Who is this Race kid, anyway?"

Rachel smiled and crossed past Jesse to her side of the bed again. Even under the loose nightshirt, he could see her slim form against the cloth. He liked to watch her. Efficient. Not a single wasted motion. Trained into her by years of practice in the ER, where every second counted.

"He's new in school this year. Just came to Paradise. Father and mother just moved in. Bought a new place. They're doing lots of renovations. I think maybe you met him recently."

Jesse got it. "Ah," he said. "I see. He's Ramsey Devlin's son."

"You should be a detective. I knew you'd find the answer if I dropped enough clues."

"And that's why you don't want me to intervene."

She was on her side, her head propped up by her arm as she stared at him.

"How would it look if the chief of police came to school to harass the child of the guy he just arrested? How do you think Devlin could *make* it look?"

"Race Devlin. Man, they did not do that kid any favors when they tagged him with that."

"Jesse. How would it look?"

"I try not to worry about appearances when I'm doing the job."

She sighed. "I've heard. That's why we're having this conversation. I don't want you going off half-cocked."

"I always go off fully cocked," Jesse said.

She rolled her eyes at him again. She pretended not to think he was funny. It was just an act. He was sure of it.

"I'm serious, Jesse. The last thing Jacob needs is the chief of police storming into the elementary school, threatening to beat up the class bully for him."

"Look. There's right and there's wrong—"

"And there are things that are *not your job*," Rachel said. "You are not the police chief of the school. I am on this. Jacob is tougher than he looks. We're handling it."

Jesse was surprised to find that that stung a bit. He took a quick moment to check in, as Dix would have said, to figure out where that feeling was coming from. "You want people to stay in your life?" Dix had said at their last session. "Then be honest with them. Stop with this strong-and-silent-type stuff. Tell them what you're thinking."

So Jesse did something he never liked to do: He talked about it.

"I might not be Jacob's father, but I care about him," Jesse said.

For Jesse, this was a huge confession. No jokes, no obfuscation. No keeping it in the vault.

Rachel's face softened. "I know you do," she said. "He knows, too. But I am trying to keep this off your plate. You don't need to worry about it."

"I do worry about it," Jesse said. Two confessions in one night. *Good Lord, Dix,* he thought, *what have you done to me?*

She smiled at him. "I know you do. And I appreciate it. That's why I'm keeping you in the loop. You're in Jacob's life now. And mine."

Jesse smiled back. "You'll tell me if it gets worse? If you need my help?"

"Absolutely," she said. She paused for a moment. "So. That book looks pretty fascinating."

"It's great."

"You couldn't possibly put it down, I bet."

"Well," Jesse said. "Maybe if there was something to distract me."

Rachel rose up and hooked her fingers under the bottom of the nightshirt. It was over her head and off in a second.

"How about this?"

Jesse tossed the book aside. "Yeah, that'll work."

SEVEN

The next day at the station, a tall, skinny man in a tight suit poked his head through Jesse's door, stooping slightly so he wouldn't hit the frame. Jesse couldn't help thinking of a stork walking through a marsh.

"Chief? Thanks for seeing me. I'm Robert Hanrahan. Deputy U.S. Marshal."

"Oh, hey, Jesse, you have a visitor," Molly yelled from outside.

"Thank you, Molly."

"U.S. Marshals Office."

"Thank you, Molly," Jesse said again, and shook the deputy marshal's hand.

"Come on in, Mr. Hanrahan. Or is it Deputy?"

"Bob is fine," he said. Jesse offered him coffee, which he declined, and a seat, which he took.

Once he'd folded his long legs and got himself situated, Jesse sat back down as well.

"You know, I thought you might wear a cowboy hat," Jesse said.

Hanrahan blinked twice at Jesse. He didn't get the joke. Or pretended not to. A lot of people reacted that way to Jesse's sense of humor.

Molly would have told him that was a sign he wasn't all that funny, but Jesse didn't really tell his jokes for any outside audience.

"What can I do for you?" Jesse asked.

"Well, I was alerted when you arrested a recent federal indictee, Ramsey Devlin."

"Drunk and disorderly. Operating a vehicle under the influence. Not exactly federal crimes."

"No, of course not." Hanrahan shook his head quickly. "But you're aware that Mr. Devlin was acquitted of multiple federal charges."

Jesse shrugged. "My deputy chief mentioned something. You're going to have to fill me in on the details."

"Oh? I thought you would have followed the news."

"I mainly watch sports."

Hanrahan's lips pursed involuntarily, like he'd tasted something bad or was about to sneeze.

But he shook off the expression quickly and resumed speaking in his calm, professional drone.

"The U.S. Attorney indicted Mr. Devlin on sixty-one counts of wire fraud for his latest investment offering, which he'd promoted as a hedge fund marketed primarily to nonprofits looking for a higher rate of return. He claimed to have proficiency and knowledge of the cryptocurrency markets, which would enable him to provide a guaranteed twenty percent increase, year over year, on investments."

"And he didn't come through?"

"To the contrary, for the first year, he was able to show thirty and fifty percent returns to his clients, even, in some cases, more than one hundred percent."

"But it didn't last?"

"No, it did not," Hanrahan said. "Because, as the U.S. Attorney's investigators found, the returns were entirely bogus. He was using fresh capital from new investors to pay the previous investors. A classic Ponzi scheme."

"Nobody noticed this?"

"The investors were not inclined to question their good fortune. A number of them were church organizations, charities, foundations. They were not terribly sophisticated, and Mr. Devlin was operating in new markets that are not well defined. Cryptocurrency and NFTs. Those can seem confusing even to experienced investors. On the financial statements, everything looked good. But eventually his investors began asking to make withdrawals."

"And the money wasn't there."

"Mr. Devlin said that an unexpected run on the assets and a downturn in the crypto market left him without the ability to meet his cash obligations. His investors lost everything."

"Sounds like an open-and-shut case," Jesse said. "Why isn't he in prison?"

Hanrahan scowled. He looked genuinely angry, but again, the expression passed almost immediately. "Mr. Devlin had access to funds I could not trace, which paid for highly competent lawyers. They were able to show that the clients were apprised of the risks when they invested. The jurors agreed. Apparently."

Jesse was curious.

"What do you think happened?" Jesse asked. "If you don't mind me asking."

Hanrahan was buttoned down so tight that Jesse thought he could hear the man creaking, but he clearly had an opinion.

"I was on the prosecution team," he said. "And I was in charge of seizing Mr. Devlin's assets, so you understand this is just my admittedly biased opinion. What I would say is that these are new markets, and not everyone understands the nature of cryptocurrency, which can be highly volatile and is untethered to anything but its own value in most cases. To a layman—say, for instance, a juror who does not even look at his own 401(k) statements—it can all seem like a scam, and it's the fault of whoever believes they can get money for nothing."

"Never give a sucker an even break, right?" Jesse said.

"Or, put another way, it's impossible to cheat an honest man."

"Probably didn't help the clients to hear that."

"No, it did not," Hanrahan said. "One in particular, a foundation dedicated to eliminating pediatric cancer and providing financial assistance to the families of children suffering from it, was forced to close down entirely."

"So where do you come in?"

"I was obliged to return to Mr. Devlin all of his assets that the federal government had seized. As a part of a settlement in his lawsuit for wrongful prosecution, I am also obligated to deliver to him a check for seven hundred fifty thousand dollars."

Jesse took his feet off the desk and leaned forward.

"You're paying him almost a million dollars because he got away with it?"

Hanrahan's nostrils flared slightly. "It was not my decision to settle."

"Do you want a police escort to his home? Do you think he might be looking for some kind of revenge against you for seizing his assets in the first place?"

"No," he said. "I am capable of protecting myself, if it comes to that."

Jesse wondered if that were true, but he let it go.

"I don't understand, Deputy—"

"Bob."

"Bob. Why are you here? You want me to harass Devlin? Figure out some kind of payback?"

Hanrahan recoiled, as if Jesse had suggested picking up dog poop with his bare hands. "That would be both improper and illegal, Chief Stone. I am simply here because I have to deliver a check. And I want you to know the history of your town's newest resident. You might not have been aware when you incarcerated him. There are other members of the law enforcement community that feel it is best to give him a wide berth. Mr. Devlin is smart, well funded, aggressive, and highly litigious. What you do with this information is entirely up to you."

Jesse sat back. "It sounds like you're saying Devlin isn't a great addition to our town."

Hanrahan frowned. "I know you're joking, Chief Stone. But you should take this seriously. Mr. Devlin is a risk to anyone who gets in his way. I would gladly testify if anyone were to bring this to a courtroom again. He is a thug who uses the financial system to rob people instead of a gun. And he will do it again."

"You'd think he already had enough money now," Jesse said.

"For men like Mr. Devlin, it's not about the money. It's about the thrill of proving he's smart enough to get away with stealing it. He enjoys it."

Jesse waited. That was it, apparently. Hanrahan nodded once, stood, and stepped to the door.

"I can promise you, if he tries to pull something here, he won't get away with it," Jesse said. "I've already put him in a cell once. I will do it again."

Hanrahan stooped at the door, halfway out of Jesse's office. A brief smile flitted across his face.

"I certainly would not be unhappy if that came to pass," he said. "Good day, Chief Stone."

EIGHT

Not long after the deputy left, Jesse came out of his office for more coffee. He stopped when he saw Rachel at Molly's desk.

"Hey," he said. "What's going on?"

"We're getting lunch," Molly said.

Jesse hesitated. "Great."

Molly and Rachel both laughed. "You worried we're going to talk about you?"

Jesse smiled. "I'm sure you have better things to discuss."

"Ha!" Molly said as she got up. "Of course we're going to talk about you."

"Have fun," Jesse said, heading toward the coffeemaker.

"I'm going to tell her lots of stories!" Molly called after his retreating back.

"I'm just getting coffee," Jesse said.

"Probably gonna go into a lot of embarrassing details! Anything I shouldn't mention? Any special requests?"

"You know what, I've had enough coffee today." Jesse turned around and went back into his office, closing the door.

Molly cackled. There was no other word. She cackled like a witch over a cauldron.

"Well, that was fun," she said. "Let's go, I'm starving."

THEY WENT TO the Gray Gull, which was really the only place to go aside from Daisy's, at least as far as most Paradise cops were concerned.

Spike, the owner, was in town and behind the host station. He looked more like a well-groomed bear with a gym membership than a maître d'. Ordinarily he was in Boston, overseeing his restaurant there.

He came around and gave Molly a big hug and a kiss on the cheek.

"What are you doing here?" she asked.

"You know I only came to Paradise because of you," he said.

"You're a terrible liar and flirt and I love it," Molly said. She introduced Rachel to Spike. "ER doctor at the hospital," Molly said. "And Jesse's girlfriend."

Spike took a moment and looked at Rachel. It was for only a second or two, but his eyes went flat, like he was scanning her for flaws. Rachel could feel it. Then he snapped back into the role of genial host.

"Well, he's a lucky man," Spike said. "But then, he always did have excellent taste in women."

"Thanks, I think," Rachel said, and shook his oversize hand.

"The best table in the house for you two," he said, and whisked them away to a table by the window. The place was half empty, so it wasn't that grand a gesture, but Spike really sold it.

"Seriously," Molly asked before he left them, "what are you doing in town?"

"Place has been running a little slack lately," he said. "Nothing too terrible yet, but if you don't watch out, before you know it, you're closing the doors, wondering where it all went wrong."

A waiter stood by the kitchen door, staring at his phone.

"Case in point," Spike said. "Hey, dummy. You looking for another job?"

The kid looked up, confused.

"Well, you're gonna be if you don't get your orders over to twelve."

"Right," he said, suddenly moving quickly. "Sorry, Spike."

Spike looked back at Molly and shrugged. "See what I mean?" He headed back to the front.

After they got their drinks—iced tea for both of them—Molly asked Rachel how things were going at the hospital.

Rachel stuffed a large hunk of bread into her mouth and chewed. She'd been up since four a.m. and hadn't taken a break in order to make this lunch work. "Sometimes it's like I don't know what I'm saving their lives for," she said. "I pulled a guy out of his third fentanyl OD this morning. If it weren't for Narcan, he'd have been dead six months ago. And I have one frequent flyer who keeps coming in with cardiac events despite being on his second bypass. He won't stop smoking or drinking, and God forbid he exercise. Heck, he won't even switch to decaf."

"I hear that," Molly said. "We have repeat customers, too. Drugs, drunk driving, bar fights. It's like they're diving headfirst into their own graves. You wonder why you try to stop them."

"Because that's the job," Rachel said.

"That's the job," Molly said, and tapped her glass against Rachel's in a kind of toast.

"You ever think about doing something different?" Rachel asked.

Molly shook her head. "What else am I going to do?"

"Anything. Sell shoes. Open a bakery. Troubleshoot people's computer problems. There's always something else."

"God, that sounds boring," Molly said. "I mean, no offense. But can you imagine working retail after cracking some guy's chest in the ER?"

Rachel smiled. "I rarely get to cut open anyone's chest."

"You know what I mean."

"I do," she said. "I get it. What you do matters."

"Sometimes," Molly said. "And with the kids out of the house, it's easier than it used to be."

"Jesse says Michael is on another trip," Rachel said.

Molly smiled, but her eyes darted away. "Some rich guy decides he wants a boat but doesn't know how to sail it. Michael brings it back from Cannes for him after the parties are done."

"Is that hard? Do you miss him?"

She shrugged. "Kids are gone, and Michael always went on long trips. Part of being a sailor's wife, he always says."

"What do you say?" Rachel asked.

"I'm getting used to an empty house."

"That doesn't sound great."

Molly sighed and looked away. "Did Jesse put you up to this?"

"No," Rachel said, genuinely surprised. "I was just wondering."

"I appreciate it," Molly said. "But I don't really want to talk about it."

Spike interrupted then. Rachel was grateful. She worried she'd overstepped.

"These are for you," Spike said. "Compliments of the house."

He put down plates of french fries, fried mozzarella, and fried zucchini. Basically, everything fried.

"Good Lord, Spike," Molly said. "Are you trying to kill us?"

Spike shrugged. "You dodge bullets for a living, Molly. A plate of fried food isn't going to be the thing that gets you. Live a little."

He winked at them both and then walked away.

"He seems nice," Rachel said.

"He is. Absolute sweetheart. Even though he could tear your head off without blinking."

"No, I can see that. Especially the way he looked at me when we came in. I thought he was going to throw me out."

"Oh, that," Molly said. "Yeah, Spike is best friends with an ex of Jesse's. He's pretty loyal to her. Even though it's been over for a while. Sorry."

"It's fine. I'm getting used to running into Jesse's past around here," Rachel said. "What happened with them?"

"Not my story to tell," Molly said, moving the plate of fries closer to her.

"Fair enough," Rachel said. "I'm sorry if I was prying about Michael. It just sounds lonely."

"That's why I'm wondering if Jesse asked you to talk to me about it. He says the same thing."

"Jesse talks about feelings with you?" Rachel put her hand to her chest in mock horror. "Do you have to use a Taser?"

Molly laughed. "It's hilarious, actually. He gets all quiet and his voice goes deep and gravelly. Like he's in a movie. I don't even think he realizes it. It's adorable."

Rachel laughed, too, but she figured she might as well ask what was on her mind.

"You two seem really close," she said. "Did you ever . . ."

She didn't get to finish the question. Molly was laughing too hard.

Rachel had to wait until Molly could breathe again.

"Oh my God, no," she said. "Jesus. Absolutely not."

"It's not that crazy a question," Rachel said, a little insulted. "He's good-looking, kind, strong, funny, decent . . ."

"Sure," Molly said. "All those things. Also: angry, bullheaded, a former addict, obsessive, and occasionally an idiot."

Rachel took one of Molly's fries and chewed thoughtfully for a second. "You're a terrible wingman," she said.

"I love Jesse," Molly said. "I do. There's no one in the world I trust more. But you have to know that he works very hard, every day, to get to the point where he can function like what we consider normal.

"He rushes in and does what he thinks is right, no matter what the cost. People near him have died because of it.

There's no getting around that. Jesse's life is dangerous. And not just to him."

Rachel considered that. "Sounds like a very lonely way to live."

Molly shrugged. "He's a hero. Heroes aren't always great at living everyday life."

Rachel took Molly's hand and squeezed it, to show her appreciation. She knew Molly didn't have to say any of this. Then she let go and took another fry.

"Maybe that means Jesse needs someone who can show him how to do that."

Molly sat back and looked at Rachel.

"You're not scared of much, are you?"

Rachel smiled. "I cut people open every day," she said. "They should be scared of me."

NINE

"So he threatened to kill you?" Dix, Jesse's therapist, asked.

"Not exactly," Jesse said. "He said he was going to end me."

Dix sat behind his desk, as usual wearing his pressed white shirt and his Rolex. His shaved head gleamed. He and Jesse did not go in for the couch or soft furnishings in their sessions. Jesse preferred to sit in front of the desk, as if it were a business meeting. When he'd started seeing Dix, this little bit of playacting helped Jesse deal with the fact that he was in therapy at all.

Now he'd been seeing Dix for years, and he was more at ease with the whole process. He would admit, if pressed, that Dix had saved his life just as if he'd pushed Jesse out of the path of a bullet.

But Jesse still liked to sit in the chair. It felt more professional somehow.

Today he'd told Dix about meeting the town's newest rich prick. Dix was an ex-cop before he'd gotten his shingle as a psychiatrist. He understood Jesse's job in a way most other therapists couldn't. Jesse liked to get Dix's take on the work; it helped him know when he might be close to crossing a line, or when a problem might be staring him in the face.

"*End* you? That sounds ominous," Dix said.

"Mostly it sounds likc something he heard in a movie."

"That, too. Did you feel threatened?"

"No," Jesse said. "Mainly annoyed."

"You didn't hit him? Bounce his head off the cell wall?"

Jesse smiled. "No."

"Then I'd say you handled the encounter successfully. Why does it worry you?"

"Who says it worries me?"

"You've had a really good run for the last few months, Jesse," Dix said. "You're healthier. You're handling your anger. Have you even felt the need for a drink lately?"

"No," Jesse said. He honestly couldn't remember the last time he'd felt the thirst bubble up in his throat.

"Good. And you didn't take out your frustration on this guy even though you had plenty of chances. So I'd say you're thinking pretty clearly," Dix said. "My point is: You wouldn't bring this up if there wasn't something about it that bothered you."

Jesse nodded. "That's why you're the shrink."

"Well. That and the diploma."

"I don't know," Jesse said. "I think I might be worried that I'm not worried enough."

Dix waited for Jesse to keep going. He did that a lot. Jesse wondered sometimes if he was paying Dix to talk or just to be quiet.

"Most people, when they come out of the cells, they're

embarrassed," Jesse said. "They want to put the whole thing behind them. So either they pretend nothing happened or they're apologetic."

"In other words, they know they screwed up," Dix said. "They feel like they're being punished."

"Right," Jesse said. "That's maybe eighty percent of the people we see here in town. It's mostly a group of law-abiding citizens."

"With one or two notable exceptions," Dix said.

"Exactly. Then you have the people who take that embarrassment and turn it into anger. They mouth off or act out. They have to be convinced they didn't do anything wrong. But deep down, they know they screwed up. So they argue loudly that they were right."

Dix nodded. "Pretty insightful for a cop."

"Maybe I've learned something from you," Jesse said.

"So do you think Devlin was just mouthing off? Trying to convince himself he was right even though he knew better?"

"No," Jesse said. "That's what bothers me. He sounded like he was absolutely convinced he was right. And I had done something against him by arresting him. Like the law should actually work in the opposite direction. He wasn't threatening. He was promising."

Dix thought about that for a second. "Like the world should work only the way he wants it."

"Yeah," Jesse said. "Just an absolute certainty in his voice. And he was going to make sure I knew it, too."

"Sounds like he's chosen you as the means by which he validates his worldview."

Jesse looked at Dix. "I was following along pretty well until just now."

"Don't play dumb, Jesse. It doesn't suit you. This guy is a Master of the Universe, right? He's beaten Wall Street and the markets and made himself rich. He's convinced people to give him millions of dollars based on the strength of his personality alone. He's even beaten the federal government. That's power. That's freedom from consequences. You know that's what most criminals are looking for. You've seen it for years."

"Of course," Jesse said. "But I didn't let him get away with anything."

"Exactly. And that's deeply disturbing to him. That upsets his whole belief in how the world works. He thinks he's on top. And you took him down to the ground, where he doesn't have any power anymore."

"That's why he's coming after me now."

Dix shrugged. "Guys like that usually have a few sociopathic tendencies. Most people in high-powered jobs do. Wall Street traders, CEOs, surgeons, fighter pilots, politicians, even some police officers . . ."

"Thankfully, nobody we know."

"Right," Dix said. "But men like that—and they're usually men—they have a deficit when it comes to seeing other people as fully human. They have a lack of affect. They're not overly concerned with empathy. It's what enables them to move millions of dollars around on a daily basis without being paralyzed by guilt or fear. Or cut people open on an operating table. Or lay off thousands of people they've never met. They do what's best for them."

"You make it sound almost normal."

"I wouldn't say *normal.* I would say *within the acceptable tolerances to operate successfully in our society,*" Dix said. "You have more experience with the violent antisocial personalities. The ones with poor impulse control. The guy who has ten drinks down at the Scupper because he can't see any reason why not."

"Hey. I've had ten drinks at the Scupper before."

Dix sighed. "And was that version of Jesse trustworthy? Did he make good decisions?"

"No," Jesse admitted. "He did not."

"Right. So let me finish. Those guys are your basic, store-brand criminals. They make dumb mistakes. They rob a liquor store in full view of the security cameras. They throw a punch at a cop. They can't hold a job. They can't keep it together long enough to do anything complex or sophisticated. But guys like Devlin . . . they can look normal to most people. Successful. Attractive, even."

"Unless something goes wrong," Jesse said.

"Exactly," Dix said. "Then they see an assault on their ego as the first step to their whole world falling apart. That's why they can't let go of the rope."

"What rope?" Jesse said.

"You said you offered this guy a chance to sleep it off. To admit he'd made a mistake and go on with his life. Instead, he escalated. You gave him one end of the rope. He took it and started a tug-of-war. And he can't stop pulling now. It would make more sense if he just quit fighting. There's nothing he can win. There's no prize, no trophy. But he won't let go."

"That sounds familiar," Jesse admitted.

Dix smiled. "You think you know someone who's behaved like that in the past?"

"Yeah," Jesse said. "Molly."

Dix actually laughed. "Right. Molly."

"So you think he's actually dangerous?" Jesse asked.

"Well," Dix said. "He's an incredibly wealthy, highly intelligent man with a vendetta against you and nothing but time on his hands. His whole sense of himself is wrapped up in beating you, and proving that he's smarter and tougher than you are. What do you think?"

"I think he's still just talking tough," Jesse said. "He has a chance to walk away from this. Find another hobby."

"And if he doesn't?"

"Then he picked the wrong fight."

Dix nodded. "Jesse. I know you're not scared of him. Because you don't really care about him. But it sounds like he's invested in this. A lot more than you are."

"Which means what, exactly?"

"It wouldn't hurt to watch your back," Dix said.

"I always do," Jesse said.

TEN

Jesse overheard Molly get the call at the front desk. There was a strange car on Seaside Drive.

"Gabe's busy with another call right now. Can you check it out?"

"What's the problem?"

"I've heard from three of the neighbors so far. They all say the same thing. It's just sitting there, parked on the side of the road."

"Public parking."

"They're all sure the driver is there to break into their homes and murder them."

"What leads them to believe that?"

"Well, for starters, it's a Toyota."

"So?"

"Jesse, anything less than a Mercedes is considered a sign of criminal intent on Seaside Drive. You know that."

Jesse sighed.

"Oh, you're not doing anything right now anyway," Molly said.

Jesse grabbed his keys and got up. At the very least, it would give him a chance to drive by Devlin's house and see what Paradise's newest resident was up to.

JESSE PULLED HIS Explorer up behind the Toyota. It was parked on the right side of the road, facing the concrete monstrosity of Devlin's house on the point. It had California plates.

The driver turned his head once to look at Jesse, and then turned around again quickly.

Jesse walked up to the side of the car, careful and slow. The driver seemed nervous, but a lot of people were nervous when dealing with the police.

When he looked inside, he could see the driver was a young man. Maybe early twenties at the most. But still basically a kid. He stared straight ahead, as if by ignoring Jesse he could make him go away.

Jesse knocked on the window.

The kid looked up at him and then rolled down the window.

"Is there a problem, Officer?" he asked, perfectly polite.

Still, his eyes kept darting away. His voice even shook a little.

"No problem," Jesse said. "Any reason you're parked here? Car trouble?"

"What? Oh, no. No trouble."

"Waiting for someone?"

"No. No, just, uh, looking at the view."

Jesse turned his head, keeping one eye on the kid. The Devlin house was framed in his line of sight.

"Yeah, it's something, isn't it?" Jesse said. "What's your name?"

"Uh, T-Thomas."

"Thomas." *Sure,* Jesse thought. "Would you do me a favor and step out of the car, Thomas?"

"What? Why? Why would you want me to do that?"

"Well, Thomas, I'd like to talk to you. And I don't really want to be looking down on you when I do. That sound fair?"

"Uh, sure. Sure. Yeah."

The kid—whose name was almost certainly not Thomas—got out of the car. Jesse stepped back and gave him plenty of room. He took a quick look inside the Toyota as the kid got out. It was filled with the debris of a long drive—empty water bottles, fast-food bags, crumpled papers, and discarded wrappers. In the passenger seat was a backpack, unzipped and half open. There was a patch sewn onto it: YOSEMITE YOUTH CAMP: OUR GOD IS AN AWESOME GOD!

There was no smell of weed, no beer cans or liquor bottles. The kid wasn't drunk or high. He was just scared.

"You on vacation, Thomas?" Jesse asked.

"Sort of," the kid said. "Road trip. Looking around the country before I go back to school."

"It's almost October. Hasn't your college started yet?"

He looked even more nervous. "Yeah, of course. I'm just taking a semester off. You know."

"Sure," Jesse said. "What brings you to Paradise?"

The kid's eyes darted to the big house involuntarily. "Nothing."

"You thinking about paying Ramsey Devlin a visit?"

The kid's eyes went wide. And he panicked and went for the gun.

Jesse cursed inwardly. He'd already spotted the object weighing down one side of the kid's jacket. He'd hoped to talk this out first.

But the kid reached for the weapon and got it halfway out before it snagged on the lining of his pocket.

Instead of going for his own gun, Jesse grabbed the kid's wrist with his left hand while he slammed his right fist into the side of the kid's temple.

The kid's skull bounced off the roof of the car. His eyes rattled in his skull and his fingers went limp on the gun as his knees pointed toward the road.

Jesse pulled the gun away just as the kid slumped to the ground.

Jesse rolled him onto his stomach. He was semiconscious.

Jesse found the kid's wallet in his back pocket. His California driver's license said his name was Tyler Stephens.

Jesse began to put the cuffs on him.

"You don't unnerstan . . ." the kid slurred. "He can't get away with it."

Jesse hauled him to his feet. "Tyler," he said, "you have the right to remain silent. I suggest you use it."

JESSE PUT TYLER Stephens in a cell. Molly followed a moment later with an ice pack.

They both watched him as he put the ice on his head and then sat down on the bunk in the cell.

Whatever fight he'd had in him before was gone.

"I'm sorry," he said, looking at the floor.

"What are you apologizing for?" Jesse asked.

"I wasn't going to hurt you. I just—I just needed to get past you. I know it was stupid."

"Tyler," Jesse said. "You do not have to talk to us. Like I told you before, when I read you your rights."

"No," he said. "I want to tell you. I can't believe I did this. My mom is going to be so ashamed of me."

He kept looking at the floor.

"You drove all the way from California?" Jesse asked. Start with the easy questions, he knew. Then move on to the harder ones.

Tyler nodded.

"I lived in L.A. for years," Jesse said. "Where are you from?"

"Bakersfield."

"Why are you here?" Molly asked.

"Wanted to see him."

"Ramsey Devlin?"

Tyler nodded again.

"Why?"

"Our church invested with him. My dad is on the governing council. He'd heard about it from another guy at a conference. He's the one who sold the rest of the council on it. He probably thought it was cool. He's always loved new stuff. Always buying the latest tech. He said he understood Bitcoin. It only goes up, he said."

Jesse didn't have to ask what happened next. He already knew. He just wanted to know how bad it was. "How much did they lose?"

"Everything," Tyler said, his voice breaking. "They lost everything."

"That must have been hard," Molly said, her voice gentle.

Tyler looked up, his face suddenly ugly and his voice sharp. "Hard? Yeah, our church is broke and filing for bankruptcy and my pastor is working as a greeter at Walmart and we're selling the building where I was baptized. Yeah, you could say that's *hard*."

He looked down at the floor.

He choked back a noise that might have been a sob.

"I'm sorry," he said. "I apologize, ma'am."

"Don't worry about it," Molly said.

"What were you doing with the gun, Tyler?" Jesse asked. Figuring it was his turn to play bad cop.

"I don't know."

"You don't know?"

"He ruined our lives. I wanted him to see. I wanted him to know."

"What did you want him to know?"

"What he did to us. The federal guys, they said he'd pay for it, but he got off. He got away with everything. That's not right. I wanted to tell him."

"Why did you need the gun for that?"

Tyler sat back, no longer looking angry or nervous. He just looked empty. Drained.

"You know why," he said.

"I really don't," Jesse said.

Now Tyler looked at the ceiling instead of at the floor.

"Because that's the gun my dad used when he killed himself. I wanted Devlin to know. I wanted him to pay for it."

He stopped talking. They were all silent for a moment.

"Tyler—" Molly began.

"I don't want to talk to you anymore," he said, turning

toward the cell wall. "You can do whatever you want. I'm done talking."

THEY SAT IN Jesse's office afterward. Both of them thinking.

"That bastard," Molly said.

"Seems a little harsh on the kid."

Molly gave him a face. "I mean Devlin. Jesse, I've been researching this guy. Do you know what he's done? How many lives he's ruined? And he got away clean."

"I know. Not much we can do about it."

"We can keep that boy from becoming another victim. We can help him."

Jesse realized Tyler was about the age of Molly's kids. She had different reflexes than he did.

"Molly, he confessed to planning a homicide."

"You think he was actually going to go through with it?"

"We'll never know. But he was there with a gun. Which he pulled on me."

"Like he's the first person to do that."

"Your concern is touching."

"Oh, don't be such a baby. You know what I mean," Molly said. "This kid's whole life collapsed in front of his eyes. He'd gone a little crazy because he thought he'd lost everything. Surely you can relate to that?"

Jesse could. But he also couldn't excuse it. This wasn't a traffic ticket.

"We can't just let this slide," he said. "You know that."

Molly's jaw clenched. She was furious.

"I know that," she said. "Of course I know that. But how many times have we done the right thing even when it might look like the wrong thing? If there was any justice, that guy Devlin would be in a cell instead of that kid. He's a piece of shit, Jesse. He's hurt people."

"We have nothing on Devlin outside of his OUI. And we are not the Feds. We don't investigate securities fraud."

"I know that, too."

"Look," Jesse said. "I'll talk to Ellis. Maybe he can cut a deal for a reduced sentence. Simple assault or something. But he's going to do some time, Molly. There's no way around that."

"I know, all right? Jesus. I know. Can't save everyone. We enforce the law. Can't fix the world," Molly said, standing up. "I just never thought I'd see this."

"See what?"

"Jesse Stone letting the bad guy get away with it."

She stomped away, back to her desk. Jesse sat behind his, feeling a bit stung.

After a moment, Molly called out to him.

"Was that too harsh?" she asked.

"Little bit," Jesse said.

"It felt a little harsh," she said. "Would a donut fix it?"

Jesse smiled, even though she couldn't see it. "I don't know. I'm pretty wounded."

Long pause.

"I'll get you one with sprinkles," Molly said.

"Deal."

ELEVEN

Jesse, I need you to come over to my place," Rachel said. "Right away."

Jesse had been catching up on sleep; today was his regular day off, but as soon as he heard her voice over the phone, he was instantly on alert.

"What's going on?" he asked, while in his mind, he was already loading his backup weapon, ready to sprint out the door. "Do you need me to call Suit? He can have people over there in a few minutes."

"What?" Rachel didn't sound scared or panicked. Just irritated. "No, it's nothing like that. Jacob is sick, and Brianna can't stay with him today. I'm pulling a double and I need you to look after him."

"Oh," Jesse said. Brianna was Rachel's babysitter/nanny/all-around helper. She was a college student, going to BU while cobbling together a living between house-sitting and other part-time jobs in Paradise. "So you want me to babysit?"

"You sound disappointed."

"Well," Jesse said. "That is a little less exciting than what I had in mind."

"Did you think I was in trouble?"

"No."

"You did, didn't you? You were ready to ride to the rescue."

"Maybe," Jesse admitted.

"So, can you do it? You don't have anything else going on right now, do you?"

In truth, Jesse had nothing going on today. But he still hesitated. A double shift meant twenty-four hours, two twelve-hour shifts back-to-back. Paradise's hospital was understaffed, like most hospitals. Rachel worked a lot of hours.

"I'm not sure childcare is in my skill set."

"Oh, for God's sake, Jesse. It's not hard. I just don't want to leave him alone. Keep an eye on him, make sure he doesn't throw up or spike a fever. And stop him from playing video games all day. Mark will come get him tonight after he's done with work."

"I can probably handle that. Is Jacob okay with it, too?"

"Of course. He likes you."

Jesse wasn't entirely sure about that, but he figured he and Jacob could handle watching TV together.

"I'll be there in ten."

"My hero," she said. "Just remember to leave your gun at home."

JESSE AND JACOB had been parked on the couch for hours, working their way through the Marvel Universe. Jesse had never been much of a comic-book reader even as a kid, so

Jacob had to fill in the backstory for him. It was surprisingly complex.

Rachel had told him when he arrived that Jacob had a stomach bug. Then she kissed them both on the cheek before she ran out the door.

Since then, Jesse had made breakfast and lunch for Jacob, who wolfed the food down like he was starving. He didn't look particularly sick to Jesse. His color was good and he seemed to have plenty of energy. He paused the movies several times to explain, in great detail, why the magic rocks were crucial to the scheme of the big purple monster guy.

Jesse would rather have been watching baseball or maybe a Clint Eastwood movie. But that was true about almost everything on TV. This was fine.

Jesse could guess why Jacob wanted a day off from school. But he didn't want to press the issue. He wasn't Jacob's dad. And Rachel had told him she was handling it.

Anyway, it probably wasn't the end of the world if Jacob stayed home. Jesse had to admit, just to himself, he was actually enjoying doing nothing.

Then came a knock at the door. Jesse checked his watch. It was almost three-thirty p.m. Jacob looked up, and Jesse noticed a sudden look of panic flash across the kid's face. "It's okay," Jesse told him, not sure why Jacob would need reassurance right then. "I've got it."

"You want me to pause?" Jacob asked. "There's a really good part coming up."

"Sure," Jesse said, and got off the couch.

He opened the door and saw a kid standing there, a sheaf of papers in his hands and a smirk on his face. He was blond and had sharp features.

Jesse was pretty sure he recognized that smirk before it vanished, replaced by a look of sheer confusion.

"What are you doing here?" he asked.

"Is that how you say hello?" Jesse asked.

The boy didn't respond. He was just a kid, Jesse reminded himself.

"You must be Race," Jesse said, extending his hand.

The boy didn't take it. "I know who you are," he mumbled.

He couldn't help who his father was, Jesse thought, or who his father was turning him into.

So he forced himself to be patient when he said, "I'm here to look after Jacob. What are you doing here?"

Race didn't look directly at him. Jesse pointed to the papers in his hands.

"You dropping off Jacob's homework?"

Race nodded but didn't hand over the papers.

Leave it to the class bully to make sure that Jacob still has to do his homework, Jesse thought. He probably wanted to make sure Jacob didn't go a full day without being harassed, either.

Jesse put his hand out. Race stood there, seemingly paralyzed.

He tried to take the papers, but as soon as his fingers touched them, Race jerked back.

"Can I have them?" Jesse asked, as gently as possible.

Race didn't answer. Jesse took the papers, and this time Race let them go after only a momentary tug-of-war.

"Thank you," Jesse said.

Race looked torn for another moment.

"Is there something you want to say?" Jesse asked.

Race looked like he was working up the courage to reply. Then a young woman in tight exercise gear came around the corner.

"Race, we need to get going," she said.

Jesse waved. "Are you Mrs. Devlin?"

The young woman laughed, then saw he was serious. "No. I'm the nanny."

"Nice to meet you. I'm Jesse."

"Uh-huh," she said, already looking at her phone. "Race, come on."

Race looked up at Jesse, tried for a glare, then turned and scurried away. He and his nanny vanished around the corner again.

For a moment, Jesse felt nothing but pity for the kid.

Then he looked down at the pages, and all his sympathy vanished.

JACOB CAUGHT A glimpse of the papers when Jesse returned to the couch. He tensed up but didn't say anything.

Jesse sat down and put the papers on the coffee table. He forced himself to be still. Jacob didn't need him to be angry right now. He'd never been a dad, not really, but he knew that much.

"Race dropped these off," he said.

"Uh-huh," Jacob said, still not looking at him. "You want to start the movie again?"

"I think we should probably talk about this."

Jesse slid the papers over on the table, closer to Jacob.

They were his homework assignments and worksheets.

But on them, someone had scrawled swastikas. Dozens

of them. And the words KITE—presumably Race meant *kike*—and JEWBOY.

"It's not a big deal," Jacob said.

"I think it is."

"Well, you're wrong. Can we just watch the movie?"

Jesse was surprised. He didn't think Jacob would talk back to him.

Jesse sighed. He didn't really know what the right thing was here. He knew what he wanted to do. And he knew how he'd handle it as the chief of police.

But he wasn't Jacob's dad, and he wasn't a cop at this particular moment. This was uncharted territory.

So he thought he should just say what was on his mind. It might even work.

"Jacob, if you want me to forget about this and just go back to watching the movie, we can do that. We've got a long time together before your dad gets here. And I don't want to make your life harder. But I think maybe you do want to talk about this. Because you and I both know this is wrong."

Jacob looked at him, his cheeks red, eyes welling. He wasn't just scared. He was embarrassed. And he was angry.

"What are you going to do about it? You think you can make it better?"

"I don't know," Jesse said. "Maybe not. But I can listen, at least. That's a start."

Jacob thought for a few seconds. Then he spoke. "I'll tell you. But you can't tell my mom."

"Can't promise that."

"Why not?"

"Because it wouldn't be right. She's your mom, Jacob.

She wants to know what's going on with you. She needs to know what's going on with you. This is a big deal."

"That's the problem," Jacob said, rolling his eyes. "I know it's a big deal! I'm not stupid."

"I never thought you were."

"But my mom will make it an even bigger deal. She's already talked to the teachers and the principal."

"What did they do?"

Jacob laughed, a surprisingly adult sound for such a young kid. "You know what they did. They didn't do anything."

"Yeah, I don't understand that," Jesse said. "How does a kid like Race get away with bullying you?"

Jacob rolled his eyes. "They keep telling me I have to understand that Race has feelings, and he doesn't know how to express them appropriately, and I have to be patient, too."

"*You* have to be patient? With *him*?"

"Uh-huh."

Jesse took in a deep breath. "Okay. How's that working out?"

"You can see right there." Jacob pointed at the papers. "He used to just say this stuff to me. Or shove me. Or hit me when nobody was looking. So I try to stay away from him, but that just makes him madder. So he started getting my homework and writing these things on it."

Jesse thought about how to ask his next question the right way. Unfortunately, what he said was "Have you tried hitting him back?"

Jacob looked at Jesse like he was crazy. "Why would I do that?"

"Well . . ." Jesse began. And then stopped. "Why wouldn't you do that? When someone hits you?"

"What good would it do?"

"You think it might stop him from hitting you? I mean, I understand if you're scared . . ."

"I'm not *scared*." Jacob's tone was withering.

"It just means we'd have to fight. And then he'd start again, and I'd have to fight him again. It wouldn't change anything."

"It might," Jesse said. "Sometimes people back down when you show them you're willing to fight back."

"Is that how it worked for you and Race's dad?"

Jesse had to admit, the kid had a point. That stung a bit.

"Okay, fair enough," Jesse said. "But sometimes you have to fight. You get backed into a corner and then you don't have any choice."

Jacob sighed heavily and leaned into the couch cushions. "You don't get it. I don't *want* to fight him. If I get caught fighting, my mom will pull me out of that school and find another."

"She might surprise you."

Jacob gave him a very weary look, as if Jesse was the dumbest human being to walk the earth.

"Race's parents are rich. The school isn't going to do anything about him. So if I'm fighting him all the time, my mom will take me out."

Jesse realized that Jacob had been thinking about this for a while. And even if Jesse could argue with him about the facts, he couldn't argue with how Jacob saw it.

"You don't want to leave? Even with Race doing what he does."

"No. I've changed schools four times already. When my parents divorced. When Mom got a new job. When she got another new job. And then another new job. I like it here. I have friends. I like Paradise. It's a pretty nice place."

"Yeah, I think so, too," Jesse said.

"I want to stay."

"I want you to stay, too. So how do we make that happen, and stop Race from bullying you?"

"I don't know," Jacob said, in the tone of a prisoner being shown to his cell. "I keep thinking about it and I can't come up with anything."

"How long has he been doing this? Writing on your papers."

"I dunno," Jacob said. "Few weeks now."

"Your mom hasn't seen the papers?"

"I haven't showed her any."

"Because you think she's going to blow everything up."

Jacob lowered his head. "She doesn't mean to. I know. But I just . . ."

"You just what?"

"I was just starting to be happy here. I'm afraid of screwing it up."

Jesse thought about that for a moment. "Yeah," he said. "I know the feeling."

They sat quietly together for another beat.

"You're going to make me tell her, aren't you?"

Jesse sat back and thought. Rachel wouldn't be home until tomorrow. He and Jacob were stuck together for a while.

He could just leave it. He could tell Rachel and let her handle it.

But he felt an obligation he couldn't quite explain. He thought about Jacob going to school every day, doing his best to stand up to this other kid and still follow the rules. To avoid bothering his mom. To keep things running smoothly. He'd painted himself into a perfect box, and he was suffering inside it.

Jesse wanted to get him out of it.

"What if I tried to talk to the school?"

"Mom's tried that already," Jacob said and groaned. "The principal says she's going to do something and then she just tells me and Race we have to get along and it starts all over again."

"The principal?"

"Right. Ms. Hawley." Jacob said her name like he was talking about a chronic disease.

"You know, I am chief of police. Sometimes people take me a little more seriously."

"Yeah, but it's not like you can arrest her."

"Good point," Jesse said. "But I can still talk to her."

"I don't know," Jacob said. "You won't tell my mom about it?"

"Either way, I'm telling your mom."

"Great," Jacob said, and sagged visibly.

"I think your mom will handle it," Jesse said. "And I'd really like to help if you'll let me, Jacob. Maybe we can settle this. I don't want to see you leave town, either."

"Well, of course you don't. You're in love with my mom."

Jesus, this kid.

"I want both of you to stay here."

Jacob looked at him suspiciously. He thought about it for a second.

"Okay," he said.

Jesse held out his hand to shake. Jacob made a face, but he took it and they sealed the deal.

Jesse felt almost like he did on the first day he'd gotten his badge, like he'd been trusted with a great responsibility and he had to do his best to live up to it.

TWELVE

Jesse sat with Suit in the front of the station. Suit was on night duty. Jesse had worked late, signing off on reports and filing them.

Now they were just talking. Jesse didn't have anywhere to be. Rachel was working another double at the hospital, Jacob was with his nanny, and there was no baseball tonight on ESPN.

He liked to catch up with Suit at least once a week. But between tourist season and Jesse's new relationship, that had been hard to do.

Suit saw things nobody else did, because people didn't think he was paying attention. They confided in him, because he had an open and honest face, and they didn't think he'd get them into trouble. He still looked like a big kid.

Which gave him the opportunity to pass those things along to Jesse, if he thought Jesse needed to hear them. Not like he was ratting anyone out. But people were often scared of Jesse. Jesse could be intimidating. And his officers were, aside from Suit and Molly and usually Gabe, afraid to disappoint him.

That made Suit the perfect conduit for important messages.

"You have to get us more help, Jesse," he said. "Everyone is tired. All it takes is one of us calling out sick or going on vacation and we're all working double shifts and overtime trying to keep up."

This wasn't a new complaint, Jesse knew. But if he was hearing it again, through Suit, it meant it was getting bad.

"I've been talking to Armistead," Jesse said. "He keeps telling me we don't have the budget now. Especially after what happened with our last hire."

"I know," Suit said. "Nobody's blaming you. But Barry and Jimmy have been making noises about going to Helton. They've got openings. Or applying in Boston again."

Jimmy Alonso and Barry Stanton hadn't made the cut the first time they'd applied for Boston PD. But now, with their training and seasoning under Jesse, he knew they'd get accepted. He couldn't afford to lose them.

But Jesse didn't think that was the main reason Suit was bringing this up. He could see it on Suit's face. He waited.

Suit let it all out in a big rush of air, like he'd been holding his breath.

"There's also a deputy chief position open in Worcester," he said. "I got a call."

Jesse took a second with that. "You interested?"

"It's more money. And it would be less time on patrol. Not like here."

"Do you want to spend less time on patrol? Getting tired of wrestling with drunks at the Scupper?"

Suit laughed. "Nah, I'm still undefeated champion."

"I can see about more money in the next budget," Jesse said. "You're all due for a raise."

"That's not really it, either. It's just . . . you know anything can happen out there, right. I mean, we've both almost died. More than once. And it's not just the really bad guys. Some night I could be writing a ticket on the side of the road and some drunk plows into me because he doesn't see my car."

"Why are you thinking about this now, Suit?"

Suit hesitated. "Jesse, Elena's pregnant."

Jesse did something that surprised even him. He stood up, grabbed Suit by the shoulders, and pulled him into a hug.

"Congratulations," Jesse said.

He felt his face split into a wide grin. Suit, on the other hand, looked a little nauseated.

"Yeah, thanks," Suit said. "I just—it's a lot, you know?"

"You don't think you're ready to be a dad?"

"Maybe," he said. "Maybe not. We've been trying for a while. I mean, we always said we wanted kids, but—well, I'd sort of given up. And now . . ."

"Now it's real."

"Yeah."

"That's why you're worried," Jesse said. "You don't want to leave your kid without a father."

"No," Suit said. "That's about the worst thing I can imagine doing. I don't want to be a story she hears or a picture of some guy she's never met."

"I hear you," Jesse said. "I wasn't there for my kid. It marked him. I didn't know, but still. I feel responsible."

"You feel responsible for everything. This isn't your

problem, Jesse. I didn't even mean to tell you. I'm going to have to make this decision. One way or another."

"I know. And you'll do the right thing, Suit. I know that, too."

"Thanks."

"Let me see what I can do about the budget," Jesse said. "I can talk to Armistead again."

"Appreciate it."

Jesse shrugged. "So you're having a girl?"

Suit smiled. "Yeah. Got the ultrasound yesterday."

"I'm trying to imagine you shopping for clothes with her."

Suit looked offended. "I'll have you know I have an excellent sense of fashion."

"Oh, and can you imagine what college is going to cost by the time she's eighteen? I'd better ask for a big raise for you."

"That's not funny, Jesse," Suit said, looking nauseated again.

Then the phone rang. Dispatch. Jesse grabbed the line first.

"Big party," he told Suit. "Lots of drunks and noise. A whole bunch of complaints in the last twenty minutes or so. I guess the neighbors tried to endure it, but it's getting even louder now."

"How many people?"

"At least a hundred."

"Thank God," Suit said. "I'd rather fight a whole pack of drunks than think about tuition right now."

THIRTEEN

Ms. Elizabeth Foley was furious. Jesse had seen her angry before, but never while holding a baseball bat.

He and Suit stood on the front porch of her big colonial on Seaside Drive.

Ms. Foley could trace her lineage back to the earliest settlers in Massachusetts. She wore her white hair short and her back was still ramrod straight at ninety. She still walked down the road to the shore every day without a cane. She had never married—God help you if you called her *Mrs.* Foley—probably, Jesse thought, because no man could keep up with her.

But now her hair was disheveled and her knuckles were white as she gripped the bat.

"I tell you, Jesse, if you don't do something about that racket, I'm going over there myself."

Jesse didn't have to ask what racket. The noise from the party on the Devlin estate rattled the windows of Ms. Foley's house in their frames.

Like most of her neighbors, Ms. Foley had been a resident of this line of houses right on Seaside Drive for decades. They were old money, or at least tasteful money. They didn't believe in showing off. Ms. Foley wore the same Hunter boots she'd had for twenty years and an old coat that had probably belonged to her father.

Devlin's giant eyesore of a house was a direct insult to the older residents of Paradise.

Having lived here for years, Jesse knew it wasn't Devlin's money the Paradise old guard objected to—they were big fans of money. But the manner in which he splashed it around made them uncomfortable. It just wasn't done. It was loud.

Very loud, in this case tonight. Jesse felt like he needed earplugs and he was still a thousand yards away.

Still, he couldn't have Ms. Foley going over and cracking Devlin's skull with a baseball bat.

"Ms. Foley," he said. "I promise you: We'll take care of it."

Ms. Foley looked at him and Suit. She didn't look convinced. "Just the two of you?" she said.

"Are you kidding? It should only take one of us. This is a show of force meant to intimidate them."

Despite herself, Ms. Foley cracked a smile. For her, this was the equivalent of falling down on the floor laughing.

"All right," she said. "But if I hear another sound from that playboy's mansion, I'll take the law into my own hands, Jesse."

"I promise you, that won't be necessary," Jesse said. He and Suit turned to go. Then he stopped.

"Would you mind if I borrowed your bat?"

"Don't you have a gun?" she asked.

"I'd rather not use it if I don't have to."

"You just don't want me bashing anyone's brains in."

"You're too smart for me, Ms. Foley." He put his hand out. "Please?"

Reluctantly, Ms. Foley handed it over.

JESSE AND SUIT walked down the lane to the Devlin house, leaving their cars in Ms. Foley's driveway.

It still looked like a monstrosity to Jesse. It was lit up from every angle, large floodlights in the gardens and landscaping illuminating all its edges and corners. It somehow managed to loom and squat at the same time against the horizon.

Cars were parked all up and down Seaside, crammed into every bit of available space, blocking driveways and the road. Jesse saw a BMW driven into a neighbor's hedge, the door open, the car's lights still on.

"Nice parking job," Suit said.

"These people have no respect for their vehicles," Jesse said. He still carried Ms. Foley's bat.

By the time they got to the front gate of the mansion, the noise was unbelievable. Jesse had heard aircraft take off that were quieter. It was easy to see through the gate and over the house's low wall to the front and side lawns. Devlin had set up speakers that looked like they belonged in a twenty-thousand-seat stadium. Jesse wasn't sure he'd call what was coming out of them music, but the people on the lawns and in the pool seemed to be dancing to it.

"You want to ring the bell?" Jesse yelled at Suit.

"What?" Suit yelled back.

Jesse walked to the gate and pressed a button. He assumed there was a buzzer or bell in the house, but he wasn't sure how anyone would hear it.

But someone must have, because the gate swung open, triggered by some kind of remote switch.

"Seems like an invitation," Jesse said.

"What?" Suit said again.

Jesse shook his head and began walking. Suit followed.

Jesse crossed the front lawn. People were dancing, walking, stumbling, and passed out all around, in various states of sobriety and undress. It seemed like Devlin had imported most of his guests for this event. Jesse didn't recognize many locals among them. The people who did recognize Jesse—a couple kids from the high school, a few of the younger members of the Paradise Country Club—quickly vanished into the crowd as soon as they saw his face.

A guy wearing only a Speedo staggered into Jesse and turned to face him, clenching a joint between his lips.

His eyes went wide when he saw Jesse's gun and badge.

"Relax," Jesse said. "It's legal here now."

The guy still ran in the other direction.

He and Suit made their way through the crowd and to the DJ in front of the speaker tower. He stared intently at his turntables and his equipment, not looking up.

Jesse tapped him on the shoulder.

The DJ twitched, then looked up, annoyed.

"Gonna have to ask you to turn it off," Jesse hollered.

The DJ smiled and cranked a knob. The noise went from deafening to apocalyptic.

The crowd roared with approval.

The DJ laughed. Or seemed to. Jesse couldn't hear what was coming out of his mouth.

Jesse shrugged, then looked around the equipment. He found a tangle of cables leading to the decks and the speakers. He smiled at the DJ, wrapped the cables in his fist, and then hauled on them.

Several things came loose at once, with loud popping and cracking noises. The speakers went dead so suddenly it was like the opposite of a bomb dropping, a silence that seemed to leave a crater.

It didn't last.

"What the fuck, man?" the DJ screamed, his voice suddenly carrying across the night.

Jesse ignored him. He turned to the crowd, while Suit stepped up to the DJ and loomed over him.

"Folks," he said, "I am sorry to tell you the party is over. You don't have to go home, but you can't stay here. If you can't drive, we will wait while you arrange for transportation. But please do not attempt to leave while intoxicated. I am sure you do not want to wake up in one of our cells tomorrow."

There was a low rumbling of discontent from the partiers. But they began to move.

Jesse didn't show it, but he felt a small release of tension in his chest. A crowd this big could always turn ugly, and it was just him and Suit here. He was relying on the power of the badge and the general willingness of the people to follow orders.

Then he heard someone yelling.

"The hell happened to the music?"

The crowd parted, opening a path from the edge of the swimming pool right up to the DJ booth. Ramsey Devlin strode forward, wearing a robe over his swim trunks, hair glistening and wet, his arm around a young woman in her twenties wearing a bikini that barely covered her impressive form.

He saw Jesse and Suit and marched right up to them.

"Mr. Devlin," Jesse said. "Looks like the missus is out for the evening."

"Chief Stone," he said. "How nice of you to show up. I didn't think you'd make it. But then, I didn't think I invited you, either."

He was performing, projecting his voice so the entire crowd could hear. People laughed.

Jesse had the sinking feeling that Devlin thought this was the perfect way to end the evening: a showdown with the cops.

"I'd heard you played baseball," he said, looking at the bat in Jesse's hand. "You come here to take a swing at me?"

"I'm afraid the party is over now. It's time for you to call it a night."

"We're not stopping until daybreak, Chief," Devlin said. "Those are the rules for a Devlin party." A couple people whooped and cheered in agreement.

Jesse stepped around the DJ's turntables so he was almost toe to toe with Devlin. Devlin dropped his arm from the swimsuit model. She shrank away from them both, melting back into the crowd.

Jesse scanned the other man quickly. He didn't think he was hiding a weapon in his trunks or the robe.

"It looks like you've had a pretty good time already," he

said, trying for reasonable one more time. "Why not give your neighbors a break? Let them get some rest."

"My neighbors? Fuck them! I'll buy their houses, too! I need more room!"

Now there were more cheers. Jesse had to put a lid on this quickly.

"Mr. Devlin," Jesse said, and took a step closer.

Devlin put his hands in front of his chest.

"You going to sucker-punch me again, Chief? I think you'd get tired of beating up on the same guy."

"As I recall, you threw a punch at me."

Devlin leaned closer. "Who gives a shit? All that really matters is what my lawyers are going to argue in court." Then he leaned back again, yelling for his audience. "So what's your answer? You too scared to take off that gun and fight like a man?"

The crowd said *whoaaaaa* like they were standing in the cafeteria of a junior high school. Jesse looked briefly to the sky, searching for patience. He didn't see any up there.

"Devlin," he said, dragging the last ounce of restraint he had from some hidden reserve. "Do you really want to find out what it would be like if I hit you?"

Devlin, even through his fog of cocktails and drugs, heard something in Jesse's voice. He dropped his hands and stepped back. Jesse thought this was the smartest thing he'd done all night. He could see this wrapping up without violence.

Then someone else stepped up.

"Shit, I'll fight him," another man said, and muscled his way forward.

Clayton Ashcraft. A great big mass of muscle and bone,

going a little soft around the edges. He was a defensive lineman back in college, and a starter at the Sugar Bowl. He had a good college career but got his knee twisted in the wrong direction in his fourth appearance with the Patriots. He'd turned his minor NFL celebrity into a half-dozen luxury car dealerships throughout New England.

Now he stood a couple feet behind Devlin, dripping wet in his own towel and robe. He and Jesse had never really squared off before. He'd played in the summer softball league and made a few comments about being the only real pro athlete in town. The usual ex-jock bullshit.

But now he looked a little more unfocused, and a lot meaner.

Suit tried to intervene. He knew Clay from the youth football programs where they both coached.

"Clay," Suit said. "You don't wanna do this."

Clay looked at Suit and tried to focus on him. His eyes were bleary and mean. "Shut up, you pussy," he spat. "Don't you tell me what I want."

Suit shrugged. "Okay. I tried, man. Good luck with that."

Clay stepped forward. Devlin, still grinning, was only too happy to step back.

Jesse had to look up at him.

"Thanks, Suit," he said, without taking his eyes off Clay. "He was trying to keep you from embarrassing yourself."

Clay looked down. "I'm not the one who's gonna get his ass beat. I always wanted to find out just how tough you really are."

He threw off his robe, standing there, all six-foot-four of him, arms and chest covered in slabs of muscle. The crowd hooted and hollered.

"You want to hang on to that bat?" Clay said. "You need an advantage?"

Jesse smiled at him. It was not a nice smile. He looked at the bat and then tossed it to him.

"No," he said. "But you might."

Clay looked surprised, but covered it well. He took a few practice swings with the bat in one hand. It looked like a toothpick compared to his bulk.

He stepped forward.

Jesse didn't move.

"How's the knee, Clay?" he asked.

Clay hesitated. He looked confused by the question.

"My knee?"

"Did it hurt when you got it torn up back then?"

Clay shrugged. "I handled it."

"Still hurts sometimes?" Jesse asked.

Jesse spoke at a normal volume. It was easy to hear him now. The entire crowd was quiet. Waiting for something to happen. You could have heard a pin drop.

Clay shrugged. "Fuck's my knee got to do with anything?"

Jesse stared right into Clay's eyes. His voice was mild when he said, "Because you can either walk away or limp away. It's your choice."

Clay might have backed down. Jesse could see the uncertainty on his face. His mouth was slightly open, his chin drooping. He was thinking about it, Jesse was sure.

But then the crowd said *whoooooaaaaa* once again, and Clay's ego got involved, and Jesse knew he wouldn't let anyone see him as weak.

Clay took a big step forward, swinging with the bat.

But Jesse was already ducking. He took the collapsible police baton from his belt and extended it with a neat *snick* in one smooth motion.

Jesse turned his body as if he was about to hit a home run and swung the baton into Clay's left knee—the one Clay was using to support all 275 pounds of his weight.

There was a crack like a tree being hit by an ax, and Clay dropped the bat as he went down, howling in pain. He hit the ground with a heavy thud.

"I told you," Jesse said.

"Shit," Clay said. "That really fuckin' hurts!"

"That's assault on a police officer during his official duties, Clay. Up to ten years in prison if we press charges. You ready to behave?"

Clay answered by making a grab for Jesse's legs and screaming, "You son of a bitch!"

Jesse sidestepped him easily. He was not a man who liked to hit people when they were down. But he'd do it, especially if those people were angry ex–NFL players who hadn't learned to stop thrashing around when they were beaten.

He handed the baton to Suit, who took it. Then he leaned over and popped Clay hard with a straight right into his nose.

Clay's eyes went unfocused. He slapped at Jesse slowly again, like he was trying to swat a fly buzzing around his head.

Jesse hit him one more time. Clay's eyes rolled all the way into his head and he sank back on the ground, unconscious.

"God*damn*," one of the onlookers said.

"He's been hit harder than that," Jesse said. "He'll be fine."

Jesse turned to Devlin. "Now," he said. "You want to tell your guests to go home?"

Devlin inclined his head, as if to grant Jesse some point. Then he turned and yelled at the crowd.

"Party's over," he shouted. "Get the hell out of here."

The partiers began to walk away, muttering to one another. They all gave Jesse and Suit a wide berth.

"Suit, go make sure nobody's driving drunk," Jesse said. "And maybe call an ambulance for Clay. He's going to be in a lot of pain when he wakes up."

"Sure thing, Jesse," Suit said.

Jesse and Devlin stood there, neither man taking their eyes off the other.

"Well, Jesse," Devlin said. "You really know how to liven up a party. I'll have to come up with something even better for the next one."

"I have a question," Jesse said.

"Shoot."

"What do you think you're doing here? Is there something you think you're going to prove? Something you think you're going to win?"

"You're damn right," Devlin said. "I haven't even started yet. I am going to do what nobody else has ever done to you, Stone: I'm going to beat you."

Jesse shook his head. "You know, we don't have to do this. It doesn't have to be a fight."

Devlin waved his arms around at everything behind him. The grounds, the house, the view. "You think I got all of this by letting go? By backing down?"

"No," Jesse said. "But I have to say: If you don't learn how, it seems like a real good way to lose it."

Devlin smiled again, cinched his robe tight, then turned his back on Jesse and walked away, crossing the lawn to his enormous, ugly house.

FOURTEEN

On his way to the station the next day, Jesse parked outside the elementary school in the space marked VISITOR.

He walked in through the front door. Ashish, the school's security guard, crossed the lobby to greet him.

Jesse knew Ashish. Paradise didn't have enough personnel to station an officer full-time at each school, so Jesse made sure that the on-site security was trained and competent. Paradise had been lucky enough to avoid the school shootings that had devastated other places. But Jesse wanted to be prepared for the worst-case scenario.

Ashish could have been a cop. He was a Marine veteran who'd come back from Iraq to a variety of jobs before landing the security gig. Jesse had asked him if he wanted to attend one of the state's police academies, but Ashish declined. "Had enough people shooting at me already, Chief," he'd told Jesse. "I'm happy to keep an eye on the kids. That's all."

Still, Jesse thought anyone trying to get past him to the children would find themselves in a world of hurt.

Even knowing Jesse, Ashish had moved forward, friendly enough, but had blocked him effectively from getting into the hallways or deeper into the school.

They shook hands. “How’s it going, Chief?” Ashish asked. “Something wrong?”

“Hoping to speak to Ms. Hawley. If she’s not too busy.”

“Nothing official?”

“No.”

That was all Jesse was willing to say. Ashish nodded. “I think I might know what you’re going to ask her about.”

That didn’t surprise Jesse, either. Ashish knew what happened in his school, and he usually had to respond to discipline problems if they got out of hand.

“Anything you can tell me?”

“Can’t talk about the kids, you know that,” he said. “Ms. Hawley, on the other hand . . . Well. She’s probably not going to want to hear it.”

“Okay if I give it a shot, anyway?”

“I wish you luck,” Ashish said. “Sincerely.”

They shook hands again and Jesse headed for the office.

The receptionist, Mrs. Curtis, had known Jesse for years and hurried to Ms. Hawley’s office to announce him. Jesse noticed the door was closed. He didn’t like that. He didn’t know how someone could expect to keep track of what was going on if they shut the door on everyone else.

Mrs. Curtis emerged and closed the door behind her again, then walked the few steps over to Jesse. “She says you can go right in.”

“She want me to close the door behind me?”

Mrs. Curtis smiled a little. “She’s kind of a stickler about that.”

Jesse walked over, knocked on the door, and opened it in response to a woman's voice within.

Ms. Hawley was younger than Jesse, hair streaked with blond highlights, and wore bright pink plastic glasses on her head and chunky costume rings on her fingers. The coffee mug on her desk said I WISH THIS WAS WINE. Jesse could relate to that. There was also a tiny hangman's noose on a little gallows that said COMPLAINTS DEPT. Jesse wasn't sure either were entirely appropriate for an elementary school principal.

"Chief Stone," she said, not smiling.

"Please. It's Jesse."

She didn't acknowledge that. "I didn't expect a visit from you," she said.

"Really?" Jesse said. "You didn't?"

That threw her for a moment. "Well, yes. You didn't call or make an appointment."

"I figured you'd know why I was here," Jesse said.

She sat and blinked at him.

Jesse took one of the visitor's chairs without being asked. Despite all the years since he'd last had to sit in front of a principal, he still didn't like the feeling.

"I'm sorry," she finally said. "I really have no idea."

Jesse reached into his jacket pocket and took out Jacob's homework papers, the ones dropped off by Race.

He put them on the desk. The swastikas and skulls were plainly visible.

Ms. Hawley did not look surprised. Or all that bothered, Jesse thought.

"I'd hoped you might be able to explain this to me," Jesse said.

Ms. Hawley frowned. "Are you opening an investigation, Chief Stone?"

"I'm reaching out to you as a concerned citizen."

"I know how you've dealt in the past with some of my counterparts at the high school and middle school. I want to tell you, I will not be intimidated. Inside these walls, I run things. And that includes protecting the privacy of the students."

"I'm not sure how this invades anyone's privacy," Jesse said. "I know whose paper this is."

"Yes. I've heard you were involved with Jacob's mother." The way she said the word *involved* sounded like she wondered if Jesse should be allowed within one hundred yards of a school.

"Right. And I also know who drew all these swastikas."

"Oh. You do?"

"You don't?"

"I'm not prepared to say."

"From what I hear, you'd have to work pretty hard not to know who's been bullying Jacob."

"Let me give you a little pushback there," Ms. Hawley said. "I'm not sure we can use the word *bullying.*"

"How about *antisemitism*? Or *bigotry*? Or *harassment*? Those aren't just words. Those are indications of a possible crime."

"I thought you said this wasn't official."

"That's what happens if this becomes official. I'm trying to avoid it."

"I am handling this situation within the school's disciplinary system."

"Oh. You have one of those?"

Her nostrils flared. "Of course."

"I wasn't sure."

"We believe in allowing children to learn from their mistakes," Ms. Hawley said. "You see, there is a spectrum of behavior. Some boys need more time to learn to adjust to the restrictions of the classroom, and how to relate to people they might not have encountered before. There are all kinds of behaviors that appear to be aggressive, or even violent, to someone who doesn't have the right training. This is a kind, compassionate, caring school, Jesse. In fact, I would say it's the most compassionate and caring place I've ever worked. I choose to treat these children with understanding rather than punitive measures."

"And you think that's working?"

"Absolutely."

"I'm not sure I agree. As I said, these could easily be considered threats."

"Frankly, it's none of your business. This is why I didn't see the point of involving any outside authorities. Especially given your . . . *relationship* . . . with the mother of one of the boys in question."

Ms. Hawley managed to make *relationship* sound even sleazier than *involved*. For all her bright colors, she seemed downright puritanical.

"So you let Race Devlin draw swastikas and harass a Jewish kid whenever he wants?"

"Without confirming the name of the student," she said, "I counseled the boy and he assured me he did not know the history of the symbol or the fraught nature of the slurs he used. He thought he was simply being insulting. And he promised that this was a onetime thing."

Jesse reached into his jacket again and came out with Jacob's math homework. And his social studies homework. And his health worksheet. He placed those papers on the desk next to the others.

All were covered in swastikas as well. Jacob had handed them over to Jesse when Jesse asked.

"No," Jesse said. "It was not a onetime thing."

Ms. Hawley's face went red. Her frown only deepened. "I was not expecting to be interrogated today."

"I imagine that if I were allowing this in school, I wouldn't want to talk about it, either."

"I am not *allowing*—"

"If you're not working to stop something like this," Jesse said, "you're allowing it."

"Look. Just because I won't give the son of your, your, *girlfriend* special treatment doesn't mean I am not doing my job."

Jesse let the tone of *girlfriend* slide. "Well, you're certainly giving someone special treatment."

"That is a completely spurious and entirely insulting allegation."

Jesse picked up a copy of the PTA bulletin from Ms. Hawley's desk. He read from the News & Notes section. "'And a special big thank-you to Mr. Ramsey Devlin, who sponsored the Faculty and Staff Appreciation Banquet, where he pledged an additional five million dollars to refurbish the Paradise Elementary gymnasium,'" Jesse quoted. "Then it says, 'Go Eagles.'"

Now Ms. Hawley hunched forward. She looked mean. Jesse suddenly understood why Jacob had trouble speaking to her.

"Are you saying I can be bought, Chief Stone?"

"Well. Maybe rented."

She didn't respond.

"Or a lease, with an option to buy."

"You're not funny."

"Look," Jesse said. "What I really want to know is why you think you're doing this kid a favor by letting him get away with this. If he doesn't ever have to deal with the consequences of his actions, he's going to keep doing it. Until it becomes something that can't be ignored. And while I don't have a doctorate in education, I am willing to bet he's acting this way because he's practically begging someone to pay attention to him before it gets to that point."

"I assure you, I am not doing Race any special favors."

"You're right. You're not. You're actually doing his father the favor. The longer you let this slide, the longer he can ignore it. And then he doesn't have to do the hard work of raising his own son."

Ms. Hawley finally raised her voice. "Why are you even here?" she snapped. "You're not Jacob's father. You're not even a parent. You're only in this school because I allow it. So what are you trying to do here?"

Jesse shrugged. "You're right. I can't do anything to stop it. But you can. And I sure hope you do. Because Race is only going to get worse. And you could spare him—and Jacob—a lot of pain if you'd just do your job."

"Sometimes my methods actually work, Chief Stone," she said, the smile back on her face. "You might be surprised."

"Frankly, Ms. Hawley," Jesse said as he got up to leave. "I would be astonished."

FIFTEEN

Gary Armistead smiled when Jesse showed up at the mayor's office. He was always in a good mood when he got to summon Jesse and force him to show up.

Jesse figured Armistead had to take the little victories where he could. They had never gotten along, and probably never would. Armistead was under the impression not only that being the mayor made him Jesse's boss—which was technically true—but that this also made him, somehow, Jesse's *superior.*

Truth be told, Jesse had never understood why he'd instinctively disliked Gary Armistead. A lot of other people liked him just fine. They seemed to buy his grip-and-grin friendliness, his instant interest in whatever they were saying. And Jesse had to give Armistead credit. He appeared to pay attention to whatever problems the residents of Paradise brought him. He could listen and nod and give the impression that they were, for that moment, the most important person in the whole world.

Jesse suspected that Armistead forgot them as soon as they were out of his line of sight, just like a goldfish swimming in a new direction. But that was an opinion he'd formed only after watching the mayor in action for a while. When they first met, he didn't think that.

But he'd never trusted Armistead, even at the beginning of their relationship. And maybe Armistead had sensed that, because he'd been equally suspicious of Jesse since day one as well. Jesse had learned that Armistead, like a lot of politicians, didn't trust anything he didn't control. And Jesse would never allow anyone else to control him.

Or maybe it was just that deep down, Armistead was kind of a dickhead, and Jesse had a low tolerance for dickheads.

Whatever the reason, every time Jesse came to this office and sat in this chair, there was now a long history of grievances and slights that would take a full mining team to excavate.

Jesse let the mayor have the little victories, like summoning him here. It saved time and it made Armistead feel better, which gave Jesse more freedom to focus on the things that mattered, like doing his job.

"So, we have an event coming up. The museum fundraiser. It's important."

The Paradise Museum of Art was not big or impressive, but it was funded by people who liked to know they could look at a Renoir when they visited their summer place if they got the notion. It was a way for the wealthy residents of Paradise to feel they still had some sophistication and class. The annual fundraiser was how they showed off a little, pulling their tuxedos and gowns out of the closet for a night.

The event would also be a way for Armistead to raise money for his campaign, but neither of them needed to say that out loud. The mayor got to walk around in his suit and discreetly accept pledges of support from the town's most prominent citizens.

"I want to talk to you about police protection," Armistead said.

"Why?" Jesse asked.

Armistead looked like he'd just sucked a lemon. "Because you're the chief of police, Jesse. I thought you knew that."

Jesse should have known not to give him a chance to be clever. "I mean, why do you think you need police protection?"

Armistead sat back and frowned. "Jesse, come on. I think you know that bad things can happen in Paradise. Especially when it's a big event like this one."

Jesse managed not to roll his eyes. "Gary. I'm well aware of when a situation can turn ugly around here. Believe me when I say this isn't one of them."

"And one of our donors has had a threat against him," Armistead said. "Ramsey Devlin is going to hand over a million-dollar check for the museum."

Jesse got it now. This was Armistead's way of helping Devlin look like a good citizen. Which also explained why Armistead was so invested in Devlin's happiness as a resident of Paradise.

He really wished Armistead hadn't known about the kid who showed up with a gun outside Devlin's house. He didn't have much choice, of course. He'd informed Devlin of the potential threat since he was the possible victim, and Devlin told Armistead. Even if he hadn't, the mayor would have known. News traveled fast in Paradise. People needed the entertainment.

But that kid was in the county lockup now. He wasn't nearly enough justification to sway Jesse into putting his whole department at the mayor's beck and call.

"Nobody's going to crash the party to steal a giant fake check, Gary. And if you're that concerned about public safety, have you reviewed my request for another patrol position?"

"That's not why we're here," Armistead snapped. "I'm talking about protecting the town's most prominent citizens. If you can't do that, why are you even in the job?"

Jesse let that sit for a long moment. "Gary, it seems like you're asking for a bunch of my people in uniform to make you look good."

Armistead leaned forward, about to spit fire.

Then he stopped himself. And the grin came back.

"Well," he said. "It wouldn't hurt."

"There you go," Jesse said. "It would save us both time if you just told me what you really want."

"Fine. I want all your people there. Shoes shined, uniforms pressed, guns loaded. Make everyone feel important and safe."

"You can have two officers. At the door."

Armistead drew himself up in his chair and put on what Jesse always thought of as his Official Mayor Face. "You're going to have the whole department there. Consider this an order, Chief Stone."

Jesse waited. Armistead kept glaring at him.

"You were never in the military, were you, Gary?"

"I don't see what that has to do with anything."

"Well, if you were, you'd know that an order carries force. You're not actually my boss. I answer to the whole Town Council. You can try to fire me, sure, but you'd have to get their approval—"

"You think I can't do that?"

Jesse ignored the interruption. "—and that would be a fight I don't think you want to start. Not over dress-up for a campaign event. So why don't you tell me why I should spend half a month's overtime on this. Since we're being honest now."

Armistead dropped his official face. He sat back in his chair.

"Do this and I'll fund the cost of a new patrol officer to replace Perkins."

That was something Jesse wanted. Peter Perkins, one of his veterans, had finally retired earlier this year after being badly injured. Even before that, Peter had been part-time, mainly doing crime scene work because he was one of the few people with any training or experience in that area. But after nearly dying, he'd had enough.

Paradise had a hard time attracting young recruits because the town didn't like to fund their retirement benefits. Those were expensive. Armistead and the Town Council wanted Jesse to do the same as other towns outside Boston, and hire veteran officers who were already qualified for pensions from other departments.

Jesse, on the other hand, wanted someone who'd live in Paradise and put down roots. Who'd care what happened here. He also wanted someone to pick up the slack on crime scene investigation. That would take even more money, for training and education.

Armistead knew all this. Which meant he knew Jesse was ready to bargain.

"I want Suit and Gabe to get certified on forensics as well," Jesse said. "We need that with Peter gone."

"Two of them, both going off to some resort where they'll drink mai tais and pretend to listen to a bunch of old cops jabbering? We're not here to pay for your guys' vacations, Jesse."

"You know that's not where I'd send them."

"Yeah, but that's how I can make it sound."

"Then I guess you'll have to settle for one officer at the door of your campaign fundraiser."

"A minute ago it was two."

"In another minute I'm going to tell you to hire private security."

Armistead thought about it. "Okay. A new patrol position, fully funded. And whatever you need to get Suit and Gabe certified. Let them drink margaritas or whatever. Who cares?"

"And I want a five percent raise for all the officers. Across the board."

"Does that include you?"

"I'm fine. This is for everyone else. Ten percent for Molly and Suit."

"Can't do it."

"Come on, Gary. It's been five years since the last raise. You've coasted on their goodwill long enough."

Armistead sighed, chewed his lip, and then finally nodded.

Jesse wasn't quite ready to shake on it. "You sure the council will go along with that?"

"I can sell it as part of my new law-and-order initiative."

Jesse hated this part of the job. But it was part of the job. And he really wanted to get a new recruit on the force. The last one hadn't worked out that well. That was the main reason Peter finally retired.

And Jesse wanted to keep Suit.

"All right," he said. "You'll have everyone out there."

"In full uniform."

Jesse nodded. "In full uniform."

"And I want you inside the event, too. With Molly. The chief and the deputy chief."

"Why?"

"People like the two of you. God knows why. I want you there, showing your support. Smiling and shaking hands."

"You might need to throw in a new patrol vehicle for that."

"I'm serious. You can tell people old baseball stories or how you've killed bad guys. They love that shit."

"Okay. We'll be there."

"Good."

Armistead looked down at his desk and shuffled papers. Jesse assumed he was dismissed. He stood up, glad to be going back to doing something useful.

"Dress like a grown-up for once," Armistead said as Jesse walked to the door. "No polo shirt and ball cap. Wear a suit and tie. Molly, too."

"Not sure Molly owns a suit."

"You're not nearly as funny as you think."

"Yeah," Jesse said as he walked out. "I get that a lot."

SIXTEEN

The next week, Gabe and Suit were at the front door of the museum in full uniform. Gabe looked professional and bored. Suit looked more uncomfortable than usual in the stiff jacket.

"You all right there?" Jesse asked as he reached the entrance.

"Fine," Gabe said. Just his tone made Jesse feel a little bad. They all knew this was a waste of time.

But a deal was a deal.

"Everyone here?"

"Yeah," Suit said. "I put Jimmy and Barry inside the lobby. Dani and Brendan are in the room. Any dispatch calls will come to me, and Gabe will handle the door."

"Good," Jesse said. "Everywhere you turn, there's a cop."

"Yeah, well, I figured people would rather see them inside. They look better in their uniforms." Suit shifted back and forth on his feet, like a kid stuck in church.

"You sure you're okay, Suit?"

Suit leaned in. "I haven't worn this in years," he said quietly.

"Doesn't fit anymore?"

"It's a little tight," Suit admitted.

"I thought it was the mother who was supposed to gain weight during pregnancy."

Suit gave him a face. "Don't have too many appetizers, Jesse. That tux looks a little snug."

Jesse smiled and briefly gripped Suit's arm. Then he turned back to Rachel.

She smiled brilliantly at him.

"You ready for this?" she asked.

She really did look beautiful. Jesse felt like a lucky man.

"How bad could it be?" he said.

Rachel rolled her eyes at him, and they walked into the museum together.

IT WASN'T THAT bad. Not at first.

Jesse and Rachel made their way through a cluster of Paradise's first citizens in the lobby. Elizabeth Foley was there, and she gushed over Jesse's handling of the party to Rachel and to everyone else within twenty feet.

"Thugs and lowlifes," she said. "Hoodlums. And Jesse sent them all packing."

"I just told them you'd come after them next," Jesse said, and everyone laughed.

Jesse and Rachel moved into the next cluster, where Gary Armistead was holding court. He smiled and grabbed Jesse's hand like they were old friends. He tried to pull Jesse into a hug, but Jesse remained still, and Armistead gave up before any strain became noticeable. He settled for a selfie with Jesse and then elegantly dismissed him to greet another new arrival, spreading his good cheer around.

Rachel looked at Jesse, sizing him up. "You're not actually bad at this. You could even be a politician if you worked at it a little more."

"You really know how to hurt a guy."

"Good-looking, funny, a dedicated law enforcement officer . . . Some men have made it to the White House on less than that."

"I'm not sure I can be trusted with the nuclear codes."

Rachel laughed. "Absolutely not. You'd order a strike on the first guy who broke the speed limit in a school zone."

"You have to admit, it would solve most of our traffic problems."

They made their way into the main gallery of the museum. It was crowded, because the museum was not really meant for large events, just small, tasteful gatherings and little groups of tourists. This was considered a problem the fundraiser was supposed to solve. The money raised tonight—aside from the checks that went into Armistead's pocket—would pay for a renovation that would increase the size and square footage of the museum.

Jesse actually preferred it the way it was, but nobody asked him.

Everyone in the room was decked out in their best. When Paradise had an occasion like this, the citizens took the chance to remind one another that, collectively, they were the elite. Other people worked. They *owned*. The cost of the clothing in the room would have paid for his department's budget for two years, easily. Jesse noticed a woman wearing an emerald the size of a baby's fist, probably something that had been handed down in her family for more than a hundred years.

Molly was already inside. She looked lovely in a simple gown in pale purple. She also looked deeply uncomfortable and had a drink in one hand. She waved them over. Jesse got the feeling that for him, at least, it was not a request.

Molly and Rachel hugged. "One lunch and you two are best friends," Jesse said.

"You're just afraid I spilled all your secrets," Molly said.

"Well, yeah," Jesse said.

"Smart man," Molly said. "But I wish you'd run this whole thing past me before you cut your deal with Gary."

Jesse shrugged. "We need the money. We need the position filled."

"I know. I just hate it," Molly said. "I mean, I hate hate *hate* it."

"You made that clear."

"Is it that bad?" Rachel asked. "I mean, we all have to suck up to the boss sometimes."

"Molly doesn't," Jesse pointed out. "I can assure you of that."

"This *is* me sucking up," Molly said, and drained her drink. "You're lucky you never get the unfiltered version."

"I count my blessings every day."

Molly stuck her tongue out at him, lifted her glass again, and then realized it was empty. "It's not just the mayor," she said to Rachel. "It's giving him special treatment for Devlin. You know what that guy did. He literally stole from kids with cancer. He destroyed that church in Bakersfield. And that's not even the end of it. He's got a trail of carnage behind him. That man is a disease."

"Believe me, I know," Rachel said. "My kid has to deal with his son every day."

"See?" Molly said to Jesse. "Another reason we shouldn't be making deals with this creep."

"Maybe so," Jesse said. "But aside from driving drunk, we don't have anything on him. We're not the Feds. And I've been told I can't solve every problem by punching it in the face."

"What happened to the Jesse Stone I used to know?"

"He's growing up," Rachel said sweetly, and put her hand in Jesse's. Jesse actually felt quite proud of that.

Molly made a face like a teenager watching her parents kissing. "Ugh," she said. "You're a good influence on him and I want you to know I think it's terrible."

They all laughed, but Jesse nodded toward Molly's empty glass. "How many drinks is that, Molly?"

"It's not the last one, I can tell you that," Molly said. "This is on you, Jesse. You told me I had to be here."

She headed off in the direction of one of the bars. "You look very nice," Jesse said to her retreating back.

"You're damn right I do," she said, and merged into the crowd.

"That's not a great sign," Jesse said.

"Didn't you tell me she's much smarter than you? She'll be fine," Rachel said. "Now, I need to do some schmoozing myself." She pointed to a group including the hospital's administrator, decked out in a knockoff gown, and the chairwoman of its board, wearing the real thing.

"You go ahead. I'll get you a drink," Jesse said.

She raised an eyebrow. "You sure?"

He didn't take offense. An open bar was a minefield for any drunk. "I'm sure," he said.

She took him at his word. "Champagne, please. And come rescue me as soon as you get it."

Jesse promised and crossed the room to the bar. A different one than the one where Molly was headed, just in case.

ON HIS WAY, Jesse was sidetracked a couple times by people he knew and people who wanted to ask him about official business, but he finally made it.

He'd just ordered—champagne for Rachel, a club soda for him—when someone tapped him on the shoulder.

He turned to see Ramsey Devlin.

"Chief, I didn't think you were supposed to be drinking," he said, his face about 90 percent shit-eating grin.

Jesse took his club soda from the bartender and held it up.

"Ah, I see. Well, good for you, staying on that wagon," he said. He shoved a hundred-dollar bill into the tip jar and ordered a Macallan neat and a glass of champagne.

Jesse figured he was supposed to be intimidated that Devlin had learned he was an alcoholic. But one thing quitting had taught him was that it was better to live with his drinking in the past than it ever was living with it in the present.

Still, Jesse reminded himself to stay civil tonight, if only for the sake of the new department hire.

"I told you before, Ramsey. You can call me Jesse."

"See, I don't get that," Devlin said. "If I were the chief of police, I'd make everyone call me that. Hell, I'd make my wife and kid call me Chief."

The mention of his son reminded Jesse again of Jacob and the problems at school. "You know, I actually wanted to speak with you about your son, if you have a minute."

Devlin picked up his drink and the champagne flute. He downed half the scotch in a single gulp. He grunted and exhaled. "That's the stuff. Boy, I bet you miss it."

"Some moments more than others," Jesse said. "Anyway. About Race."

Devlin ignored him and gulped another drink. "I hear you played baseball."

"I did."

"Minor-leaguer, right? Never made it into the big show?"

"Yeah. That's right."

"That's a shame," Devlin said. "I imagine washing out like that, losing out on your biggest dream. That must keep you up at night."

Jesse heard Dix's voice in his head: *Don't let him provoke you. Let go of the rope.*

"So you're a baseball fan?" he asked.

"I admire excellence in all its forms," Devlin said. "I collect it. In my house, I keep a little trophy room. You should come by and check it out. See what you're missing. I have a jersey that Kobe Bryant wore. I have a game ball from the Super Bowl signed by Tom Brady. And I have Mark McGwire's sixty-ninth home run ball from right before he broke the single-season record."

"I would have thought you'd want the actual seventieth home run ball."

"Ah, some comic-book guy has that. Besides, sixty-nine is funnier. And it's still part of the legend. You must have watched when it happened."

"I did," Jesse said. "But he was on steroids at the time."

Devlin shrugged. "Doesn't matter. No such thing as cheating, as long as you win."

"I just thought that might lessen the resale value."

"Well," Devlin said, grinning again. "Even if it did, you'd never be able to afford it."

Jesse smiled back. "Good thing I don't collect other people's trophies."

Devlin's grin vanished. Jesse sipped his club soda.

"You're funny, you know that?" Devlin said.

"Tell my deputy chief. She doesn't think so."

"No, I don't mean ha-ha funny. I mean funny-strange," Devlin said. "I told you what I'm going to do to you. I mean, you have to know I was serious about that. Before I'm done, you're going to be ruined."

Jesse sighed. "Ramsey—"

"No, no," Devlin interrupted. "I'm not like you. You don't get to use my first name."

"You know," Jesse said. "We don't have to do this. We can just . . . let go of the rope."

Devlin laughed, and this time it sounded genuine. "Is that some faggoty New Age therapy shit? Sounds like loser talk to me."

Jesse really was doing his best to let go, but Devlin kept picking up the rope and throwing it at him. He tried again anyway.

"Look. You can live here happily in Paradise and never have to deal with me or my department again. Just stop talking like a James Bond villain and show a little courtesy to your neighbors. That's all it takes."

"That's all, huh? That's what you suggest?"

"That's right," Jesse said. "You'd be surprised how big an asshole you can be here without breaking the law."

Devlin lost any pretense of good humor. He looked like he was about to say something in reply when a stunning woman in a sleek silver dress joined him.

"Ramsey," she said. "I thought maybe you got lost on your way to bring me that champagne."

She turned toward Jesse without waiting for a response. "And you must be Chief Stone," she said, putting her hand forward. "I'm Janis Devlin."

Jesse took it. "A pleasure to meet you, Janis. Please call me Jesse."

"I'm so glad to meet you, too, Jesse, because I have been dying to ask you a question," she said, her smile bright and wide.

"Go ahead."

She leaned in close, giving him the full sparkle of her white teeth and big blue eyes. "Don't you have anything better to do in this shitty little town than to bother my husband?"

Jesse laughed. Her smile never faltered.

"I have plenty to do, Janis," he said. "I was just telling your husband we literally never have to speak again if he doesn't want that."

"Oh, I would love to believe that. But it seems like you're hell-bent on harassing him even at a fundraiser where—not to brag—we have agreed to put a million bucks into this dump."

"That's very generous," Jesse said.

"Isn't it, though?" Janis sipped her champagne. "I mean,

you'd think with all we're paying, we could qualify for better treatment from the town's rent-a-cop."

Jesse thought, all things considered, he'd rather have Devlin throw more punches at him than verbally spar with his wife.

At that moment, Rachel came to his rescue. "Why, Janis," she said happily. "So nice to see you again."

Janis looked momentarily lost. "I'm sorry, do we know each other?"

"Oh, that's right," Rachel said. "You don't know me. I'm Jacob's mother. You haven't been to any of the parent days at the school. Or the class presentations. Or the science fair, come to think of it. I always see Race there. Alone."

Janis's eyes went cold and hard. "I have better things to do with my time."

"Who doesn't?" Rachel said. "I mean, I literally save lives at my job, and God knows they need me there. But I try to show up for my son anyway."

"Oh, I know you now. You're that . . . doctor who keeps complaining about our son." She half turned to Devlin but kept her eyes on Rachel. "You remember, darling. The little crybaby who keeps whining about Race."

"Oh, is that what you wanted to talk about, Jesse?" Devlin said. "You going to arrest my kid because you can't touch me?"

"You think it's funny?" Rachel asked. "It's pretty clear that Race is picking up some dangerous ideas. It's not going to end anyplace good for him."

Devlin bristled at that. "My son is a winner. If your kid can't handle that, it's on him."

Rachel tried again. "Race is just a boy acting out right now. But it will get worse if it's not stopped."

"You just raise your kid, okay? We know how to raise ours."

"I sincerely hope that's true, Mrs. Devlin," Rachel said, her tone still courteous. "But it doesn't seem like you do."

She turned to Jesse. "You have my champagne?"

He gave it to her.

"Then let's move on," she said. "Well, this was lovely."

"I'm sure it was for you," Janis said.

"No," Rachel said. "I was lying. To be polite. If I were being honest, I'd tell you that everyone can see your thong through that dress and you have spinach in your teeth."

Janis's eyes went wide.

Jesse took Rachel's arm, and they walked away into the crowd.

"I thought you said fighting doesn't solve everything?"

"I did say that," Rachel admitted. "And I hope you noticed: I used my words instead of knocking that skank's teeth down her throat."

JESSE AND RACHEL got pulled into different conversations, and he lost her in the crowd. He wondered how long they'd have to stay. The room only got louder and more crowded as the night went on and the bartenders kept serving drinks.

Jesse really appreciated sobriety on nights like this: He got to see how he'd made a complete ass of himself before he quit.

Even the people who drank only socially became bigger, sloppier versions of themselves. They crossed lines. Jesse saw Brett Summerlin stare down Merilee Winthrop's low-cut dress to get a good look at her new implants. Paul Hailey accidentally shoved his wife into a table as he gestured while telling a story. Layla Kendrick berated her husband, Frank, in a corner, where she thought no one could see them.

The club soda went down a little easier after that.

Jesse was about to search for Rachel and make his exit. It was almost midnight, and he'd reached his limit on small talk for the next six months.

Then he heard something crash to the floor and voices raised in anger.

Jesse's eyes immediately found Brendan Murphy and Dani Collins, the uniforms Suit had put inside the room. They were already on alert, moving through the crowd toward the disturbance.

Jesse moved in the same direction, people automatically parting in front of him as he went. He had his small backup piece, a Glock .32, in a concealed-carry holster under his jacket. But he'd rather not pull it here and start a panic.

Then he stopped when he saw the source of the noise.

Molly Crane was standing in front of Ramsey Devlin, a tray of spilled drinks on the floor near them.

And to one side, a young waitress looked down, ashamed and embarrassed.

"You clumsy *bitch*," Devlin spat at the waitress. "You did that on purpose!"

"I am really sorry, sir," the waitress said, her face bright red, eyes still stuck on the floor. "I will pay for the cleaning."

Jesse could guess what was happening. He was relieved it was nothing he'd need the Glock for.

But even as he waved off Brendan and Dani, he worried things might escalate. Most people probably wouldn't have been able to tell, but Molly was drunk. She still carried herself well, but Jesse could see the difference between her usual self-control and the deliberate effort she made now.

"What did you just say to her?" Molly demanded, her voice carrying loud and clear through the room.

Devlin, however, was too busy wiping at the front of his tux with one of the ridiculous little cocktail napkins to pay attention to Molly.

Jesse recognized the girl now. She was one of the kids from the same class as Molly's youngest daughter. Barely into her twenties. Jesse couldn't recall her name, but Molly thought of all of her daughters' classmates as part of her extended family. She'd known them since they were kindergarteners.

"You absolutely *will not* pay for the cleaning," Molly said. She smacked the napkin out of Devlin's hand, forcing him to look up at her.

"And you," Molly said to Devlin. "You will apologize for the horrible thing you just said."

"Jesus Christ," Devlin said, the familiar smarmy grin back on his face now. "Is this how you people police this town? You want to arrest me for my language?"

Everyone in the museum was riveted. This was quality entertainment right here. People would be talking about it for months—maybe all the way until next summer.

Molly took a step closer to Devlin. "Look, you might be able to lie and cheat and steal your way everywhere else, but you are absolutely not going to speak that way to this young woman here—"

Jesse stepped over to the conflict. Gary Armistead got

there at the same time and, unfortunately, started talking first.

"Okay, okay, let's all just take a minute here. Molly, I think you need to step back and maybe reconsider your tone."

Oh, no, Jesse thought. *Armistead, you idiot.*

"My tone?" Molly said. "Gary, I know you've got your nose up this guy's ass, but don't expect the rest of us to pretend it smells like roses, too."

A lot of people in the room laughed at that. Jesse tried not to join in.

Because he could see the hate in Devlin's eyes. This was deadly serious to him.

"Gary, you better get your people under control," he said, his voice trembling.

Jesse inserted his body into the middle of the group. If anything was coming, he figured he could be a human shield. He looked at Armistead, hoping to God the mayor wouldn't make things worse.

No such luck. "Absolutely, Ramsey," Armistead said. "Crane, you are out of line."

"Oh, for Christ's sake," Molly said. "He's a thief and a con man, Gary. I think he's heard worse."

"Molly," Jesse said, trying to keep his body between her and Devlin.

But Devlin didn't throw a punch or lunge at her. He got very still and waited for the laughter to die down so he could speak in the quiet that followed.

"No wonder your husband spends all his time in a boat on the other side of the world," he said. "If I were him, I'd fucking drown myself."

Molly's eyes went cold. She took a step forward. Jesse turned so he could keep her from making a big mistake.

But she slipped under his arm and took another step toward Devlin, her fists clenched.

Devlin saw the look on her face and took a quick step back.

Molly threw her drink instead of a punch.

It hit Devlin right in the face, blinding him. His foot came down on the puddle of champagne behind him. And slid out from under him, immediately dumping him on his ass.

It was the perfect slapstick ending to the whole farce. The entire room roared with laughter.

Except for Devlin, Armistead, and Jesse.

Devlin because he was furious, his jaw clenched and his face beet-red with rage as he tried to slip and slide his way back to his feet.

Armistead because he was angry, too, his mouth pinched with worry as he glared at Jesse with a look that said *This is all your fault.*

And Jesse wasn't laughing because he knew everything had just gotten so much worse.

SEVENTEEN

Jesse woke early the next morning, showered and dressed, then made a pot of extra-strong coffee and poured it into a thermos. He drove downtown and stopped at Daisy's for turnovers, then turned around and drove back to Molly's house.

He had a key, just like she had a key to his place. He let himself in, pretty confident she would not be awake yet.

He was right. He made it into the kitchen and poured the coffee into two cups without any sound coming from her bedroom. He was able to get all the way to her side of the bed, coffee cups in hand, before she opened one eye to look at him.

"Oh, God," she said. "For a minute I thought you were here to shoot me."

Jesse put the coffee down on the nightstand. "Nope. Just coffee."

She hauled herself upright, then groaned. "Did you make it?"

"I did."

"I might want the bullet instead."

She took the cup anyway and sipped at it. Jesse then placed three Advil on the nightstand. She took those, too.

He noticed Michael's side of the bed was empty, still neatly made, the sheets tucked in tight. Even when he was gone on one of his ocean voyages, Molly stuck to her side.

He'd been traveling more and more lately, but Jesse didn't ever bring that up.

He pulled over a chair she kept in the room for Michael to hang his clothes on and sat down.

"I brought food from Daisy. Turnovers."

She gave him a hard look.

"Maybe later, then."

Molly closed her eyes again. "God. I feel like death. I do not know how you did this for all that time."

"Well, I had you to take care of me."

"I can't imagine you ever felt this bad."

"You get used to it."

"I sincerely hope not." She sipped coffee. Then winced. "Oh, God."

"Starting to come back to you?"

"In big, bright flashes."

"So what was that about last night?"

"Do I need to have a reason? Like my dad was ripped off by scammers and we didn't have Christmas one year? Well, he wasn't. I just can't stand con artists. Liars who steal from people by preying on their hope and their trust."

"And their greed, don't forget greed."

"Kids with cancer, Jesse. He emptied a teachers' pension fund. He destroyed lives, like that dumb kid you arrested.

And then he spoke that way to a girl I've known since she was five years old. He's lucky I only threw a drink in his face."

"Don't worry about it right now."

"I'm not worried. I should have slapped the son of a bitch."

"See, it took me a lot longer to get to the level of belligerent drunk."

"Ah, bite me."

"There you go."

"I mean it, Jesse. Go ahead and suspend me."

"I'm not suspending you. Don't be an idiot. Armistead will calm down. Just avoid him for a while."

"Oh, I plan to," Molly said. "I have a crapload of vacation time coming. Here's my official notice. I'm taking it."

"Right now?"

"Starting today. Just as soon as I can get out of bed."

"You might want to take it easy for a while. Takes practice to ride out what you did to yourself last night."

"I'll be fine. Just need to gather my strength," Molly said.

Jesse sipped his coffee. "You sound like you've decided on something."

"Maybe."

"You want to let me in on it?"

She thought about it. "Not yet."

"Any reason why?"

"Then you don't have to pretend you don't know what I'm doing when someone asks," Molly said. "No offense, Jesse, but you're a terrible liar."

"I'm not that bad at it. I just rarely see the point of lying."

"Same difference."

"So you're going to do something I might need to cover

up? You plan on going after someone? Like, say, our newest resident asshole?"

"No. At least, not like you're thinking. I'm not going to hurt anyone. Well. Not the way you're thinking."

"That doesn't really comfort me."

She opened her eyes again and gave him a too-sweet smile. "That's because you don't know if I mean it or not," she said. "See? That's what I mean by being a good liar."

"Molly," Jesse said. He waited until she looked him in the eye.

"I don't want to hear it, Jesse. I've covered for you for years, the least you can do is trust me on this—"

"I was just going to say, whatever happens, you know I have your back. There's nothing you could do that would change that. Nothing at all."

"You mean that, huh? You don't even know what I'm going to do?"

"If you do it, it's probably the right thing."

Molly pressed her lips together and looked away. "Damn it, I hate being hungover. You get all emotional about the stupidest stuff."

"Yeah, I remember."

She sniffed loudly, then looked back at him. "This doesn't make us even, you know. I cleaned up way more of your messes. I counted them all up somewhere."

"I know," Jesse said.

"You going to be okay on your own? I can stick around for a bit if you want."

"I can handle it."

"Don't do that thing where you try to take care of everything alone. Don't be afraid to ask for help. You're not Batman."

Jesse looked a little offended. "I could be Batman."

"I'm just saying: You've got Suit, you've got Gabe. They'll back you up," Molly said. "And please. If anyone is Batman around here, it's me."

Molly took another drink of her coffee, then began to sit upright.

"You're going to want to eat something," Jesse said.

"No. Possibly never again."

"Well, you say that, but when the acid from that coffee hits your stomach . . ."

Molly's eyes snapped open and she hopped out of bed, shoving past Jesse on her way to the bathroom.

"See, that's what I was talking about."

EIGHTEEN

Jesse went back to Daisy's for lunch after a morning at the station, where he filed Molly's approval for vacation. She'd earned it, and he didn't want anyone—well, Armistead—saying he hadn't done things through proper channels.

He read the paper. An actual physical newspaper. It wasn't that Jesse didn't know how to read it on his phone. He just didn't like it.

Then Ramsey Devlin entered.

Everyone turned and looked, first at him, then at Jesse.

Jesse clocked him the minute his McLaren pulled up outside, of course. The car was guaranteed to attract attention.

But Jesse kept his eyes fixed on the paper until Devlin stood right at his table.

"Hello, Jesse," Devlin said, giving Jesse's name an extra little twist, like they were both still in high school. "Got a minute to talk?"

Using his foot, Jesse pushed out a chair on the opposite side of the table.

"Sure," he said. "Have a seat."

Devlin sat down. He looked right at Jesse. Jesse had been mad-dogged by scarier people.

"You want something to eat? Coffee?"

Devlin snickered. "This won't take that long. I want you to know, if you don't fire that bitch—"

Jesse put down the paper and was suddenly, quickly, very close to Devlin's face.

"I know you're not talking about Molly," he said. "Because if you were using that word about Molly, this conversation would be over a lot quicker than you think."

Devlin sat back. It took him a moment to pick up where he'd left off.

"As I was saying, if you don't fire your deputy chief for her assault on me in public, I am going to sue the Paradise Police Department and the Town of Paradise—"

"Go ahead," Jesse said.

"What?"

"Whatever you're going to do, do it. I'm not going to fire Molly. Or anything else you want me to do. You might as well get started. It's going to save us both time."

Devlin looked impressed. "You really don't give a fuck, do you? You're ready for a fight."

"Actually, I'm ready for lunch. You going to get to the point anytime soon?"

"You really play the good guy well," Devlin said. "But you're not a good guy."

"Never said I was."

"Oh, but I bet you think it. See, that's the one thing I do better than almost anyone: I read people. That's how I got rich. I mean, sure, I'm good at the math, and I can predict the market as well as anyone—"

"Modest, too," Jesse said.

"—but mainly, all investment comes down to sales, and sales all comes down to one thing: knowing people. Who they really are. I watch what they do, not what they say. That's how you know a person. Like you. I have you all figured out, Stone."

"I should have you talk to my therapist. He'd love to hear this."

Devlin ignored that. He preferred talking to listening.

"Like the other night at my place," he said. "During the party. I wondered why you tossed that bat to that dumb fuck, Ashcraft. I mean, why would you give a guy like that an advantage? I thought you'd have to be smarter than that."

"Guess you were wrong."

"No," Devlin said. "I wasn't. Because you already knew what he would do. He'd take a swing. And you already had your baton ready to go. You gave him a deadly weapon so you could justify the use of force. You planned the whole thing."

Jesse just looked at Devlin for a moment. "You think I wanted a three-hundred-pound former NFL lineman to swing at me with a baseball bat?"

"See? It sounds crazy. But you made it work for you."

"Just one problem with that plan," Jesse said. "Clayton could have spoiled the whole thing by backing off and putting the bat down."

"Surrender? Not on your life. You know a big meathead jock like that can't resist a challenge. It's how alpha males like us are wired. We take it to the limit. We never back down."

"Is that how you see yourself? How you see this—I don't know what you want to call it—conflict between us?" Jesse really wanted to know.

"Yeah. Don't you?"

Jesse told the truth: "To be completely honest, Devlin, when you're not right in front of me, I try not to think about you at all."

All the delight went out of Devlin's face.

"Let me ask you a question," Jesse said. "I wanted to talk about this at the party, but, you know, you were busy falling on your ass."

Devlin scowled. "What do you want to know?"

"I was wondering, why would your kid think swastikas and other Nazi shit is cool?"

"No idea what you're talking about, Chief."

"I just wanted to ask, because he keeps drawing them on the homework of my girlfriend's son. He had to get the idea somewhere."

Devlin smirked. "Who can say where kids pick up stuff now? The Internet, you know."

Jesse leaned forward again. "Can we cut the crap for a second? What do you think this is going to do to your son? Do you think this is going to be good for him?"

Devlin struggled to look innocent. It wasn't an expression he was good at. "I don't know what you mean."

"I think you do," Jesse said. "He's a seven-year-old boy, Ramsey. He probably thinks his dad is the greatest guy alive.

So when I see him doing this stupid, obscene shit, I know he's got to be doing it to impress you. I just don't think you realize the damage you're doing to him."

"Please," Devlin said. "Kids bully each other all the time. It's nothing."

"You really believe that? You think this is just another insult, like calling someone names? Do you have any idea where the swastika comes from? What it stands for? It's a symbol that was built on bodies and blood, Ramsey. It's an infection, and you're willingly exposing your kid to it."

Devlin looked at him blankly. He didn't know or care. It simply didn't register. It bounced off him completely.

Jesse tried one more time. "You're teaching him to hate. Where do you think that ends up?"

"I'll tell you what I've taught my kid," Devlin said. "You use any tool to get what you want and any weapon against the people who get in your way. They're going to be stuck with their beliefs and their ethics. There's always things they won't do, lines they won't cross. And that's why we win and they lose."

Jesse was pretty sure Devlin had practiced that line in the mirror.

Devlin stood up and nodded, looking satisfied. "See you in court, Jesse."

He turned to go.

"Ramsey," Jesse said.

Devlin looked back at him.

"I know you think you know who I am. You don't," Jesse said. "But you keep pulling this crap, you're going to find out."

Devlin looked uncomfortable. Then his face lit up and he yelled, "Don't you dare threaten me, Jesse! I don't care if you are the chief of police, you still have to follow the law! You don't scare me!"

He stomped out of Daisy's.

Jesse wondered for a minute why he put on the performance.

Then he saw everyone in the café looking at him.

Oh, Jesse realized. *That's why.*

NINETEEN

"He intends to sue," Gary Armistead said, tossing down a sheaf of papers on his desk. He stood behind it, nostrils flared, glaring at Jesse.

Jesse sat in the visitor's chair in Armistead's office and tried to look appropriately concerned. He wasn't doing a very good job.

He picked up the papers and scanned them. Devlin's lawyer, Wilkes, had put it together very quickly. Lots of intimidating legalese on his firm's letterhead. But nothing Jesse hadn't seen before. Jesse was familiar with lawsuits. He'd been threatened by much scarier people. Wilkes didn't even make the top fifty.

"Okay," Jesse finally said.

"That's it?"

"What do you want me to say, Gary? The guy was out of line. I know he's your new best friend, but you've known Molly for years. Whose side are you on?"

Armistead flushed red but ignored the dig. "We're not talking about me."

"He was an asshole. And he's lucky Molly didn't deck him."

"Molly was drunk."

Jesse shrugged. "It was a party. You insisted she attend."

"She was inebriated on duty. You might have gotten away with that for years, but I'm not going to let your whole department use it as an excuse."

Jesse took a deep breath. "I had my problems. Molly made a onetime mistake. They're not the same thing."

"I want her suspended. On administrative leave. Whatever the hell you call it. Without pay."

"Going to be hard to do that."

"I don't want to hear any excuses, Jesse."

"She's on vacation."

"What?"

"She had a bunch of PTO coming. She decided to take it."

"Goddamn it. And you let her?"

"You just said you wanted her suspended."

"I want her punished. Not out taking a spa day or whatever."

Jesse smiled at him. "I think she's going to be gone longer than a day. She's got months of vacation time built up."

"How did you let that happen?"

"I think I've mentioned our staffing issues. Several times."

Armistead sat back down heavily in the chair, his jaw clenched. "You think this is funny, don't you? Enjoying yourself?"

"I've had worse mornings," Jesse admitted.

"I am trying to head off a disaster here, Jesse. You think

your budget is tight now? Imagine what it'll be like if we have to ask the good people of Paradise for a tax increase or a bond measure to pay off a multimillion-dollar lawsuit."

"She threw a drink in his face."

"While she was acting in her official capacity as deputy chief."

"He had it coming."

Armistead laughed. "Yeah. Let's see how that stands up in court."

"How much of this is you worrying about the town, and how much of this is you worrying about your contributions from Devlin?"

Jesse expected Armistead to explode again, but instead he smiled. "In this case, they're the same thing. If Devlin's happy, Paradise is fine. If he's not, we're in trouble."

"You really that scared of him?"

Armistead rubbed his eyes. "Jesse, I know you lack the part of your brain that enables you to see a threat when it's staring you right in the face. But yes, I am worried about the angry multimillionaire with nothing but free time on his hands. I would rather have him look for other hobbies than sue the shit out of us."

Jesse had to admit that was a pretty good point. But keeping the citizens of Paradise happy wasn't Jesse's job. He was just supposed to keep them safe.

"Gary, no offense, but you wanted to be mayor," Jesse said. "You're supposed to handle guys like Devlin. I only deal with these people when they break the law."

"Well, Jesse, that's actually what I'm trying to do here. I was hoping the suspension would be enough to satisfy him. Toss him a little red meat."

"No, that's like cutting off your arm to feed a shark. He'll come back for more."

Armistead actually looked impressed. "Damn, Jesse. For you, that's almost poetry."

"I'm not firing Molly."

"Then I'll do it."

Jesse made sure his voice was level and controlled when he spoke again. "You prepared to get in a patrol car and police the whole town yourself?" he said. "Because we will walk. All of us."

Armistead looked at him carefully, measuring. "You're bluffing."

"Try me," Jesse said. "You fire Molly, you might as well start putting up want ads for a whole new department. Not a single person will remain on the job. I can guarantee that."

Armistead smirked, as if he'd found pocket aces in a poker game. "Suit has a baby on the way," he said.

There really were no secrets in Paradise, Jesse thought.

"Where did you hear that?"

"I play golf with his wife's OB-GYN."

"I'll tell them to get a new one."

"Either way, you think they can afford a kid on a teacher's salary?"

"Suit has offers. He'll be fine. He'll be second out the door, right after me."

"Your other people have obligations, too. Child support. Alimony."

"You think that matters? Compared to what we all owe Molly? You think you're going to win reelection if the entire police force quits?"

They stared each other down across the desk. Stalemate.

Armistead looked away first. "I have to give him something, Jesse. He will tear this town apart if I don't."

Jesse looked at the ceiling and thought for a second. He knew Armistead was right. It was all about ego with these guys. Armistead and Devlin. Everyone like them. Usually men, but he knew women like that, too. Win at all cost, because if you don't, you have to think of yourself as a loser. And then the whole wall of your ego, your *self*, comes tumbling down. Nothing matters so much as keeping that wall standing.

Jesse knew this because there had been times in his life when he was that guy as well. So what do you give a guy like that?

Again, he thought about what Dix said before. He could almost hear the shrink's voice in his head: *What if you let go of the rope?*

"How about I apologize?" Jesse said.

Armistead actually looked surprised. "Seriously?"

"Yeah. Give him a victory. Tell him I'm sorry. He can tell everyone he made me grovel or whatever helps him feel better. But he gets the win. Without any actual admission of liability. Or any money."

And, though he didn't say this out loud, it wouldn't cost Jesse a thing. Not really.

He could go back to his job, and Molly could go back to hers. And they could both get on with the real work: keeping Paradise safe.

Armistead looked at Jesse like he suspected some kind of trick. "You'd really do that?"

"Why not?"

"Well . . . because then he'd *win*."

Jesse smiled and shrugged. He knew he had Armistead figured right. Which meant he was right about Devlin, too.

Jesse suddenly got it. Now he knew what Dix meant. You're struggling and straining in a game of tug-of-war, and the other guy is pulling as hard as he can. But if you let go, then he just . . . falls on his ass. And you're still standing.

"Honestly, Gary," he said. "Who gives a damn?"

TWENTY

Armistead negotiated the meeting like the surrender of a foreign power. Jesse was supposed to go up to Devlin's ugly concrete house and make a show of delivering his formal apology for Molly's behavior.

And then, after that, Devlin promised not to sue. He'd even sign a formal release of any claim against the department and the Town of Paradise for his arrest when Jesse had found him drunk behind the wheel.

Jesse had insisted on that last part. He didn't want to bend the knee to Devlin just to have the moneyman turn around and file a lawsuit anyway.

Jesse parked his Explorer on Seaside. The gate to the big, ugly house was open, unlike on the night of the party. Jesse figured that Devlin didn't want anything to slow him down on his way to the ritual humiliation.

The thing was, Jesse didn't really care. Honestly. He'd searched his soul for irritation or anger at this move by Armistead and Devlin, and couldn't find any. Which puzzled him a little. He'd gotten a lot angrier in his life about a lot less. And he'd had times when he'd refused to budge from a position even if it meant pain and suffering for him down the line.

But this . . . This just didn't seem to matter that much to him. There were fights worth fighting. This wasn't one of them. If an apology would protect Molly and the department, then Jesse figured his ego could take the hit. Devlin cared about this a lot more than Jesse did.

Maybe Jesse was learning, like Dix said. Maybe he was even maturing. Growing up.

Okay, maybe that was going a little too far. But still. Jesse was willing to give Devlin the win, if that's what it took to end this.

He waited at the front entrance for a full three minutes before he rang the bell again. Again, there was no answer. That's when Jesse noticed that the big swinging door, which went all the way to the top of the vaulted eaves at the entry, was slightly ajar.

Jesse wasn't sure if this was a mistake—the door was big and ridiculously heavy, it could easily be left open by someone who didn't put their back into closing it—or something worse.

He usually suspected something worse.

Jesse snapped on the blue nitrile gloves he always kept in his pocket to avoid contaminating a crime scene. He pushed the door open. It swung inside. No alarm beeped. It remained open, too heavy to swing shut again on its own.

Jesse didn't like this at all.

He remembered that Devlin had lost a lot of money belonging to a lot of people, and that at least one kid—a good, churchgoing Boy Scout—had been angry enough to come after him with a gun.

Jesse took his sidearm from his holster. Rather than call out and reveal his presence, he stepped through the door quickly and moved to the side of the wall.

The interior of the house was completely lit up. No shadows where anyone could hide. The foyer opened into a great room. That extended into a dining area and kitchen that could have fed a Marine battalion. Apparently Devlin's architects didn't like the idea of walls. Every space ran into the next, until Jesse saw a hallway leading deeper into the house.

Moving quietly, he walked down the hall.

He knew that Devlin would probably have a heart attack if he saw Jesse stalking through his house with a gun. But if Devlin was in trouble, then it was Jesse's job to protect him, no matter what he thought about the guy personally. Jesse had walked into enough shoot-outs to know he'd rather feel stupid with a gun in his hand than feel stupid for not having one.

Jesse checked the bathroom off the corridor. Small for the house. It was only as big as his condo's living room. But no one could hide in there. It was done in blinding white tile and marble. Jesse briefly pitied the staff that had to keep it clean. He couldn't imagine Devlin would have chosen the color scheme if he'd ever had to mop his own floors.

Jesse moved on and found a man cave at the end of the corridor, a combination den and office with a poker table and massive TV screens. Leather couches and chairs were arranged around the room. There was a massive desk in front of a wall covered with tributes to Devlin's ego: photos of him with politicians, celebrities, and athletes; plaques and awards; framed headlines and portraits.

On the desk, on its own stand, was the baseball, McGwire's number sixty-nine, that Devlin had bragged about. And on the desk itself, Devlin's motto, CUI BONO, carved into the front with the Devlin logo.

But Jesse's attention was mostly on the expensive rug. It stretched across half the floor, interwoven with a pattern of large dollar signs and cryptocurrency symbols. It must have been custom-made and cost a fortune.

It had been completely ruined by the large pool of blood soaking into it.

The blood looked fresh, but there was no one around.

Jesse moved to the spot, checking behind the furniture, waiting for someone to jump out.

The room was as empty as the rest of the house.

Kneeling down, he tested the edge of the stain with one gloved finger. It was fresh but not warm. And rapidly congealing. Which meant that whoever lost this much blood was not here, and had not been here for a while.

It was a mystery. Someone bleeding this badly shouldn't have been able to walk away without leaving a trail. Unless someone else had taken them away.

Jesse didn't have any more time to think about it.

A woman entered the room and immediately began screaming.

It was Devlin's wife, Janis.

And she kept shrieking, over and over, "What did you do to him?"

JESSE CALLED DEV Chada, the medical examiner, and Suit and the State Homicide Division from outside Devlin's man cave. Mainly because Janis Devlin began hitting him when he tried to speak to her, and wouldn't stop until he'd retreated from the room.

He wished Molly were there. He could have used her. For that matter, he would have liked to see Peter on the job again. Peter Perkins was always good at reading a crime scene, and this one didn't make a lot of sense to Jesse. That one bloodstain, in the center of the room, like it was waiting for him.

But Jesse had to make do with what he had. He was sure Dev would figure it out.

He was surprised, then, when Ellis Munroe stepped into the Devlin house before Dev arrived—even before Suit could get there.

"Ellis," Jesse said. "What are you doing here?"

Ellis looked annoyed, and Jesse knew he'd gotten off on the wrong foot. Ellis still liked to think of himself as the chief law enforcement officer in Paradise.

"Janis Devlin called Gary," Ellis said. "Gary thought I should come over. And take charge of the scene until the State Homicide guys get here. You know. Because of your history with the victim."

"What victim?" Jesse asked. "You mean Devlin?"

"Who else would it be? This is his house."

"Ellis, we don't even know if there's been a crime yet."

"Janis says there's a giant pool of blood in the den."

"I don't know that I would call it 'giant.'"

Ellis narrowed his eyes at Jesse. That's how Jesse knew it was probably not a good time to try to lighten the mood.

"Just stay here," Ellis said. "I'll go talk to her."

"I need to do my job," Jesse said. "If Devlin is hurt, or missing, then I need to get to work."

"Jesse, please," Ellis said, his face pained. "You know she's not going to want to talk to you, right? Let me speak to her first. Maybe I can get something coherent out of her. And save you some time."

Jesse didn't like it. But given how Janis had reacted, he didn't know that he had much choice.

"All right," he said, and it felt like a surrender.

"Thank you," Ellis said, and went down the hallway.

Jesse couldn't make out the actual conversation. Janis began by screaming again at Ellis, but soon he managed to get her talking. He did hear the words "that son of a bitch." He assumed that she was referring to him. After that, they spoke in normal tones, with only occasional obscenities from Janis.

It was taking Ellis a long time to return. Jesse was about to go down the hallway himself when Brian Lundquist, the State Homicide Division chief, showed up.

"Jesse," he said, shaking Jesse's hand but not quite looking him in the eye.

Again, Jesse was surprised. Lundquist ordinarily would not show up for something like this. It was clearly Jesse's jurisdiction and the state crime scene team knew how to do their jobs without him. Dev Chada would handle any details that Jesse couldn't.

But Lundquist was there anyway.

Which finally got Jesse to understand what was going on.

"Janis isn't going to cooperate with Paradise PD on this, is she?"

"She doesn't want you here," Lundquist said. "You had a history with her husband, right?"

"I arrested him for drunk driving. And broke up a party here last week."

"But that's not all, is it?" Lundquist gave him a look.

Jesse stared right back. He and Lundquist had never been friends, not the way Jesse was with his predecessor, Healy. But they'd worked together well, and they respected each other.

At least Jesse thought so, before Lundquist came in tonight.

"What exactly are you asking me, Brian?" Jesse said.

"Come on, Jesse. The wife says you and her husband have been locking horns since you met. Sounds like a personal conflict."

"Yeah, I can see how you'd think that. What I'm wondering is where you heard it."

Lundquist had the decency to look uncomfortable. "We got a call."

"From?"

"Armistead. He said the wife might be upset by your presence."

"So you want me to let her run the investigation?"

"Jesse, come on."

"Is that how we do it now? Did it occur to you that she might be a suspect in whatever has happened here?"

"What did happen here, Jesse? You want to tell me?"

"I don't know," Jesse said, biting off each word. "I haven't even looked at the crime scene because she went berserk until I left the room."

Lundquist put up both hands. "Hey, I'm just trying to smooth the way a little here. Ellis and I can handle the questioning and do the preliminary work until the technicians get here."

"Where's Dev?"

Again, Lundquist looked away. "He's not available tonight."

"Right," Jesse said.

And turned away from Lundquist and walked down the hallway.

"Jesse," Lundquist said. But didn't stop him.

Inside the den, Jesse found Ellis comforting Janis Devlin, kneeling by her side as she sat on one of the couches.

"You're disturbing the scene, Ellis," he said. "And you need to get her out of here."

Janis stood up, her face instantly contorted and red. "I will not be ordered around my own house by this man, Ellis!" she shouted. "I told you, I saw him—"

"Janis, please," Ellis said, sounding like he was begging, struggling to his feet.

"Ellis, I'm not going to tell you again," Jesse said.

"You son of a bitch!" Janis said, and began stalking toward Jesse.

Ellis managed to intercept her and, as Jesse watched, herded her out of the room, half pushing, half carrying her, as she shouted curses at Jesse.

Most of them were insults, but one of the phrases leapt out at him. "I know you did it!" she yelled. "I know what you did!"

Jesse took a deep breath as soon as she was gone. Lundquist entered the room just after she went down the hallway.

"This is unbelievably screwed up," Jesse told him. "The scene's been compromised. She needs to be questioned. And we need a forensic detail in here."

"All the more reason you should step back and let me and Ellis handle this, Jesse," he said. "It's pretty clear that you're not going to get cooperation from her."

"I don't care what grudges Janis Devlin is carrying," Jesse said. "This is still my town and my case. I'm going to do the job."

"I'm not sure that's a great idea," Lundquist said.

Jesse couldn't understand why Lundquist, who was a good cop, was being so uncertain. Or why he was giving Janis such a free pass.

But he didn't let it stop him from surveying the crime scene. He saw, for the first time, a broken window on the side of the room facing the ocean. It extended from floor to ceiling, framing the sea like a picture.

Jesse looked at the pool of blood again, now completely soaked into the fiber of the rug. But no tracks. No visible blood spatter on the walls or any of the furniture. And most important, no weapon that could have caused the injury.

Jesse also saw some of the items in the room on the floor, in disarray—books from the shelves scattered, a laptop computer by the desk, a bowl of chips knocked over. Jesse assumed that this wasn't normal, but he'd seen Devlin at a party, so maybe the man was just a slob.

Ellis returned to the room. He spoke to Lundquist first. "Brian, would you please go interview Mrs. Devlin? She's willing to talk now."

"How kind of her," Jesse said.

"You're lucky she hasn't called her lawyer, Jesse," Ellis snapped. "Then how much information you think we're going to get from her?"

Lundquist looked at Jesse. "At least this way we get a statement, okay?"

"Sure," Jesse said. "Go ahead."

Jesse and Ellis both waited until Lundquist left the room.

"Why is he here, Ellis?" Jesse said.

"You know why," Ellis shot back. "You can't be trusted to view this case impartially."

Jesse shook his head. "You know that's crap. I have run investigations into a lot of people here in Paradise who have grudges against me."

"What if you're the one carrying the grudge, Jesse?"

Jesse didn't bother to reply to that. "What do you think is happening here? Because it's pretty clear you've got some idea. You're just not telling me."

"I took a look around while you were outside," Ellis said. "This looks staged to me."

Jesse tried to keep any tone out of his voice. "Staged?"

"Yeah. Like someone wanted us to think this was a break-in."

"Why do you think that?"

"There's a broken window but no glass on the inside," Ellis said. "Which means it's on the outside. Whatever broke the glass did it from in here, not out there. That's clearly someone trying to make this look like a break-in."

"Or—and hear me out—someone just broke the window from inside," Jesse said. "There could be other explanations."

"Like what?"

"Like Devlin was having a fight with Janis and he threw something. Or his kid was in the room and tossed a video game controller at the window when he lost. Or Devlin was drunk and ran into the glass."

"All of those explanations are pretty unflattering to the whole Devlin family."

"Yeah, well. I've met them."

"Mrs. Devlin said the window was unbroken when she left earlier to go shopping in Boston."

"Which, even if you discount her as a possible suspect in this case, doesn't mean anything. Whatever happened here, it obviously happened when she was gone."

"You think she's a suspect?"

"You don't?" Jesse could not keep the disbelief out of his voice any longer. "Ellis, you know that when there's violence against a husband or wife, the spouse is always the most likely suspect. That's if this wasn't an accident. Or a suicide attempt. There are too many possible explanations to narrow it down to one explanation yet."

"Right," Ellis said. "Because you'd know so much more about what a crime scene should look like. Because you've seen so many."

Jesse didn't understand that statement. Or the tone Ellis had used to deliver it.

"Yeah," Jesse said. "I do know that."

"So tell me what you see here, Jesse." He crossed his arms and stared at Jesse, waiting.

Again, Jesse didn't understand the sudden change in Ellis's demeanor. But he wouldn't let it get in the way of the job.

"I see signs of a struggle, and maybe some attempts to clean up afterward. There's a broken window, which could be someone trying to indicate a break-in, sure, but it's more likely that there was something thrown or someone shoved against it from inside. Maybe Devlin and Janis fought. Maybe he fell and cut himself. Maybe he was drunk and didn't realize it until he was bleeding over here."

"Or that's what someone *wants* us to think," Ellis said. "An intruder, making this look like an accident."

"Sure," Jesse said. "I even thought that at first. Devlin has enemies. He lost a lot of people a lot of money. But looking at this, I don't see it. How would someone get into this place without triggering an alarm? Or being seen on one of the security cameras?"

"You seem pretty determined to look at this as something the Devlins did, Jesse," Ellis said. "Something they caused, instead of something that was done *to* them."

"Yeah. That seems most likely."

"Based on the crime scene. Which you know because, again, you know how they're *supposed* to look."

Jesse realized Ellis was using his courtroom voice. He'd slipped into the tone he used when he was making an argument.

"Ellis, what are you trying to say? I thought we were past this kind of petty bullshit."

Jesse and Ellis used to fight all the time, back when Ellis was trying to convince Jesse that he was Jesse's boss.

"I did, too," Ellis said. He looked a little sad, Jesse thought. But it was gone in a moment.

"Wait a minute," Jesse said. "You're not taking what Janis said seriously, are you?"

Ellis didn't reply.

"Give me a break," Jesse said. "She was looking for someone to blame. That's all."

"Everyone knows you and Devlin didn't get along, Jesse.

He was trying to get you fired, and from what Gary tells me, this time it was going to stick. And he was threatening Molly. Everyone knows how far you'd go to protect a friend."

"I was here to apologize," Jesse said. "You can ask Gary."

"Mrs. Devlin said she saw you with your gun out and your hand in the pool of blood. Gloves on. Is that how you apologize?"

"I came in to what looked like a break-in," Jesse said. "The door was open. I didn't know if there was an intruder in the house."

"Where's Ramsey Devlin, Jesse?" Ellis asked.

"How should I know?"

"It looks like you were the last person who would have seen him."

Jesse finally understood what Ellis was saying. He had been slow on the uptake because he simply couldn't imagine Ellis believing anything so insane before.

But now it was quite clear.

Jesse was amazed how quickly the rage came back to him, after all his best efforts to move on, to get past his anger. How familiar it seemed, like an old friend.

His fists clenched and he stood there, stock-still.

"Are you accusing me, Ellis?" Jesse said, his voice carefully under control. He was afraid that if he lost his focus for a second, he'd begin shouting and wouldn't stop.

Ellis turned away from him. "I'm going to need you to leave the crime scene, Jesse," he said.

"That's how you got here so fast," Jesse said as it dawned on him. "Someone called you and gave you this idiotic fucking idea—"

"Jesse, I am telling you this as a colleague and a friend: Shut up. You have rights."

"You think I don't know my rights?"

"I'm going to need you to go outside," Ellis said. "Right now. As of this moment, I'm asking Lundquist to take over."

"I want to hear you say it, Ellis. Tell me. You think I'm a suspect?"

Ellis glared back at Jesse. "I'm saying you had motive and means," he said. "You're the chief of police, Jesse. You don't need me to spell it out."

Suddenly Jesse understood Ellis's attitude. He wasn't just angry with Jesse. He was upset with himself. He hated this almost as much as Jesse did.

"Ellis," Jesse said. "Do you really think I did something to hurt Devlin?"

Ellis looked at the floor, then around the room, anywhere but at Jesse. He looked a little lost.

"It wouldn't be the first time you took the law into your own hands," he said. "Would it, Jesse?"

TWENTY-ONE

Salazar and his men camped out in a suite of temporary offices near Logan airport. It had all been arranged over the Internet by Salazar's assistant, just as if he was the businessman he pretended to be. The keys were in a lockbox that opened with a code from Salazar's phone. On the door they plastered up a decal with a generic logo that had been generated by Salazar's assistant as well. It was the same logo they used on their fake business cards. They had cabinets for their weapons, and fast-food restaurants nearby to feed them. They'd taken a six-month lease to avoid suspicion, but Salazar didn't expect this to take more than a couple days.

There was a shower and a private bathroom in one office, and they slept on the couches and the floor. They'd all lived in much worse conditions. Salazar himself had stayed on a rooftop, under a tarp, for three days when he was twenty-one. He'd been waiting for a man to appear in a doorway. He'd pissed in a can and ate protein bars and amphetamines. The man finally showed up on the evening of the third day, on his way inside to visit his mistress. Salazar fired his sniper rifle and put a bullet through the man's skull, then walked down the stairs and went home.

They were preparing to drive to Paradise the morning after they'd arrived, late at night, from Florida. Salazar was at his laptop at a rental desk, going over the town's layout on Google Maps.

Arturo came into the office. He waited, and Salazar looked up at him.

"What's wrong?" Salazar asked.

Arturo was afraid of Salazar—any sane man would be—but he also knew that Salazar was not a movie bad guy. He wouldn't like hearing the news, but he wouldn't punish him for it.

"Devlin. He's gone."

"Gone? Gone where?"

"It's on the news," Arturo said. That was his job, because he had the best English and he was probably the smartest of Salazar's crew. Watch the news, keep an eye on local conditions, assess any problems. "He's missing. They think maybe dead."

Salazar immediately clicked over to a local news website. The story was there, at the top of the page: NOTORIOUS INVESTMENT BANKER MISSING FROM $23 MILLION MANSION.

Underneath a large photo of Devlin, smiling, was a news story filled with holes. There were clearly things the police weren't sharing with the public.

But even so, there were details that leaped out at Salazar. The local police chief was named but not quoted. The State Police would not rule out any suspects or even say if Devlin was dead.

Salazar didn't believe it. Even if he did, he wanted to see the corpse himself. And then he would begin on Devlin's family until they paid what he owed.

He'd met with Devlin once. The man was a snake, but that's the risk you took in any business. No one was trustworthy, no matter how expensive their suits were. The more money they had, the more they wanted.

But he didn't think Devlin was stupid.

And he still did not.

He suspected the banker was still out there, somewhere. Probably close by, since it would be difficult to walk away from a crime scene like the one described in the news with no witnesses.

Salazar didn't want to waste time looking around Boston for Devlin. He didn't know the area. He didn't know the people. It would be pointless and foolish.

Instead, he wanted someone who was already motivated to look for Devlin. Someone local. Someone who could be pressured or bribed into finding Devlin and then making a call to Salazar.

He read the story again, more carefully.

Arturo still stood at the door, awaiting his orders.

Salazar looked up at him.

"I want you to find out everything you can about this local cop in Paradise," he said. "Tell me about Jesse Stone."

TWENTY-TWO

"Jesse, I'm sorry to tell you, but I've got to suspend you from duty," Armistead said.

The mayor didn't look sorry. He'd walked into the station and gone right past the front desk where Suit was sitting, and then past Molly's desk, which was empty because Molly was on her secret mission. There was a distinct spring in his step.

Jesse didn't bother to get up from his chair. This was hardly the first time Armistead had made this threat.

"Why do you say that, Gary?" Jesse asked.

Armistead sat down in one of the visitor's chairs without being asked. "Jesse. Come on. Be reasonable. You're under investigation by the State Police."

"That's news to me."

"Is it?" Armistead said. "Well. I hate to be the bearer of bad tidings. But Brian Lundquist has told me that he is looking into the disappearance of Ramsey Devlin. And that you were at the scene of the crime."

"I'm often at the scene of a crime. That's a big part of the job."

"Jesse. This is not a joking matter. It's serious. And in fact, it's quite sad. For you and for me."

Armistead did not look remotely unhappy. In fact, he looked happier than Jesse had ever seen him. Like he was animated from inside by a warm glow.

"Lundquist is going to find out that I had nothing to do with Devlin's absence. In the meantime, there's still plenty to do around here."

Armistead tried to put on a solemn face. It almost worked. "I'm afraid I can't allow that, Jesse."

"It's not up to you, Gary."

Armistead couldn't help smiling as he put down a piece of paper. "Today it is," he said. "The Town Council passed a motion this morning in closed session. Because we didn't want to embarrass you."

Jesse picked up the paper. It was an order, signed by the town clerk, declaring that the chief of the Paradise Police Department should be placed on a temporary leave of absence.

It had passed unanimously.

Apparently Jesse didn't have the support he thought he did.

Jesse thought Armistead could have called him over to the mayor's office for this, but he didn't. He couldn't wait.

"So who's supposed to run the department while I'm gone?"

For an instant, Armistead's face went blank. Jesse was amused—but not surprised—that he had not thought this through.

"Call Molly. Get her back here. That's why she's deputy chief, isn't it?"

"Molly is on vacation. And isn't she supposed to be a person of interest in this investigation as well?"

"Fine," Armistead said. "Who's the next highest-ranked officer in the department?"

"That would be Suit."

"Then Suit will be the acting chief of police."

Suit appeared at the door then, nearly filling the frame.

"No" was all he said.

Armistead turned in his chair. He was back to normal, or at least how Jesse thought of him as normal. Annoyed and impatient.

"You don't want the job?"

"Jesse is the chief," Suit said. "I work for him."

Armistead got up and faced Suit. "Is this your 'I am Spartacus' moment? You prepared to walk out the door with him? Because I can promise you that's what's going to happen."

Suit didn't look the least bit threatened. "We were all prepared to walk out when you wanted to suspend Molly. What makes you think this is any different?"

"You listen to me, Officer Simpson—"

"Detective," Suit said, interrupting Armistead before he could reach full volume on his rant.

"What?" Armistead looked confused.

"It's Detective Simpson, Mr. Mayor," Suit said mildly. "Jeez, you want to rearrange the whole department and you don't even know the command structure?"

Even sitting behind them, Jesse could see Armistead's

posture lock up with anger. He had to admire that. But he also felt like it was time to intervene, before Suit talked himself onto the unemployment line.

"Gary," Jesse said, before Armistead could wind up into a full-throated rage at Suit. "Can you give me a minute with Detective Simpson?"

Armistead spun around, jaw clenched. That good mood didn't last long.

"Please," Jesse said, knowing that he didn't hold any leverage over the mayor at this moment.

"And why the hell should I do that?"

"I'm going to tell him to take the job," Jesse said.

Suit looked shocked. Armistead calmed down a little. "Sure, Jesse. All right," he said. "But your entire department needs to remember who's in charge in this town."

"Of course," Jesse said.

He walked out. Jesse waved Suit inside, and Suit closed the door.

"What the hell, Jesse?" he said. "I'm trying to stand up for you here."

"I appreciate that," Jesse said. "I really do. But I need you to do this."

"Is this because Elena's pregnant? Jesus, Jesse, I didn't tell you that so you'd take pity on me. I can find another job. I don't want you to treat me like I'm the same dumb kid you first met."

"I'm not, Suit. I promise you."

"Then why are you doing this?"

"Because I know two things," Jesse said. "One, I know I didn't have anything to do with whatever happened to Devlin. Lundquist will see that, too. And that means I'm going to be back on the job before long. I'm going to want you here when that happens. And while it takes the whole Town Council to fire me, Armistead can dump you anytime he wants, just like any other city employee."

"I'm prepared to take that chance," Suit said, chin out, shoulders squared.

Jesse felt proud of him for a moment. He looked like a recruiting poster. He'd come a long way from the patrolman he'd met on his first day.

"That's the second thing: If Armistead really does succeed in getting me out, then I want to know the department has a chief who can do the job."

Suit was speechless for a moment. Then he looked away. "There's always Molly."

"Molly's not here. I need you."

Suit thought about it for another moment. "Okay," he said. Then he cleared his throat.

"Okay," Jesse said.

He stood up and went around the desk. He opened the door and waved Armistead inside.

Suit stood up. "I'll do it," he told Armistead. "But I'm doing it for Jesse, not for you."

"Terrific. Whatever," Armistead said. He looked at Jesse. "That's settled. You can go now."

Jesse grabbed his jacket and began to walk out, but then Armistead spoke up again.

"Oh, I'll need your badge and gun, Jesse," Armistead said.

Jesse couldn't help laughing. "Seriously, Gary? You've seen too much TV."

"You're a private citizen now," Armistead said. "I don't

want you running around out there pretending you're still representing Paradise."

"So what are you going to do with them?"

"What?" Armistead said.

"What are you going to do with them? You going to put them in a drawer in your office?"

Suit looked down, hiding a smile.

"Give them to Suit. He'll hold them."

Jesse sighed. He took the badge and his holster off his belt, then placed them on the desk.

He was surprised that he felt lighter. And a little emptier, too.

Suit nodded at him. "I'll hang on to these for you."

"Thanks," Jesse said.

"Okay, Jesse. Time to go," Armistead said. "I have some police business to discuss with Suit. That doesn't include you."

"Careful, Gary. I'm a private citizen now," Jesse said as he walked out. "You keep acting like this, you just might lose my vote."

TWENTY-THREE

"So did you kill him?" Molly asked.

"I was just about to ask you the same question," Jesse said as he walked away from the station.

Molly's laugh came through loud and clear across the phone. "Imagine if someone was recording this conversation."

"You wearing a wire, Crane?"

She laughed again.

Jesse unlocked his Explorer. Armistead had wanted to take it away—it was an official Paradise police vehicle, after all—but Suit had reminded him how many of Jesse's personal vehicles had been shot, blown up, and crashed in the line of duty. Then he told Armistead Jesse would keep the Explorer as long as he needed it.

Armistead, probably not wanting to lose two police chiefs in one day, had agreed.

"I thought you were on vacation," Jesse said as he got behind the wheel. "Don't you have better things to do than keep up with the local gossip?"

"I do," Molly said. "I'm just not doing them right now. Suit called me as soon as Armistead suspended you."

"Did he beg you to come back?"

"I wouldn't say *begged*. More like pleaded."

"But you're still on your secret mission."

"That's right," Molly said. "Besides, if I wanted your job, I would have taken it years ago."

"Can't argue with that."

"What do you think happened to Devlin?"

"I'd have a better idea if they'd let me examine the scene, but I'm certainly not the only person in town who might want to get rid of him. There was that kid, Tyler Stephens," Jesse reminded her.

"He wouldn't really hurt anyone."

"I know you keep saying that, but he's proof that Devlin has enemies."

"He's in jail. I don't see other church groups sending any assassins."

"Yeah," Jesse said. "Me, either."

"So do you think someone actually grabbed him?"

"Same question applies. Who'd want to do that?" Jesse said. "Who's got the motive?"

"His neighbors hate him, but I don't see them killing him or kidnapping him," Molly said.

"Ms. Foley might."

"Maybe her," Molly said. "The others would just say mean things about him at his parties."

"While drinking his booze and eating his food."

"That's how the better half does it."

"I'm starting to see the appeal," Jesse said.

"Yeah, it's definitely safer."

At that moment, Jesse felt an itch at the back of his skull. A feeling like someone was focusing on him. There was no rational reason for him to believe that, but he'd learned to trust those feelings over the years. They'd saved his life on more than one occasion.

Jesse adjusted his mirrors to check the street behind him.

He caught sight of a black BMW, just sitting at the curb opposite the police station. No way to see who was inside. The windows were too dark.

But Paradise was a small town. He knew most of the residents' cars by sight. It was possible this was a tourist. Or someone passing through.

That didn't explain why there was another black Beemer on a side street ahead of him, parked in the opposite direction, however.

And both BMWs had Florida plates.

A little too late for tourist season.

"Jesse?"

"What? Sorry, Molly. Got distracted."

"Something wrong?"

"No," he said. "I'm fine." He didn't want her to worry. There was nothing she could do about it, anyway.

"So what do you think? Is there anyone who'd want to kidnap Devlin or hurt him?"

"I don't know," Jesse said. "I think maybe there are more players involved in this than we might know."

"What makes you say that?" Molly sounded suspicious.

Jesse watched the cars. Neither one moved.

He started his engine.

A second later, the headlights on both cars lit up and they began spewing exhaust.

"Just a hunch."

"You want to let me in on it?" she asked.

"You going to tell me what you're doing?" Jesse replied.

"And spoil the surprise? No chance."

"Well. Call if you need me."

"You sound like you're up to something," Molly said. She really did know him well. "What are you up to, Jesse?"

Jesse put the Explorer in gear, then pulled away from the curb.

The black BMWs both started up and began following him at the same time.

"I think I'm going to get lunch," he said.

TWENTY-FOUR

The man sat down at Jesse's table, uninvited.

Jesse was at lunch at the Gray Gull. He'd said hello to Spike, who was behind the bar today. They were still friendly, although Spike had never really forgiven Jesse for not making it work with Sunny. In his mind, Sunny could do no wrong, and any straight man who didn't stay with her was an idiot.

There were times when Jesse thought Spike had a point.

A couple people saw Jesse and whispered when he sat down. The rumors about Devlin and Jesse were going around Paradise. He wasn't sure if people were taking sides, but he'd dealt with whispers and gossip before. He ignored them.

That had been the only drama Jesse had faced until the stranger joined him without asking.

He was tall and well-built, with strong features. His eyes and hair were light, but his skin appeared deeply tanned. He had a pleasant look on his face, completely at odds with his sudden intrusion into Jesse's meal.

This had to be one of the people from the BMWs, Jesse knew. They'd followed him, not very discreetly, all the way to the Gull. It didn't take long. He'd parked like he hadn't seen them and had gone inside.

If someone is looking for you, sometimes Jesse thought it was best to let them find you.

Spike noticed the new guy. He looked over the man's shoulder at Jesse, a question on his face. Jesse shook his head no with a very slight movement of his chin and his eyes.

Spike stayed where he was, behind the bar. But he watched and listened without making it obvious.

"Jesse Stone," the man said. His voice was deep and lightly accented. Jesse couldn't place it.

"Have we met?" Jesse asked.

"We're meeting now," he said.

"Usually that involves you telling me your name."

The man smiled with his teeth. It didn't reach his eyes. Jesse tried to identify the color and had trouble. They were pale blue to the point that they were almost silver.

"Alberto Suarez. I'm sorry to interrupt your lunch, Jesse," he said. "May I call you Jesse?"

"Most people do," Jesse said.

He offered his hand. The man shook it with a firm grip.

"How can I help you?"

"I have a couple questions for you. And I wanted to get a look at you. See the man himself, in person."

So it was going to be one of those things. There was always a guy who wanted to meet Jesse across a table before he did something stupid in Paradise. Jesse understood the impulse—he liked Westerns as much as anyone—but he always wondered why they didn't recognize the difference between movies and real life.

Jesse's Glock was in the station armory, thanks to Armistead, so there was nothing at his waist. But he had his .32 backup from the Explorer in his pocket.

He also knew Spike kept a piece under the bar. But there were a lot of bystanders in the Gull for lunch today. The place was packed.

He decided to sit tight. He kept his voice calm and his eyes steady on the visitor. "What kind of questions?" he asked.

The man put a card on the table. "I'm an investigator with Global Alliance Insurance Company. I am looking into the disappearance of Ramsey Devlin."

"Of course you are." Jesse didn't bother to look at the card. If this man worked for an insurance company, Jesse would eat the tablecloth.

"Oh, please don't worry. I am not blaming you for his sudden vanishing act. I've heard the rumors, but I assure you, I don't believe any of them."

"You're very well informed already, Mr. Suarez."

"I'm good at my job. And from what I've learned, so are you. It doesn't make sense to me that someone with your distinguished career would suddenly break the law to hurt a man. Even someone as pathetic and dishonorable as Ramsey Devlin."

"Well, you seem to be in the minority right now."

The man laughed. It sounded rehearsed. "No. I cannot imagine you had anything to do with Mr. Devlin's sudden absence. If you were going to get rid of a man, I imagine there wouldn't be any traces left."

"You run into a lot of murder and kidnapping in the insurance business?" Jesse said.

"You'd be surprised how often it comes up."

"And here I thought insurance was boring."

"You've probably heard that Mr. Devlin owed a great deal of money to his investors when his previous fund went bankrupt."

"I have."

"I represent some of those investors," the man calling himself Suarez said. "And they believe there are assets they might recover for their losses. But first, of course, they need to find Mr. Devlin."

"Why come to me? I don't know where he is."

The man leaned in, showing his teeth again. "But I believe you could find out, Jesse. In fact, looking at your history, I believe that if anyone can find Mr. Devlin, it would be you."

"Well, unfortunately, that's not my job now. Sorry to disappoint you, Mr. Suarez."

For a split second, the man's façade vanished and the rage appeared on his face, ugly and immediate. He was not used to anyone telling him no.

Jesse picked up his fork again. He could use it to continue eating lunch, or he could jam it into the man's face. Could go either way.

The man recovered. He looked calm and collected again. "Sadly, I cannot accept that answer, Jesse. The interests I represent—"

"The Global Alliance Insurance Company?" Jesse interrupted.

Another flicker of rage. "Yes. My employers. They need a resolution of this matter. I also believe that it is in your best interests to find him as soon as possible. Your career and your reputation depend on it. I think that would be enough of an incentive. If there is anyone who can find Mr. Devlin, I believe it will be you. All I ask is that you call that number on the card when you do. Before you call anyone else."

"And if I don't?"

The man shrugged. "That would be a grave disappointment," he said. "For both of us. But especially for you."

"Well, I'd hate to disappoint the Global Alliance Insurance Company," Jesse said. "But I am not currently looking for Devlin. I'm suspended. Right now, all I'm going to do is finish my lunch."

"Please," the man said. "You'll find him. It's what you do."

"You seem to think you know me pretty well for a guy I just met."

The man pushed the card across the table to Jesse with another big smile. "I recognize your type," he said. "One professional to another."

He stood up. "I sincerely hope you will call that number."

Jesse smiled back at him for the first time. "Everyone has dreams."

The man's face curdled into pure hate for a second, then he got it under control again. He even made a small bow before he turned and left.

Spike came around to Jesse's table, watching the man's retreating back go through the exit.

"Who the hell was that?" Spike asked.

"Latest member of my fan club."

Spike looked at him. "You just win friends all the time, don't you?"

Jesse dug his fork into his pasta. "Well. I'm a people person."

TWENTY-FIVE

"Is there some reason you haven't gotten a lawyer?"

Cole Slayton, Jesse's son, had that tone in his voice again, the one where it sounded like he was barely able to keep from calling his father an idiot. Jesse tried to ignore it. He'd had plenty of practice.

"Mainly because I'm not guilty."

Jesse heard Cole sigh heavily over the phone.

Cole lived in Los Angeles, where he was an assistant United States Attorney. For most of his life, Jesse didn't know he existed. Cole's mother had split up with Jesse before he knew she was pregnant, and she chose to raise him without Jesse's involvement. After her death, he'd come to Paradise, angry and lost, and somehow they'd managed to forge a relationship. Cole had followed Jesse into law enforcement, then decided he could do more good as a prosecutor. Some people would say that was a compliment to Jesse—that his son had wanted, in some small way, to be like him.

They still had their problems. Cole also had Jesse's

temper, and a lifetime of hurt to work through. Sometimes Jesse thought it was best they were on opposite coasts. Other times, he thought they could be in the same town again and still be thousands of miles apart.

But Jesse made an effort to call at least once a week. Cole had asked him what was going on. Jesse told him. And they started arguing almost immediately.

"Jesse," Cole said, speaking with exaggerated patience. He rarely ever called him Dad. "What's the first rule every suspect should know when they get questioned by the police?"

"Look, Cole, it's not an interrogation. It's an interview. Lundquist is going to ask some questions. We're going to clear it up. Ellis will be there. We've had our problems, but he's not going to build a case against me if the evidence isn't there. Then I can get back to work and start looking for the real answers."

"I'll repeat the question: What's the first thing any suspect should know?" Cole said.

Now it was Jesse's turn to sigh heavily. But he answered: "The first rule is shut the fuck up."

"Exactly. How many times have you nailed someone because they thought they were smart enough to talk to you and get away with it?"

"Too many to count."

"Right," Cole said. "Which is why you always try to get the suspect talking."

"I am aware of that," Jesse said. "As you've mentioned, I have done this before."

"Then what makes you think you're the exception to the rule, Jesse?"

"Well, I was smart enough to catch all those people."

"You think that's how it works? Oh, Christ, they are going to love you in the interrogation."

"Interview," Jesse said.

"It's *always* an interrogation," Cole snapped. "I was not a cop as long as you, but give me some credit, will you? I have been in that room, too, and it is always a mistake for the suspect to talk."

"You keep calling me a suspect."

"You think you're not?"

"Do you seriously believe I committed a crime?"

"That's not the point and you know it," Cole said. "The point is they think you did. They're not interested in finding the truth. They want to make a case. And you should know the truth comes in second if they're motivated enough."

"I am innocent. Or doesn't that matter when you make cases?"

There was a pause on the line. "Jesus Christ, Jesse. You do not make it easy to try to help you."

Jesse felt like an asshole. He immediately regretted what he'd just said.

"Look," he said. "I'm sorry. I appreciate it. Armistead is only using this as a way to get at me. They're flailing around, looking for a scapegoat."

"And they've found one."

"They won't be able to use me. Because I didn't do anything."

Another pause. "Can you at least call Rita Fiore? Have her sit in with you?"

"Rita's still mad at me," Jesse said. "Or she's mad at the department, anyway."

"Is there a difference?"

"Funny. She hasn't made up her mind about suing us for that incident earlier this year."

"Can't really blame her," Cole said.

"Me, either," Jesse said. "Look, it's going to be fine. I appreciate your concern, but I've got it under control."

"So that's it, huh? You're just going to walk in there tomorrow with nothing but the truth as your guide."

"You almost sound worried," Jesse said.

"I'm not," Cole said. "But you should be."

TWENTY-SIX

Jesse walked into the station and saw Ellis Munroe standing outside the conference room in his best suit. That was his first indication that something was wrong.

Jesse had shown up with a box of muffins from Daisy's.

Ellis looked behind him and then hurried over to Jesse, intercepting him before he could get too far inside.

For once, though, he didn't seem to know what to say.

"You okay, Ellis?"

Ellis nearly looked over his shoulder again. "Jesse," he said. "We've had our differences, but—" He stopped himself. "Do you have a lawyer?"

"What? No, of course not."

Ellis sighed. Then he offered Jesse his hand. "Okay. Good luck."

Jesse shook it, and Ellis turned and walked away.

Jesse followed, and went into the conference room behind him.

Inside were Lundquist and two people Jesse didn't recognize, a man and a woman, both wearing off-the-rack suits that pegged them as cops immediately.

Jesse looked at Lundquist, who would not meet his eyes.

"Have a seat, Chief Stone," the man said, pointing to a chair on the opposite side of the conference table. There was a video camera set up on the table and aimed at that place.

Jesse suddenly understood he was not there for a friendly chat.

"It's Jesse," he said to the man. "And you are?"

"Chief Stone, I'm Special Agent Kirkpatrick with the State Internal Affairs Section." He nodded at the woman, who was short and blond and stared at Jesse as if he were a particularly uninteresting section of a brick wall. "This is Special Agent Hodges."

"Internal Affairs?" Jesse said. This was directed more at Lundquist than at Kirkpatrick or Hodges. Lundquist finally looked at Jesse and shrugged.

"They're taking over the case," he said. "Since we have a history. It was thought that they would be more impartial. To avoid the appearance of any favoritism. Or a cover-up."

"We handle all allegations of police misconduct, Chief Stone," Hodges said. "Before we begin, do you need your rights explained to you? Or would you like a lawyer to be present?"

Jesse got it now. He had thought they were doing this at the station because it was informal. His home ground.

But now he understood they'd wanted him off guard. If they'd asked him to the DA's office, he might have realized what they were doing.

This wasn't up to Lundquist and Ellis anymore.

Cole was right. They were treating him like a suspect.

"Chief Stone," Kirkpatrick said. "Are you still willing to cooperate?"

Jesse looked back at the two agents.

He sat down in the chair. The camera was pointed at him.

"Of course," he said. "I take it you guys aren't going to have any muffins?"

Neither of them cracked a smile.

It didn't matter. He hadn't done anything wrong. And Jesse knew these intimidation tactics as well as anyone else did.

He would clear this up and get back to work.

Ellis and Lundquist both sat down at the other end of the table. They found other places to look, instead of at Jesse. Ellis shuffled papers. Lundquist checked his watch.

But Kirkpatrick and Hodges sat down right across from him, staring at Jesse coldly.

"Will you please state your name for the record," Kirkpatrick began. His tie was blood-red. Jesse tried not to think of it as a sign.

"Come on," Jesse said. "Everyone in here knows who I am."

Now Ellis looked at him. "We need to do this right, Jesse."

"Jesse," Lundquist said. "It'll go a lot faster if you just jump through the hoops. Let's get it over with and we can all go back to normal, right?"

He smiled a little.

Jesse shrugged, even though he suspected normal was a long way in the rearview mirror now.

"My name is Jesse Stone."

"And you are currently the chief of the police department for the Town of Paradise?"

"Yes."

"And you are appearing here today of your own free will, and you have waived your right to counsel?"

"Yes, I am. I have nothing to hide."

Kirkpatrick might have smirked a little bit at that. "How long have you been chief?"

"At the moment, it feels like forever."

"Chief Stone," Hodges said, her tone sharp. "Will you at least try to take this seriously?"

"I'm doing my best."

"On the night of October twenty-first, do you recall where you were?" Kirkpatrick said.

"Yes. I had a scheduled appointment with Ramsey Devlin, at his home on Fourteen Seaside Drive, overlooking the point. Mayor Gary Armistead had arranged for us to meet."

"What was the purpose of your meeting?"

"I was there to apologize," Jesse said. "Mr. Devlin had been involved in some conflicts with my officers and the department, and we were trying to resolve our differences amicably."

Hodges leaned forward. "You say 'my officers,' but in fact you had conflicts with Mr. Devlin personally, didn't you?"

"No."

"No?" Kirkpatrick looked at his notes. "You and your current girlfriend didn't have an argument with him and his wife at a public event at the museum? You didn't stand by as your deputy chief insulted and threatened him? You didn't threaten him again at a local restaurant in front of a dozen witnesses? You didn't get into a physical fight with Mr. Devlin and assault him while arresting him for driving under the influence?"

"That's not what happened," Jesse said. "Mr. Devlin had conflicts with me. I didn't have any personal feelings toward him. I was doing my job."

"Of course you were." Kirkpatrick was definitely smirking now. "So when did you see Mr. Devlin on the night in question?"

"I didn't," Jesse said. "I found the front door open and made my way inside. In the house, I discovered Devlin was missing, and there was a bloodstain on the carpet."

"Did you call for backup?"

"I didn't have time."

"Why not?"

"Janis Devlin, Mr. Devlin's wife, came into the room and became upset. She began screaming at me, telling me to get out."

"I've got a transcript of our interview with Janis Devlin here," Hodges said, tag-teaming in again. "She told us you had your gun drawn. She says you were the one who was upset, and you screamed at her to leave the room."

"That's not true."

"Are you calling her a liar?"

"I'm telling you what happened."

"Did you record your initial interview with her?" Kirkpatrick asked.

"No."

"Take any notes?"

"No."

"Do you ever record your interviews?"

"Sometimes, sure."

"But not that night."

"She was a little busy hitting me and screaming at me," Jesse said. "It was not an ideal situation to interview a witness."

"Why did you have your sidearm drawn?"

"I noticed the door was ajar, and I thought there might be an intruder in the house."

"An intruder. Right," Kirkpatrick said. "We'll come back to that. Did you use your gun to threaten Mrs. Devlin?"

"What?" Jesse was genuinely taken aback. "No. Of course not."

Hodges looked at a sheet of paper in front of her. "Would it surprise you to hear that she has said you pointed your gun at her? That she began screaming in fear for her life? That you told her to shut up if she—quote—'knew what was good for her'—unquote?"

"At this point, nothing Janis Devlin could say would surprise me."

"Jesse," Ellis said. "Just answer the questions yes or no. Please."

Kirkpatrick looked at Ellis coldly. "Mr. Munroe," he said. "I'd like to remind you that you are not Chief Stone's attorney here today."

"Right," Ellis said, sitting back in his chair. "Sure."

Kirkpatrick and Hodges turned to Jesse. "Are you prepared to continue, Chief Stone?"

"Look," Jesse said. "I can't tell you what Janis Devlin is thinking, or why she said what she said. You know as well as I do you don't always take notes or record every interaction. I was trying to understand what happened, and I wanted to get the information from Janis. I thought it was possible Devlin was hurt or in trouble."

"Why would you think that?"

"Maybe because of the giant puddle of blood in the room."

"You thought that was Devlin's blood?" Hodges said.

"Why would you assume it was his?" Kirkpatrick asked. "Did you have some reason to believe he was hurt? Or perhaps you *knew* he was hurt?"

Jesse looked at them both. He knew what they were doing. He'd done it himself, hundreds of times, even thousands. Shifting the conversation. Hitting from both sides. He knew how it looked and how it was meant to look.

"You don't want to answer that question, Chief Stone?" Kirkpatrick asked.

Jesse took a deep breath. "Maybe this will go faster if you both tell me what you think happened."

They both leaned back, putting on looks of saintly innocence.

"That's why we're here, Chief Stone," Kirkpatrick said.

"We're trying to figure it out," Hodges said. "And, frankly, you haven't given us much to go on so far."

They could be a comedy team with that timing, Jesse thought. He took another deep breath.

"I'm sure the security cameras can tell you exactly what happened and when."

"Someone disabled them," Kirkpatrick said. "But you don't know anything about that."

"I don't."

"Could you disable a security system, though? If you really had to?"

Jesse wasn't dumb enough to answer that.

"So you were there, what? Five or ten minutes before Mrs. Devlin arrived?" Hodges asked.

"Five at the most."

"And about how long before Mr. Munroe and Mr. Lundquist arrived?"

"Maybe another five," Jesse said. "And about that—"

He turned toward Ellis and Lundquist. "Who called you and told you to be there? Have you told them that part yet?"

Kirkpatrick and Hodges frowned, almost in unison. "They're not being interviewed here today," Hodges said. "You are."

Kirkpatrick said, "You insisted that the scene looked like a break-in. That Mr. Devlin had made some enemies, and that it was some mystery intruder who had committed the crime."

Jesse let that pass. "I said that's how it appeared at first."

"You weren't trying to mislead the investigation, were you, Chief Stone?" Kirkpatrick asked.

"Of course not."

"Did you know that we were able to type that blood and match it for DNA?" Hodges asked.

"Nobody's told me anything about the investigation, Agent Hodges."

"Uh-huh." That sound of disbelief again. "Well, we did. And you know whose DNA turned up?"

"Devlin's?"

"That's right," Kirkpatrick said. "How did you know that if you didn't know anything about this investigation?"

"Agent Kirkpatrick. It's his house. It's not exactly rocket science."

Kirkpatrick ignored that. Hodges picked up the questioning instead.

"You've broken a lot of rules over the years, haven't you, Chief Stone?" she said. "You're known as something of a loose cannon?"

"Excuse me?"

"Do you need me to repeat the question?"

"No," Jesse said. "I am comfortable with what I have done to keep this town safe and protect people's lives in my time here."

"I'm sure you are," she said. "Who's Vinnie Morris?"

"What?" Jesse was actually blindsided.

"He's a mobster, isn't he? A figure who's been involved with organized crime for decades."

"I don't know what that has to do with this investigation—"

"He helps you out on cases sometimes? Gives you information?"

"Do you tell people all about your confidential informants?"

"He's more than just a CI, though. He's your friend, isn't he?" Hodges said.

Jesse looked at Lundquist, who would not meet his eyes. Lundquist had always objected to his relationship with Vinnie. Cops and crooks were always supposed to be on opposite sides. Even though Vinnie had helped close a dozen cases over the years. And sure, Jesse had problems with it himself sometimes; it didn't take much imagination for Jesse to guess what Vinnie did when Jesse wasn't around.

But Vinnie had also saved his life. He trusted the man. He had to admit it, even though it made him look bad. He would never turn his back on Vinnie. No matter what.

He looked Kirkpatrick and Hodges in the eyes when he answered.

"Yes. I'd call him a friend."

Lundquist shook his head. Ellis looked down at the table.

Then Kirkpatrick said: "He ever help you dispose of a body before?"

Jesse felt as if he'd been sucker-punched. Kirkpatrick's voice had never changed, staying in the same monotone even as he'd asked.

"What the *hell*?" He stood up without even realizing it. "Are you serious? What the hell are you asking me?"

"Here's what we've got, *Jesse*," Kirkpatrick said, using his first name for the first time. "We've got a missing man with a history of conflict with you personally, who's been causing problems for you since he showed up in what you call 'my town.' He threatens to sue you and your best friend and deputy chief, Molly Crane. You've arrested a young man with a grudge against Mr. Devlin. That gave you an idea. What if an intruder were to remove this individual for you? That would solve all your problems."

"Where is Deputy Chief Crane, by the way?" Hodges said.

"She's taking personal time—"

"Sure she is."

Kirkpatrick continued: "And lo and behold, Ramsey Devlin disappears and you are the only one on the scene at the time. There's broken glass. There's a crime scene that looks staged. There's a pool of blood from the victim—"

"What victim? You don't even have a body."

Hodges smiled, as if Jesse had just confessed. "And there's the police chief who has a relationship with a known criminal who specializes in making the Mob's problems disappear."

Jesse realized that he needed to shut up now. They were working him like any dipshit who'd robbed a liquor store and didn't realize the whole thing was caught on camera. And he'd walked right into it.

"Nothing to say to that?" Hodges asked.

"That's all right," Kirkpatrick said, his voice calm and level again. "I believe we know what happened. But it will save you some time and buy you some leniency if you tell us how it actually went down."

For the first time in his life, Jesse felt what it was like to be a suspect. He'd done plenty wrong in his career. He knew that, and was working to make his peace with it.

But he also knew he was absolutely innocent of what he was being accused of, and it didn't matter to his accusers.

They didn't need to find someone else. There was enough pointing at him. And if Jesse had been in their shoes, he'd probably consider himself the prime suspect as well.

He was in trouble.

Then the conference room door slammed open. Cole, Jesse's son, walked through, wearing a suit and carrying a briefcase. He hadn't shaved, but his tie was knotted tightly and his shirt was pressed and white.

"This interview is over," he said.

TWENTY-SEVEN

Kirkpatrick didn't know Cole. "What are you doing in here?" he demanded.

Lundquist did, however. He'd worked cases with Cole when Cole was still a state trooper.

"Cole? What's going on?" he asked.

"I'm formally entering my appearance as attorney for Jesse Stone," Cole said. "Anything you have to ask him, you come through me."

Jesse got over his surprise. "Cole, I told you—"

Cole turned to him, his face more serious than Jesse had ever seen before, even when they'd been fighting all the time.

"Jesse, *shut up*," he said.

And then, a little more softly, "Please, Dad."

It was the *Dad* that got Jesse to listen. He closed his mouth and sat back down.

"Wait a second," Ellis said, starting to catch up. "Jesse, this is your son? I thought he was an AUSA. That doesn't mean he can come in here and start playing defense."

"Hey," Cole said, slapping his hand down on the table loudly enough to get everyone's attention. "I'm going to warn you again not to speak to my client without my permission, Counselor. You have a question? You talk to me."

Hodges shook her head, as if this was all too funny to believe.

"Oh, okay, *Counselor*," she said, laying the sarcasm on pretty thick. "You mind telling me how you think you're allowed to practice here in the Commonwealth? Since, as far as I know, you are not admitted to the bar here? This isn't California."

Cole popped open his briefcase and slid a stack of papers onto the table.

"This is my application to practice pro hac vice, sponsored by a local member of the bar, Ms. Rita Fiore," Cole said. "You'll see that she had a judge expedite the order. There is no current case against my client, but since you are clearly treating him as a suspect in an ongoing criminal investigation, the judge has admitted me to appear on his behalf."

Ellis read the paperwork. "Seems to be in order," he said.

"Glad you agree," Cole said. He pointed at Kirkpatrick and Hodges. "Since you are recording this, I want to state it clearly: As his attorney, I am instructing Chief Stone not to answer any further questions to assist you with your inquiries."

"Well, that's one way to go," Hodges said, leaning back in her chair. "But if he walks out the door, that's his last chance to make this go away."

"I think that's actually up to you, isn't it?" Cole said. "Jesse's already given you plenty of time to figure out his involvement—which is to say, none. Maybe you should work a little harder and keep looking for clues."

Kirkpatrick tried the oldest trick in the book. "You know this looks pretty bad for him," he said. "Only guilty people ask for their lawyers."

Cole laughed out loud. "Jesus. Really? I have the least experience as a cop in this room, and even I wouldn't fall for that. Besides, if you were really interested in solving this case, you'd have Jesse working on it. His track record is a hell of a lot better than yours."

Kirkpatrick flushed red, from his collar to his ears. But he closed his mouth and kept it closed.

"Anything else? No?" Cole asked. "Okay. Unless you're going to charge my client, I think we're done here."

He looked at Jesse. Jesse looked at Lundquist and Ellis. Neither of them looked at each other.

Kirkpatrick and Hodges only glared.

"All right, then," Jesse said as he stood up. He nodded at Lundquist. "Brian. Always a pleasure."

They opened the door of the conference room. Jesse and Cole were about to leave when Hodges spoke up again.

"You got this done pretty quick," she said. "Did Rita call the judge or just deliver this with his morning coffee?"

She had a little grin on her face. Cole turned and faced her, leaning on the table to look down at her.

"You saying something about Rita Fiore? Keeping in mind that we're on camera here, and this is all on the record."

Hodges shut her mouth.

"You done with your jokes? Great. Now you can listen to me. The judge wasn't terribly pleased to learn you were questioning a decorated law enforcement officer without the benefit of a lawyer," Cole said. "He said it sounded like you were trying to take the dirt road instead of the high road."

Hodges's eyes went wide. "Are you implying something?"

"Not at all," Cole said. "Unlike some people, I only make accusations when I can back them up with evidence."

Kirkpatrick shook his head, admiring the touch. "You're a lot like your father, aren't you?"

Cole smiled at him, showing his perfect white teeth. "Oh, no," he said. "Sadly for you, I am so much worse."

TWENTY-EIGHT

"So," Cole said. "Still think you can explain everything and make it go away?"

Jesse sipped his coffee. "Maybe not."

They sat together at Daisy's in a corner booth, away from the other people at the tables. Daisy had been overjoyed to see Cole, who'd worked for her when he first came to Paradise. She hugged him and fussed over him like she was his mother.

"I haven't been able to find anyone to replace you worth a damn," she'd said.

"I am *right here*," Jordyn, Daisy's latest employee, had said with a hurt look on his face.

"And there are three customers who need coffee *right over there*," Daisy had shot back, before leaving Jesse and Cole in their corner to talk.

Cole wolfed down his breakfast like he hadn't eaten in days. "I tell you, I missed this. They really seem to hate food in California. They do something to leach the taste out of it so you won't get addicted."

"You must have been on the first flight out."

"I took the red-eye and changed into my suit in an airport bathroom," Cole said. "I stopped to see Rita before I came to see you."

"I'm surprised she'd go to bat for me," Jesse said. "Sponsoring you with the judge like that."

"Oh, she's still pissed at you," Cole said. "But she was able to justify it by saying she was helping me, not you."

"You lawyers are great at finding loopholes."

"Lucky for you."

"You came an awfully long way to say 'I told you so,'" Jesse said.

Cole gave him a look. "Jesse," he said. "I came here because otherwise you'd be in a cell right now."

Jesse nodded. Cole was right. Still, he felt he had to defend himself to his son. At least a little. "I didn't realize it was going to go that way."

He'd already explained to Cole about Janis Devlin's statements and Devlin's blood on the floor.

"Well, the good news is they don't have your prints or your DNA," Cole said. "I'm sure they couldn't resist bragging about that if they did. Still, I'm a little surprised Dev Chada didn't give you a heads-up. Or Suit."

"They're keeping Dev away from it. The whole scene, the whole investigation, has been quarantined. I didn't hear a thing. I think Ellis tried to warn me. But there's only so much he and Lundquist can do without compromising the investigation."

"You think Lundquist is on board with this?"

Jesse thought about it. A day ago, he never would have considered that. But after that scene in the conference room, he had to go over the possibilities.

"No," he said after Cole spent a long time chewing his food. "Lundquist and I don't always agree on how to handle a case. And he's not like Healy. We're not friends. But he would never come after me."

"That's not very comforting," Cole said. "He's not exactly standing up for you."

"In his defense, I have given him reason to believe I would handle some things outside of proper channels."

Cole didn't look amused. "Yeah, I'm not really worried about his defense right now, Jesse. I'm worried about yours."

"You think those agents will be able to make a case?"

"I don't know," Cole said. "I won't get access to anything they've got until they get an indictment and then we enter discovery. You know how it works."

Jesse had never considered that there might be an indictment. He didn't believe it would actually go that far.

"But what do you think?" he asked. "If you had to make the case yourself."

"That depends. How much do those agents hate you now?"

"I don't think I made any friends in there before you showed up."

"Yeah, I figured. You're batting a thousand so far, aren't you?"

"I appreciate the baseball metaphor," Jesse said. "You trying to talk at my level?"

"I've even been to a couple Dodger games," Cole said. "But that's not the point. The point is, the best way for them to make a case is for you to do something stupid. And you've been giving them what they want."

Jesse felt his jaw clenching. "It's hard for me to think of myself as a defendant. Those are my colleagues. They're on the same side."

"No, they are not," Cole said. "They are the people trying to put you in a cage. And you need to stop helping them. You're not a cop now, Jesse. You're a suspect."

"You really think I don't know that?"

"You're sure as hell acting like it. Because you never should have walked in there, and you know it. Are you so dedicated to being right that you won't even look out for yourself?"

"That's not it," Jesse said.

"Then please explain it to me. You knew they were gunning for you. Or you should have. What made you think you could talk your way out of it?"

"I didn't," Jesse said.

That stopped Cole. He even paused in his eating, his fork frozen on its way to his mouth. "What?"

"I knew I couldn't talk my way out of it. That's not why I went into the room."

Cole's eyes were wide open. He looked completely baffled. "Then why?"

"Because I know the truth. And the truth is, I didn't do anything to Devlin. I had nothing to do with this."

He tapped the table with one finger so Cole would pay attention. This was important.

"The truth ought to be enough," Jesse said.

Cole put down his fork and sat back. "You know, sometimes I forget, with everything you've done, everything you've had to do—you really are an idealist, aren't you?"

"No," Jesse said. "Not really. I know how the world works. I just think it should be better. When it's not, you try to push it in that direction. And when you can, you behave as if it was."

"You really believe that?"

"You don't?"

"I'm a lawyer, Dad," Cole said. "I've seen way too many cases where the truth is not nearly enough."

"Jesus," Jesse said. "Things must be grim. That's twice in one day you've called me Dad."

"If you get convicted, I'll even give you a hug."

"Let's hope it doesn't come to that."

"It won't," Cole said. "You've got a great attorney."

Jesse took out his wallet to put money down. He had to leave it on the table before Daisy noticed, because she never gave him a bill, and she'd yell at him if she caught him. It also gave him something to do while he told Cole the most important thing:

"Thank you for being here," he said.

"Yeah, well. Just don't forget: I told you so," Cole said.

Jesse laughed.

"Now. We should probably talk about my fee."

"You can stay in your old room. Rent-free."

"Gee, thanks. You're gonna have to do better than that," Cole said.

"I'm also paying for breakfast."

"In that case, I want a muffin, too."

"Deal," Jesse said, and waved Jordyn over for more coffee as well.

TWENTY-NINE

Molly had a nice hotel room near Times Square. She didn't actually know New York very well, and she figured she might as well do some tourist stuff if she was burning her vacation days.

The hotel, which adjoined a Broadway theater on one side, turned out to be *very* nice. The concierge, a stunning Black woman in a sharp suit, gave her free chocolates when she checked in and upgraded her to a better room without asking. The hotel didn't even charge her for Wi-Fi. Definitely a step up from the motels where she used to stay on vacation.

But she and Michael had been saving and scrimping for years, and with the kids out of the house now, they had more money than she knew what to do with. Michael was paid frankly ridiculous amounts for his services by the billionaires who hired him to sail and service their yachts. Most of Molly's salary went into the bank now. After being the primary breadwinner for so long, she figured she'd earned a little luxury.

The next morning, the bellman hailed her a cab and she traveled downtown to the U.S. District Court for the Southern District of New York.

After surrendering her gun at the security checkpoint and showing her badge, she was allowed inside. She went upstairs, where she was parked in a seat in the offices of the U.S. Marshals Service.

After a few moments, Deputy U.S. Marshal Robert Hanrahan stork-walked out in his tight gray suit to greet her.

"Deputy Chief Crane," he said.

"Deputy Hanrahan," she said. "I'm surprised you remember me."

"You make quite an impression," he said, shaking her hand in a gentle grip. She wondered: Was this tall, oddly formal weirdo flirting with her?

He guided her back into the Marshals offices. They had to walk a long way, past lots of other desks, with some places in the corridor blocked by cardboard boxes and old office equipment.

When they got inside his office, he offered her coffee and a seat. She took both.

"What can I do for you today, Deputy Chief Crane?"

"You can call me Molly, for starters."

He nodded. "Molly." He barely seemed to fit behind his own desk, all folded up like a paper clip, but he didn't seem the least bit uncomfortable. He reminded her, in fact, a little of Jesse in that way: totally at ease in his own skin, even though he looked completely rigid from the outside.

She sipped her coffee. "You have your own office and a door that closes," she said. "Pretty fancy."

"One of the few perks of being in this courthouse. They didn't have cubicle farms when it was established, and I've been exiled to the back rooms."

"Because of what happened with Devlin?"

He tipped his head forward slowly, and now Molly couldn't help thinking of a flamingo. "Yes," he said. "I was involved in the case, and it ended very badly for the government. People worry that failure is contagious, and so I've been put out of sight."

"That's shitty."

He shrugged. "That's government work. You should see where they put the lawyers."

"That's the reason I'm here," Molly said. "I want to talk to you about Devlin."

"I thought as much. However, I am afraid I cannot be of much help to you. I told your Chief Stone—"

"Jesse. Everyone calls him Jesse," Molly interrupted.

"—Jesse—everything that I was allowed to tell him. My activity on the case is over, or so I have been told by my superiors. I am not to investigate Ramsey Devlin, or make inquiries about his activities, or be seen anywhere near him, or even speak about him again."

"That's pretty thorough."

"When you have been forced to settle out of court with a man you've prosecuted for a crime, you tend to be very shy about drawing his attention again. We had the complaints of his clients, and we had the financial transactions, and we had the collapse of the fund. We thought that was enough. It was not. We got, as they say, our asses handed to us. We are many things here, but we are not foolish."

"So if I were to ask you anything about the case—say, about any leads or ideas that didn't get explored, anything that might lead to another indictment against him—"

"I would be sympathetic," Hanrahan said. "And then I would apologize and decline to comment further."

Molly sort of liked the way he talked. It was weird and old-fashioned, but it was polite.

Wasn't particularly helpful, though.

"There's got to be something," Molly said.

"Deputy Chief—"

"Molly."

"Molly. Believe me. I can tell you: We investigated this case thoroughly. Why, I even took the file out to show you how thoroughly."

He put his hand on a stack of file folders and papers that towered precariously on his desk.

"Can I read that?"

"Of course you cannot. This is all off-limits, since Mr. Devlin beat us so thoroughly. As I told you. We are like a whipped dog, Molly. We have our tails tucked between our legs, and we are cowering in a corner of the yard."

Molly wanted to ask, *Then why am I here?*, but Hanrahan seemed to be building up to something.

He took a paper off the top of the stack.

"I can tell you we tried to interview employees of the Devlin Fund, who refused to meet with us. They had lawyers before we could even get them in a room. No doubt they might have been able to enlighten us about the crimes being committed by Ramsey Devlin, if only we'd been able to question them. But sadly, we did not."

He carefully put the paper down on the desk between them.

"If only we could have spoken to *any one of these people*," Hanrahan said. "If only there were a formidable, intelligent, and determined investigator who would be able to run them down and question them again. It might have made all the difference. Ah, well. Nevertheless."

Molly sat where she was.

"Okay," she said. "Thank you for your time, I guess. I'll just keep looking into him. See what I can find."

"I truly regret I cannot help you. If I were allowed to say anything about Ramsey Devlin—"

"Which you're not," Molly said.

"—which I am not," Hanrahan agreed. "I would say he is a world-class scumbag. Now, I am afraid my presence is required in another meeting. I am sorry again I couldn't be more help."

They sat looking at each other for another minute. Hanrahan smiled at her. It was a nice smile.

He stood up, rising up like a skyscraper over the stacks of papers on his desk. "And may I say, it was a distinct pleasure to see you again, Molly."

He left the room.

Molly leaned forward and looked at the paper, still sitting where he'd put it.

She got out her phone and took a picture of it.

Then she finished her coffee and left.

Yeah, she decided on her way out. He was definitely flirting with her.

THIRTY

"Damn it, Jesse, why are you so stubborn?" Cole said.

"I'm not stubborn," Jesse said. "I'm just right."

Cole rubbed his face with both hands and let out a deep breath.

He and Cole were at his condo, seated at his dining table to discuss strategy. It was not going great. Cole had a yellow legal pad filled with his notes and ideas. Most of them were crossed out.

"If we file suit demanding an end to your suspension, they will have to show cause why you shouldn't be on the job," he said.

"I get that," Jesse said. "But you take this to court, and then it's in court."

Cole looked at Jesse. "Yeah. That's how it works."

"And then it's out of our hands entirely. We put this in front of a judge, and then it becomes a public fight. Right now, it's still just behind the scenes."

"Where Kirkpatrick and Hodges can do whatever they want with no oversight."

"Maybe. But if you file a motion, then maybe they decide they can't wait any longer. And they indict me."

"They're going to do that anyway," Cole said. "These two special investigators are not looking for any other suspects. They are after you."

"I don't think so," Jesse said. "I don't think it will get that far."

"Jesse, wake up: They will do whatever it takes to nail you to the wall."

"They don't have enough evidence."

"You think that would stop them? The guy told you his whole case already."

Cole began ticking points off on his finger, as he'd been doing for most of an hour already.

"One, they've got you at the scene. Two, they've got motive. Devlin hated your ass and was making your life miserable. Three, they have you *standing over a puddle of the victim's blood*. I could indict you on any one of those things."

"Well, it's a good thing you're on my side," Jesse said, deadpan.

"Not a time for jokes."

"I've done what Kirkpatrick is doing," Jesse said. "He told me the whole case because he wants me to think he's got it locked up. But he knows there are holes in it. We push him, and he has to go ahead before he can find the real answers."

"You honestly think those two give a damn about the real truth?"

"They're good cops. I know what they'll do."

"Jesus Christ," Cole said, standing up from the table. "You are not playing the older-and-wiser card here, are you? I am an actual lawyer, Jesse. I went to law school and everything."

"I know," Jesse said. "And I am proud of you. You've become a hell of a lawyer."

"Oh, don't do that. Don't patronize me. That's not what I'm saying."

Jesse started to get frustrated, like he did when Cole first came into his life, when they would go around in circles like this. He bit back his temper and asked, as quietly as he could, "Then what are you saying?"

"If I'm going to be your lawyer, then let me do the damn job. You need to believe me when I tell you that I know this better than you do. But you can't do that, can you? You still think I'm just a screwup who turned up at your door."

Jesse was genuinely surprised. "Good God, Cole. I didn't say that."

"But you were thinking it."

"No. Absolutely not."

Cole turned away.

Jesse stood up and went around the table to face him. "Cole," he said. "I am truly proud of you. And I could not ask for a better lawyer. You've stood up for me, even though I was never around for you. I am grateful. And if I didn't say it enough, I am sorry."

Cole swallowed. Looked away. Then looked back at Jesse.

"Yeah. Me, too. Lost my temper there. Sorry."

"Well," Jesse said. "You've got an exceptionally pigheaded client."

"Yeah, that's the truth."

They both laughed.

"You want to know one reason I'm angry about all this?" Cole said. "Those guys are assholes. Kirkpatrick and Hodges. They're throwing everything they have at you. And I want to hit them back."

"Believe me, I understand the impulse. I've been there."

"Then why don't you? Why aren't you throwing punches? You should be fighting for your life, Jesse. How are you so calm?"

Jesse looked at his son. "Because I didn't do it."

Cole sighed and sat back down. "I wish that was the only thing that mattered, Dad. But most people only care about how it looks. They don't care about the truth."

"Then we make them," Jesse said. "Any way we can."

Cole couldn't help rolling his eyes. "That's why I want to file the motion—"

Just then a key rattled in the front door and it banged open. Jacob came rushing inside, dumping his backpack on the floor, skidding into the living room in his untied sneakers.

"A little help here?" Rachel called from the door, where she stood with grocery bags in her arms and at her feet.

She was there to make dinner and to spend time with Cole, to get to know him a little better. Jesse was glad she'd arrived in time to break up another fight.

Jesse and Cole both went to the door to help her. Jacob, meanwhile, went straight to the TV to begin hooking up a video game console he carried under his arms.

"Hey, I said, 'a little help,'" Rachel called after him from the kitchen.

"I'm *busy*, Mom," he said, fiddling with the cables. "Jesse, you're going to love this. You can play as any player, like, almost ever."

"I don't know," Jesse said. "I've only ever played baseball in real life."

Cole smiled at him. "Wait. You're not scared to lose at a video game, are you, Jesse?"

"Of course not."

Rachel stopped unbagging groceries. "Oh. I think you're right, Cole. I think he's a little nervous."

Jacob turned from the screen and came to Jesse's defense. "He's not scared," Jacob said fiercely. "Jesse just doesn't know how to play. And it's easy."

Cole looked at the kid, and then at Jesse.

"Wow," he said quietly.

He had a strange look on his face. "What?" Jesse asked.

Cole blinked, then looked away. "Nothing," he said. "Just thinking something."

"Okay," Rachel said, handing over a cutting board with steaks. "Jesse, put these on the grill. Make yourself useful."

Jesse went outside to his small balcony, where he kept his propane grill. Cole went with him.

Jesse fired up the grill. He waited. If Cole wanted to share something, he would.

"That kid thinks you're pretty great."

"He's a pretty great kid. Been dealing with this stupid situation with Devlin's son since school started, all on his own. He's been trying to protect his mom. I tried to help, and I found out . . . Well, there's some stuff you can't protect kids from. But he's managing. It sucks, but he's managing."

Cole cleared his throat. "I was just thinking, maybe my

mom was wrong about you. You would have been a good dad."

Jesse smiled, but he shook his head. "No," he said gently. "The guy she knew—he was a drunk. I would have been a disaster."

"Maybe so."

"Trust me."

Cole looked inside, at the boy in front of the TV, carefully entering Jesse's name on the screen. "Well," he said. "I think Jacob would disagree."

Jesse did something unusual for him. He reached over and put his hand on Cole's arm so the younger man would look at him. "I'm doing my best to be a better father."

Cole smiled.

"Never too late to learn, I guess," he said.

Jesse said, "I hope so."

From inside, they heard Jacob call through the open door. "Hey, Jesse! Did you know you can play as Ozzie Smith?"

"Really?" Jesse said. "Well, in that case, I'm going to demolish all of you."

Cole smirked. "Bring it on, old man."

THIRTY-ONE

Suit was trying to figure out how to complete the weekly time sheets when Bill Fawcett, the chief of police in Helton, walked into the office uninvited.

"You look like a kid who doesn't want to do his math homework," Fawcett said, grinning.

Suit looked up at him and suddenly had a lot more sympathy for all those times Jesse said he wanted to shoot people who interrupted him.

Fawcett was a big guy, and he looked like a cop—even more than Jesse did, Suit thought. That was probably why he kept the job. He looked the part of a police chief, all square-jawed and solid.

It was actually being a good cop that Fawcett had trouble with.

"What do you want, Bill?" Suit asked.

Fawcett sat down. "I was in the area. Thought I'd stop by and see if it was true that they left you all alone and unsupervised."

"Jesse and Molly will be back. I'm just holding down the fort."

"Yeah, that's not what I hear."

"Well, you hear wrong."

Fawcett put on a look of innocence. "I mean, you can say that," he said. "But I'm hearing it from the mayor."

That made Suit pause. "You've been talking to Armistead?"

"He asked me to come out and discuss taking over the job."

"What job?"

Now Fawcett looked contemptuous. "The chief's job. What else?"

"They want you to take over for Jesse?"

"Did you think they were going to ask you?"

Suit hadn't really thought about it. But he couldn't say he was surprised.

"So why are you here? Measuring for new curtains?"

"Maybe you ought to be nicer to me," Fawcett said. "Since I'm the one who's going to decide if you work here."

Suit laughed. "You think I'd stay?"

"Why not?"

"So many reasons, Bill," Suit said. "You don't want to hear them all. Believe me."

"Let's cut the bullshit, huh? You need a job. And I'd need a deputy chief. You might not like me as much as your hero Jesse, but you'd still be doing good here. People would still need you."

"You know Gary would only hire you because he thought you'd do as you were told."

"Yeah, they thought that about Jesse, too. How'd that work out?"

"I don't want to be any part of it," Suit said. "I wouldn't give him the satisfaction."

"So what?" Fawcett said. "Armistead is an asshole. Big deal. You get a new title, more pay, and you still get to do the job. There's no reason for you to make your life worse just to make a point. Couple more years, I retire, and you get the chief's job for real."

Suit had to admit: He'd thought about it. He'd always assumed that one day, when Jesse finally retired, he'd be the one to take over.

But Robin never gets to be Batman, does he?

Suit pushed the thought away. Jesse wasn't going to quit anytime soon. Probably not ever.

"Why would you want me here?" he asked Fawcett. "You don't care about Paradise."

"You're right about that. But I'm not an idiot, no matter what you or Jesse think of me. I'd rather have someone like you doing the hard stuff for me."

Suit sat back and looked at him. "If you hate being a cop so much, Bill, why the hell do you still wear that badge?"

Fawcett made a face. "Police work doesn't have to be as hard as you guys make it," he said. "Look at your board over there."

Suit really didn't want to. In the conference room, Jesse insisted they keep a tally of cases and tasks on the dry-erase board hanging on the wall. Crimes that hadn't been cleared by an arrest, or complaints from citizens that hadn't been resolved, were written in red. Cases and problems that had been handled were written in black. And problems that were completely resolved were erased altogether.

Every day, there were new complaints and problems. People in Paradise called the station for everything from domestic violence, to lost pets, to stolen bikes. Jesse insisted on putting everything up there. That way, if someone called and asked him what was going on with, for instance, the missing stop sign at the intersection, Jesse could look at the board and have an answer. He took it all seriously.

Even in just a couple days, the amount of red had been growing.

"Yeah?" Suit said. "What about it?"

"You think we have something like that in Helton?"

"I don't know. I guess?"

Fawcett shook his head. "We take the calls from dispatch. That's all. If it's not an emergency, we don't even take those."

"Kind of a loose definition of *protect and serve*, Bill."

Fawcett shrugged. "We're not obligated to wipe people's asses. They think cops are some kind of customer service for them. But if there's no crime, then it's not worth our time."

"You should put that on a T-shirt."

"Beats the hell out of the alternative," Fawcett said. "You run all around this town, scrambling after every little problem. I know Jesse has you all do it. You do traffic duty and you break up bar fights and you listen to the tourists when they come every season and whine. But what do you get out of it?"

"I don't know," Suit said. "But I figure you're going to tell me."

"Ask your friend Jesse. See how much loyalty doing the job like that bought him."

Suit sat back in Jesse's chair. He'd had about enough of Bill Fawcett.

"Well," he said. "Thanks for stopping by, Chief."

Fawcett wasn't offended. "You know I'm right, Suit," he said. "You think about my offer."

"Jesse's going to be back."

"Maybe," Fawcett admitted as he got up out of the chair. "Maybe not. That's the thing about guys like Jesse, Suit. Eventually, people get tired of having a hero around. It reminds them of everything they're not."

THIRTY-TWO

Lundquist heard Jesse's voice over the phone and made a noise—half groan, half growl.

"Is that how you greet people?" Jesse asked.

"I'd think you'd be used to it by now," Lundquist said. "I can't talk to you, Jesse. You should know that."

Jesse had called Lundquist this morning to see how the investigation was going. Kirkpatrick and Hodges hadn't made any more inquiries into him—or at least none they'd made public. Cole still wanted to file a motion in court to force them to end Jesse's suspension, but he'd agreed to wait.

Jesse had to give him a reason to wait, though. He needed to do something, to make some kind of progress. So he called Lundquist. Maybe the Homicide commander could provide some leads, or at least an update.

But now Lundquist didn't want to talk.

"I'm just looking to find out where things stand," Jesse said.

"I'm sure Kirkpatrick and Hodges will give you a heads-up before they get an arrest warrant."

"That's hilarious."

"Now you know what it's like talking to you."

"I'm funnier than that," Jesse said. "Come on, Brian. I gave you a lead on other people looking for Devlin. I know there's more to this. What's going on over there?"

"I'm telling you, I don't know," Lundquist snapped. "And if I did know, I wouldn't say. I should hang up on you right now. How would you feel if another cop was talking to the suspect on one of your investigations?"

"I'm not really worried about Hodges's and Kirkpatrick's feelings," Jesse said. "I'd think that with all our history, you'd give me a little consideration."

Lundquist laughed. "History. Yeah, that's part of the problem."

"What's that supposed to mean?"

"Look at it from my perspective, Jesse. I only know about half of what you've done here when you think it's necessary. Is it that crazy to think you might have gone too far this time? Because you just know you're right?"

Jesse didn't know what to say. He and Lundquist didn't always see eye to eye. But to think Jesse would lose control, would actually disappear a guy—well, he thought Lundquist knew him better than that.

But apparently that was the problem. He didn't.

"Maybe you got angry, Jesse," Lundquist said, and now he actually had the gall to sound sympathetic. "God knows you get angry."

Jesse felt his shoulders tense and his fists ball up, almost like a reflex. "Yeah," he said. "I am angry."

"I'm not saying you did it," Lundquist said. "I'm trying to tell you how it looks. And it looks bad. You were there. You were known to have a beef with the guy. That's motive and means. And you've got no other suspects to point at. Unless you want to tell us where Molly Crane was that night?"

Jesse snorted. "Now you're saying you think Molly did it?"

"No, damn it. I'm telling you to think. Why do you think this is happening? If you didn't step in this shit, it wouldn't follow you all around."

"Have you even looked into the guys I told you about?"

"You mean the insurance guy? And the cars that you say were following you?"

"They're not insurance guys."

"Yeah, that's what you said."

"Have you even checked the number he gave me?"

"No. Not yet."

Jesse was aware he was raising his voice. "You think you're going to get around to it anytime soon?"

Lundquist sighed. When he spoke again, he sounded old and tired. "Do you think this is my only job? You think I have nothing better to do than patrol this little stretch of beach for you? I'm a commander in the State Homicide Division, Jesse. That means the whole state. I'm running a dozen different investigations right now. I have corpses piling up in the morgue. So you're going to have to wait your turn."

Jesse was ready to snap back, to tell Lundquist this wasn't just an investigation, this was his *life*—

And then he stopped himself.

Like Lundquist had said, this wasn't his mess. He'd just stepped in it.

Let go of the rope, Dix had told him. Which could also mean *Don't pick a fight with your friends.*

Jesse took a breath. He unclenched his fists.

"You're right. Sorry," Jesse said.

Lundquist paused on the line, as if trying to scan the words for sarcasm. When he spoke, his tone was quieter. "I get it. This is your reputation on the line. I'd be pissed, too."

"I'm more worried about who actually took Devlin. And the people running around my town while your IA friends have me on the bench."

"I know," Lundquist said. "I know you care about Paradise. For what it's worth, that's why I don't think you did it. You wouldn't do anything that would leave the town without you."

Jesse gave a small laugh. "Thanks for that. I think."

"You're welcome. I'll try to get Booker to pick up some of the slack on this, okay?"

Booker Mays was another investigator in the State Homicide Division. He was a good cop. Just overwhelmed with cases, like Lundquist and everyone else.

It wasn't enough. Jesse knew it. But he said, "Sure."

He and Lundquist said a few more things, just to be normal with each other again. Lundquist hung up and probably went on to the next thing on his to-do list.

He was doing his best. But it wasn't his case. Lundquist wanted to help, but he'd only confirmed what Jesse already suspected: Kirkpatrick and Hodges were in charge of his fate.

That wasn't going to work for him.

This all seemed like a plan to Jesse. He couldn't see the objective yet, but he could see it moving around him. Like when he was still playing ball. There were times he could read the field and see something right before it happened.

There was some purpose to all this. It felt intentional.

There was a reason, Jesse was sure of it.

He just didn't know what it was. Not yet.

Jesse knew that if he was going to get out of this hole, he'd have to build his own ladder.

THIRTY-THREE

Jesse had been around a lot of dead bodies, but he was still sort of amazed how Dev Chada was completely unfazed by them.

He found the medical examiner in one of the exam rooms at the Boston facility, working on an autopsy. There were four other tables, and four other corpses waiting for him like cars on an assembly line. Dev had told him there was a shortage of trained forensic pathologists. Everyone in the office worked multiple cases at once. They were always knee-deep in dead people, Dev said.

Dev had the skin of the head peeled back to see the skull and tissue underneath. The ribs were already cracked open.

Dev barely looked up when Jesse entered the room.

"You know we're not supposed to be talking, Jesse," he said.

"Maybe I'm just here for the ambience."

Now Dev looked at him. "Right."

In truth, Jesse had come to the autopsy rooms because

he knew people would notice if he visited Dev in his office or approached him at a crime scene. He didn't want to get Dev in any more trouble than necessary. He figured the presence of corpses would keep any casual observers away.

It was easy to get past the front desk. He still knew most of the staff, and he went past the security guard with a wave and a smile.

Dev sat on a stool and peeled off his gloves.

"Kirkpatrick and Hodges told me to stay away from the case and from you," he said. "Apparently we're too friendly for me to be trusted."

"Is that true?"

Dev smiled. "Absolutely," he said. "Come with me, you're going to want to see this."

He walked back into a side office adjoining the autopsy suite, only a little bigger than a closet, with a computer on the counter and cabinets full of supplies.

"It's not that they're bad guys," he said. "But they're Internal Affairs. They think everyone they meet is lying to them, or covering for someone else, or both. And they're usually right."

"Are they good at their jobs?"

"Yeah," Dev said. "Very. It's why they're not wildly popular with a lot of cops."

There was a coatrack by the door. Dev rummaged in a pocket of his coat and came out with a sheet of paper.

"But you're still willing to help me," Jesse said. "You're not worried they're right?"

Dev looked at him. "I think I know you better than that," he said. "And then, to make sure, I looked into it. Even though I wasn't supposed to."

He handed over the paper.

"Turned out I was right to trust you."

Jesse read it. Or tried to. There was a lot of technical language and raw data. This wasn't one of Dev's reports where he translated his findings into plain English.

Still, Jesse knew a blood pathology report when he saw one.

"You ran tests on the blood?"

"Well, there was a lot of it," Dev said. "I was able to sneak in and get a look at the samples. The bad news, for you, is that the DNA match is one hundred percent. That's Ramsey Devlin's blood. They took samples from multiple areas in the rug and checked them all, just to be sure that it wasn't mixed with cow's blood or something else. It's all his."

"So it wasn't faked. That was definitely Devlin's blood."

"Yeah, but I was a little suspicious. I mean, that's a lot of blood, but I looked at the photos and the report. There were no spatters, no trails, no tracks or footprints. It doesn't match the scene. All of the furniture gets tossed around, but there's not a single drop anywhere but in that big puddle. It's like someone had a massive head wound—head wounds are bleeders—and hit the floor. Except there's no drag marks outside of the puddle, and no smears or anything else. It doesn't make sense."

"Maybe I cleaned it up," Jesse said. "If I was trying to cover my tracks."

"No presence of cleaning agents or even water. The rug was dry except for that puddle. And if you lifted up a body that was bleeding like that, you'd have stains on your clothes and you would have had drips as you moved. You're pretty good, Jesse, but you're not magic."

"Then why are they still looking at me?"

"Well," Dev said. "There's a great big pool of blood and you were in the victim's house with a gun. I mean, that's pretty hard to argue with."

"Good point."

"So I looked a little deeper. I took a look at the blood samples under the microscope. That's when I saw it."

Dev pointed at the paper in Jesse's hand. His finger tapped a single sentence that he'd helpfully highlighted.

"Red cells are convex, rather than concave, and show signs of lysis and bursting from crystallization, most likely due to freezing . . ." Jesse read. "You're saying the blood had been frozen?"

Dev nodded. "Nobody really bothered to look, but that blood had definitely been on ice for a while."

"Does anyone else know this?"

Dev looked a little embarrassed. "That's where we run into a problem. I don't know if this is enough to get you free and clear of this whole mess. This is the kind of thing a defense attorney could use for reasonable doubt. But blood testing and crystallization, that's something Hodges and Kirkpatrick aren't likely to give a damn about. They'll probably still be gunning for you."

"Probably," Jesse said. "Once you get a suspect, you tend to stay on that suspect."

"Yeah," Dev said, looking at the floor. "That's not the real reason, though. The real reason is I'm not supposed to be anywhere near this case."

Jesse got it. "If you tell anyone, you'll get fired."

"Exactly. I can tell someone to do the same tests I did, but . . ."

"They'll still know you're interfering in the case, and you'll still get fired."

"Yeah." Dev was having trouble meeting Jesse's eyes. "I'm sorry, Jesse. I'm scared. I hate like hell to say it, but I am."

Jesse knew that if he asked, Dev would speak up. But he'd lose his job.

And Jesse didn't want to be the reason a good pathologist like Dev was out of a job. For one thing, he wanted Dev on his cases when he got back to work.

Dev was also a friend. That had to count for something.

"Don't worry about it," Jesse said.

Dev looked both surprised and relieved. "Seriously?"

"Seriously," Jesse said. "You've stuck your neck out far enough for me. I appreciate this."

"Jesse, I'll tell them if you really need me to. I mean, they're probably going to get around to doing the tests themselves, but if it comes down to it, I will tell them."

"I know you would. But now that I see this, I don't think it's going to come to that. You've done enough, Dev. Really."

Dev let out a deep breath and his shoulders relaxed a full inch. "I'm sorry, man. I know this is bullshit."

"Don't apologize," Jesse said, holding up the paper. "None of this made sense until now. This is the right clue. I know where to go from here."

Dev looked curious. "Where's that?"

Jesse smiled.

"Back to the scene of the crime, of course."

THIRTY-FOUR

Jesse drove his Explorer over to Seaside Drive and parked down the street from the Devlins' house on the point. It looked worse in the daylight, like a big container washed up from the wreck of some cargo ship.

He sat and watched the house. At just after three, the gate opened and a Range Rover went up the drive and parked in front of the house. Race came bursting out of the backseat and ran through the front door, not waiting for the nanny, the same young woman who'd been at Rachel's door, when she got out of the driver's seat. She went to the back of the SUV and got out bags of groceries.

After several trips, she closed the front door. *A lot of food for just three people,* Jesse thought.

Jesse waited some more.

Nothing happened for a long time. He saw Ms. Foley walk down the road on her way to the beach, and then back. She waved at him. He waved back.

The sun was on its way below the horizon when Janis Devlin came racing up the road, too fast, in an Audi R8 coupe. She had to slam on the brakes to avoid hitting the gate, which moved at a slow crawl.

While she was waiting at the gate, Jesse could see her face through the windshield. She scowled.

He waved like he had to Ms. Foley. He wasn't trying to be inconspicuous.

When the gate had finally opened enough for the Audi, she hit the gas. The engine sounded like a growl of frustration. She zipped up the front drive and went around the side of the house to the garage.

Jesse waited again. This time, he didn't have to wait long.

Another Paradise PD Explorer came trundling up the road, obeying the speed limit. It pulled alongside Jesse, driver's window by his driver's window.

Gabe, behind the wheel, rolled down the window. "Hey, Jesse," he said.

"Hey, Gabe. Janis Devlin give you a call?"

"No," Gabe said. "She called Armistead. Who called Suit. Who called me."

"That's pretty good response time, considering."

Gabe looked away. "Jesse," he said. "You know this looks a little creepy, right?"

"I'm just watching the sunset."

Gabe made a face. "Let me ask you a question," he said. "Would you accept that answer if you were me?"

Jesse considered it. "No. I would not."

Gabe looked pained. "You're not helping your case here, you know."

"Come on, Gabe. You don't honestly believe that I did something to Devlin."

"Of course not," Gabe said. "But I think you're making

things harder for yourself. And for us. We still have to do the job."

"That's what I'm trying to do here."

"Yeah, but you're not on the job right now, are you?"

Jesse didn't like it, but Gabe had a point.

"I just wanted to check something about the house."

"You get a good look?"

"Yeah. I did."

"You want to tell me what you're looking for?"

Jesse thought about it for a moment. And thought about the position he'd be putting Gabe in. "No. Not yet."

"Okay," Gabe said. "You know we're there for you. All of us. When you're ready."

"I do," Jesse said.

"Then can you please move on? As a favor to me? Just so I don't have to hear about it again from Armistead?"

Jesse nodded.

"Thank you," he said, and hit the gas, made a U-turn, and drove away.

Jesse took one last look at the house and then started the engine. He was making his own U-turn when he hit the brakes.

Janis Devlin was marching down the drive, coming right for him.

He stopped at the gate, put the Explorer into park, and rolled down his window. He wasn't about to run away.

She waited again, for the gate to open, and then stomped to the side of his car.

"What the hell do you think you're doing?" she said.

"I was just leaving, but it looked like you had something you wanted to say."

Her chin wobbled. Her eyes filled with tears. She seemed to become smaller, more frail, as she crumpled in on herself. "Why are you attacking me like this?" she wailed. "Why can't you just leave my family alone? Haven't you hurt us enough?"

Jesse waited a moment.

Janis looked up. The tears rolled down her cheeks, but her eyes were clear. "Well, you're a coldhearted son of a bitch, aren't you? You're just going to sit there and watch a woman cry?"

Jesse shook his head. "I'd heard you were an actress. You're very good."

She preened a little at the compliment. "A couple soap opera appearances. One pilot that didn't go anywhere. I was lucky to get married when I did. Before everything started sagging."

Jesse didn't say anything.

"That's where you say I still look great, you prick."

"I think you know exactly how you look."

She made a face. "Well. It never hurts to hear it."

"I was hoping I could ask you a couple questions while I've got you."

She snorted. "You've got some balls, you know that? Asking me for favors after what you did to my husband."

"I never touched your husband, Janis," Jesse said quietly. "But you know that, don't you?"

She crossed her arms and stepped back. "You trying to get me to change my story?"

"Wouldn't dream of it. I know you've made your choices. I just don't know why."

"I imagine there's a lot you don't know."

"Help me out, then. Explain it to me."

She shook her head. "Nothing to explain."

"Let me try: I think I know why you're doing this. You thought it would be the best thing for your family. A way to get clear. To solve all your problems at once."

"No idea what you're talking about."

"I also know it's not going to end well for you."

"Is that some kind of threat?"

"No. It's the truth. I can understand how you wouldn't recognize it."

Her face went as cold and flat as concrete in winter. "Well, aren't you so fucking clever," she said.

"I actually feel a little slow. I shouldn't be in this situation," Jesse said. "And neither should you."

"You keep jabbering on as if it makes any difference," Janis said. "As if you can just talk your way out of everything you've done."

"No," Jesse said. "That's your husband's trick."

She shook her head. "Like I said: very clever."

"Okay," Jesse said. "I'm going to offer you one final chance, right here. You don't have to stick with this. It's not beyond fixing. I will help you as best I can. I can promise you that."

She shrugged. "Is this how you talk to suspects? Because I'm starting to see how you lost your job."

Jesse took the Explorer out of park. He had one more question. He didn't know if it would work, but it was the one answer he really wanted from Janis Devlin. "When this is all over, no matter how it goes," Jesse said. "What do you think your son is going to say?"

Janis's eyes went narrow. He'd think she was faking the rage on her face, but nobody was that good an actor.

"I will do whatever it takes to protect my son," she said. "Now, get the fuck away from my house."

Jesse nodded and pulled away.

He looked in the rearview once. Janis still stood in the road, watching him go.

Almost like she was waiting for him to come back.

THIRTY-FIVE

Jesse's phone buzzed. The caller ID listed a local bowling alley.

"I heard you've been taking my name in vain," Vinnie Morris said when Jesse answered.

"Is there some kind of bell that goes off whenever you're mentioned inside a police station?" Jesse asked.

Jesse heard the little exhalation of air that meant Vinnie laughed. "Something like that. You should come by. I got something you're gonna wanna know."

"Right now?"

"Yeah, why not?"

"I could be working."

"From what I hear, you got lots of time on your hands. I'll see you soon."

Vinnie hung up.

Jesse thought about waiting to leave, just to make a point.

But then, he knew Vinnie wouldn't reach out if he didn't have information.

And Jesse really didn't have anything else going on at the moment.

JESSE SOMETIMES WONDERED why Vinnie dressed so well when his office was in a bowling alley. Today his jacket alone would have been more than a mortgage payment in most parts of Boston. It was a fawn-soft cashmere in blue over a hand-tailored blue shirt with a white spread collar and a red tie. His gray wool slacks had a knife crease, as always.

The bowling alley itself never looked as good. The exterior was crumbling, and only the bar area ever seemed to be cleaned regularly. Jesse had never seen anyone actually use the lanes.

They sat at one of the booths in the bar, Vinnie with a Coke, Jesse with a club soda and lime. Vinnie usually had a real drink. That told Jesse this was business.

They hadn't spoken much in the past few months. Vinnie had been out of town a few times on mysterious errands, and Jesse had been busy with the usual distractions of the summer people. But they'd also been giving each other some time after their last serious discussion, which brought them up against the main issue in their relationship. Vinnie was a criminal, and Jesse was a cop. As Kirkpatrick pointed out, that tended to be a conflict of interest.

But Jesse liked Vinnie. He trusted him. Vinnie had risked his life to help Jesse more than once.

And he had to admit he missed talking to Vinnie sometimes. Jesse didn't talk much to anyone, outside of Molly and Suit. Vinnie was one of the few people who understood him.

They both held fast to a code. And they might have different subsections of the code, and some different rules, but they agreed on what really mattered.

Not many other people did. And even fewer had been tested the way he and Vinnie had.

It was hard to find people who belonged to their particular club.

"So what's it like to be a dangerous criminal suspect?" Vinnie asked.

Jesse sipped his club soda. "They've got the wrong guy."

"Oh, sure. Everybody says that."

"You're enjoying this, aren't you?"

"Just wondering what it's like for you on the other side of the law. Are you going to make a run for it? Go down to the border and change your name? Do you need a new passport?"

"If I do, I'll come to you first."

"I can't promise you a discount."

"Well, then what am I doing here?"

Vinnie took a sip of his Coke. "I thought you should know about something I heard from Florida."

"What's that?"

"There's a local gang down there, does business with the Colombians. Import only. More like customers than partners, you understand. Six of their guys got pulled out of a car in a parking lot last week. Head shots, every one."

"There's a pretty high mortality rate in the pharmaceutical business."

"True," Vinnie said. "But I was asked to keep an eye out for the possible shooters. The gang was maybe looking for some payback, if someone could keep it quiet. So it wouldn't get back to the Colombians."

"Someone wanted to hire you to hit the guys who hit their guys?"

Vinnie made a face. "For chrissakes, Jesse. I go to a lot of trouble to find other ways to say these things, and then you just blurt that shit out."

"Sorry."

"Without admitting to anything illegal—"

"You know I'm not a cop right now."

"Yeah, like you ever stop being a cop . . . Without admitting anything illegal, I might have heard that the people who killed these guys were in the area. Specifically, Paradise."

"Why are they here?"

"I'm told they're looking for a guy named Ramsey Devlin."

Suddenly Jesse's involuntary lunch meeting made more sense.

"You're telling me Devlin lost money that belonged to a Colombian drug cartel?"

"Yeah," Vinnie said. "I did a little checking. Not all of his customers were church funds and charities. That was just to look good. Devlin invested in cryptocurrency. That stuff is the greatest thing that ever happened for drug trafficking. Totally changed the game. You can convert millions in dirty money into untraceable digital currency and transfer it anywhere in the world. Then you take it out again as cash, the proceeds of a totally legitimate investment. You can even report it on your taxes."

"Not that you would know anything about money laundering."

Vinnie took another drink of his Coke. "I read a lot."

"But if the exchange where you invested the money collapses . . ." Jesse said.

"Well, some investors just have to take the loss and get nothing more than a valuable lesson," Vinnie said. "Other people, like the Colombians, they don't take the loss as well. They can trace a hundred bucks that goes into a dealer's pocket when it shouldn't. Then they make that guy extinct. You think they're going to let Devlin walk away with millions of dollars?"

"Who did they send to get it back from Devlin?"

"The main guy is named Salazar. He's a heavy hitter, Jesse. No joke. Takes big swings. Has never been touched."

"Why didn't you take the job?"

"Couple reasons. First, I am a legitimate businessman, as I keep telling you."

Vinnie was repeating that a lot. Jesse thought someone must have wired the alley recently. Maybe a new warrant for a wiretap.

"But if someone were to take out a contract on Salazar, the Colombians would be unhappy. He's connected way up in the hierarchy. And he's valuable. They've been using him to settle accounts for years, and he never fails. He's like a cruise missile. They just aim him and the problem is solved."

"I think I met him."

"Then you're lucky he didn't decide you were a problem that needs to be solved."

"Why didn't the Colombian cartel reach out to someone local in the first place? Why go to all the trouble of sending their own guy?"

"Who would they call? You know this city is full of competing interests. We're way too independent here in Boston," Vinnie said. "We don't do what we're told. We have our own ideas about what's good for business."

"And some of you even talk to cops."

Vinnie grinned. "That, too."

"Thank you, Vinnie," Jesse said. "Seriously. I owe you."

Vinnie shrugged. "Nah," he said. "I feel like I owed you one. From the time with that thing. Couldn't help you then. I thought you need to know this."

That was as close as they were going to get to talking about it. Which suited Jesse just fine.

He offered his hand and Vinnie shook it.

"You need someone watching your back?"

Jesse thought about it. If Vinnie was offering, it meant Salazar was dangerous.

But Paradise was complicated right now, to say the least.

"Nah," Jesse said, making it sound like Vinnie had offered to pay for a pizza. "I've got backup. And it probably wouldn't be a good idea for you to show up in Paradise right now. For you or me."

Vinnie nodded. "Still. If you need me."

Jesse got up to go. "I know where to find you."

Before he got more than a couple steps from the table, Vinnie spoke again.

"Hey. I heard the IA guy asked if you and I were friends."

"Yeah. He did."

"And you told him yes."

"I did."

"Would've made your life easier if you'd said no."

"Probably."

"A lot of people pretend they don't know me when they're being questioned by the cops," Vinnie said. "It wouldn't have bothered me."

"I know that," Jesse said. "But it would have bothered me."

Vinnie shook his head and smiled.

"You're too honest for your own good, Jesse," he said. "It's gonna cause you problems someday."

"Yeah," Jesse said. "But who ever said life was supposed to be easy?"

THIRTY-SIX

Molly waited on a bench in the lobby, sipping the terrible coffee from the chain shop right outside. She'd heard that workers were reluctant to go back to the office, but she couldn't tell from this building. People had been streaming in and out of the doors all morning: heading to the elevators, dropping packages with the front desk, smiling and greeting one another, or scowling with their eyes aimed at their phones.

It took about an hour before the security guard got curious enough to notice her. He'd walked over, hand on the Taser in a holster on his belt.

This told Molly a couple things. One, he wasn't an off-duty cop working a second job. Even an off-duty cop would carry an actual gun. And two, he wasn't terribly confident or well trained, because he thought he'd need a Taser for a small, well-dressed woman sitting on a bench.

"Excuse me, ma'am," he'd said.

She pulled back her coat. It revealed her badge and, not

coincidentally, her gun. Then she covered them quickly again. She let him draw the wrong conclusion, that she was NYPD and she belonged there.

"Oh, jeez. Sorry, Officer," he'd said quickly, and went back to his position behind the desk.

Nobody had bothered Molly since.

She didn't know why Jesse complained about stakeouts. This was almost peaceful. She got a chance to watch people and let her mind wander on autopilot. It was a nice change from the controlled chaos and paperwork of the station.

Then Molly felt her pulse quicken a little. She looked around the lobby and tracked the person who'd crossed her field of vision, almost without her consciously noticing. He must have arrived earlier in the morning and was now on his way out for an early lunch or a late coffee.

Patel Shirani. He was in his late twenties, wearing expensive slouchwear, which was what Molly called athletic gear that was only ever worn by people who didn't exercise. He had his head down, his eyes fixed on some internal problem.

She got up and intercepted him before he reached the doors.

"Patel," she said.

He stopped and looked up at her, confused. "Yes?"

She flashed her badge and gun again. He froze up for a second.

"Can we talk?" she asked.

"Uh, what's this about?"

"You used to work for the Devlin Fund. I'd like to ask you a couple questions."

Patel's eyes narrowed. "I've told you all before: I have nothing to say about that. You can talk to my lawyer."

Molly had done her homework. She'd been running down names on Hanrahan's list for the last couple days. Most of the names were high-level execs with his hedge fund. Most of them had, predictably, taken the Fifth. She found she couldn't get near most of them. The ones who hadn't taken their ill-gotten gains and run out of the country had private security and lived in high-rises with locked front doors. She and Jesse usually just barged into whatever places they needed to go into back in Paradise. That tactic wasn't going to work here.

But she'd also looked through the org chart of the Devlin Fund. And she found someone who was underneath everyone else, but who also carried a lot of responsibility.

Patel Shirani had been a software developer for Devlin. From what she could gather online, looking at his résumé on LinkedIn and other websites, he was responsible for a lot of the fund's algorithmic trading programs, and also the operations of the hedge fund's electronic transfer systems. Which meant he knew where the money came in from, and where it went out to.

He was her vital Jenga piece: You pulled on him, the whole thing could come down.

Molly smiled at Patel, which seemed to confuse him. "I am not with the FBI or the U.S. Attorney, Patel."

He frowned. "Are you NYPD?"

"Nope," she said. "I am Deputy Chief Molly Crane of the Town of Paradise Police Department."

Patel looked at her blankly.

"That's the place your old boss moved. In Massachusetts. He's my problem now. So I was hoping you could help me fill in a little background on him."

"Wait," he said, catching up now. "You're not even a New York cop?"

"That's right."

"So you can't arrest me or anything?"

"Of course not."

"Well, then there's absolutely no reason for me to talk to you," he said, and walked out through the doors.

Molly let him go.

She didn't need to force a confrontation.

Not here, anyway.

"Son of a bitch," Patel said in a tone of complete disgust.

Molly smiled at him again, standing outside his apartment door.

"How the hell did you get in here?" he snapped.

He looked tired. It was past seven, and his clothes were rumpled now and his eyes were red, probably from staring at screens all day.

Molly, on the other hand, was feeling pretty fresh. She'd gone back to her hotel, had a nice lunch, done more research on her laptop, and then gone to Patel's apartment building at five p.m.

A flash of her badge and a confident wave got her past the doorman. She'd waited in the hallway since.

She'd had to do a few yoga stretches when her back started bothering her—she wasn't as young as she looked—but overall, she'd passed the time easily, reading some of the information she'd found on her phone.

"We should probably talk inside your apartment," Molly said.

"Absolutely not."

"Are you sure?" Molly asked. "I just thought you wouldn't want your neighbors to know YOU'RE BEING QUESTIONED IN A POLICE INVESTIGATION."

Molly was a mother. She could bellow at the top of her lungs until the nearby doors shook in their frames.

Patel winced. "All right, all right. Damn. Just . . . be quiet, okay?"

He unlocked his door and Molly followed him in before he could close it on her.

She looked around. After the short entry hall, the apartment opened into a wide space with an open view of the streets below. It was a big place, recently redone. The living area was covered in thick white carpeting and the kitchen area gleamed with new appliances. Another hallway led to what Molly assumed were the bedroom and bathroom.

She'd looked up the apartment online when she found the address. Patel had bought it only last year. Even if she didn't know how much he'd paid, she could have guessed: A place like this in New York City went for millions of dollars.

"Pretty nice place," she said.

"Gee, thanks, Officer," Patel said.

Molly didn't care for the sarcasm. "It's Deputy Chief."

"Right. Of Podunk, Massachusetts. How could I forget?"

"I don't think you did. I think you know exactly who I am and why I'm here."

Patel went into the kitchen and opened the fridge. He got out a beer and twisted the cap off. "Sorry. You're going to have to tell me. I don't get many crazy women with guns in my life."

"That's funny," Molly said. "I told you. I want to talk to you about Ramsey Devlin."

Patel took a long drink, then belched. He was at least polite enough to cover his mouth. Somewhere along the way, someone had taught him manners. "Look. I will tell you what I told everyone else. I had no knowledge of any illegal activities at the Devlin Fund. Beyond that, under advice of my attorney, I reserve my right against self-incrimination as stated in the Fifth Amendment of the United States Constitution."

He sounded bored, like he was reciting it from memory.

"Nice speech. Is that what your lawyer told you to say?"

"Yes," Patel said. "As a matter of fact, I called him today after you showed up. He said I might have a great case for malicious harassment. How's the Town of Paradise's budget for lawsuits?"

"You called your lawyer?"

"Yeah. So, you know, you're welcome to keep bothering me. If you want to pay me a lot of money in the future. I heard your little department is already in enough trouble. But if you want to leave now, I'll let it slide."

Molly ignored that. "Is that the same lawyer you used when Devlin was arrested?"

Patel frowned. "Yeah."

"Oh, I've met Mr. Wilkes. He's a real charmer. He represents you as well as Devlin. Seems like a conflict of interest to me. Like, how can you be sure he's not looking out for Devlin and leaving you to twist by your undies if he has to choose between you?"

Patel shot her a worried look but didn't take the bait.

"What do I know? I'm just a cop from Podunk."

Patel faked a yawn. "Look. I'm tired. And I've told you I don't have anything to say. So why don't you just leave?"

"Sure. In a minute," Molly said. "I just think it's interesting. You kept your mouth shut. You didn't testify against your boss. And then, a few months after the case was resolved and he walked, you bought this lovely apartment."

Patel stopped looking bored. "You know what? You can go now."

"I mean, what does a place like this go for? A lot more money than even a guy with your job can afford, I'll bet."

"You'd be surprised how much I make."

"I don't think I would, actually."

"I'm not going to say it again: Get out," Patel said.

"Sure," Molly said. "I don't want to upset you."

Just then, both Molly and Patel turned. There was a scraping noise from Patel's door.

And then the sound of it opening, and footsteps in the entry hall.

Patel suddenly looked worried. Much more worried, Molly thought.

Two enormous men appeared in the hallway. They filled the entry like a newly installed wall. They both wore black, like some kind of thug uniform.

The bigger of the two, the one with the dyed-blond hair and beard, took another step forward, smiling.

"Hey," he said, stepping forward.

"Who the hell are you?" Patel said, his voice a couple octaves higher than usual.

"Your lawyer called us," the blond thug said. He did not appear anything but relaxed and pleasant.

Molly had to admit they were a better class of goon than she was used to seeing. Their clothes and haircuts were immaculate. Even Devlin's henchmen looked like they'd stepped out of a catalog.

That didn't mean they weren't dangerous.

"How'd you get in?" she asked.

"Door was open."

"No, it wasn't."

The blond thug ignored Molly. "We're here to help you, Mr. Shirani," he said. "We understand you've had a little trouble with someone harassing you."

He turned to Molly, an easy smile on his face. "I assume that would be you."

Molly turned and planted her feet. She put her hand on her waist. Ready, but not tense.

"You can assume that, yeah," she said.

"If you'll just come with us, Mr. Shirani. We can guarantee your safety," he said, turning back to Patel.

But Patel didn't move. He'd gone quite pale.

"I, uh, I'm fine," Patel said. "I can handle this. You can go."

"No, sir," the blond said. "We can't. Not without you."

He took another step forward. Patel shrank back, almost hiding behind the kitchen counter.

Molly swung her coat back and put her hand on her holster.

"That's far enough."

"Look," the blond said. "This doesn't have to get complicated. We're just going to take Mr. Shirani with us. That's all."

"No," Molly said. "You're not."

The big men looked at each other and laughed.

"It's really not up to you," the blond said. "Now, you step aside and nobody gets hurt."

Molly drew her pistol and aimed at him. She could hardly miss at this range. He was an enormous target.

"Take another step," she said, "and find out who gets hurt."

The blond didn't look scared. "You're just going to shoot me? Without any provocation or cause?"

Jesse probably would've bantered with these two. He could back someone down from a fight with a few well-chosen words. He made them realize they had no chance. She'd seen him do it.

Molly didn't banter.

"Yup," she said.

The blond stopped with his foot in midair. His smile vanished. He stayed where he was.

"You have a permit for that thing?"

"Not sure that's really the question you should be asking right now." Molly's aim didn't waver in the slightest.

"I don't think you really want to hurt anyone. You shoot that, someone will call the police, then we'll press charges—"

Molly sighed. She was the mother of three daughters. She knew that a lot of times, when you start arguing, you've already lost—because you're conceding there's something to argue about.

"I'm going to count to three," she said. "If you're still in the way when I finish, then you're going to also be in the way of some bullets."

The blond hesitated. He looked like he was trying to do a math problem in his head.

"I think you're bluffing," he finally said.

"One way to find out."

Both the thugs put their hands up, but they didn't back away. "Come on," the bearded one said. "You're not being reasonable. Patel, come on, talk to this crazy bitch."

Patel remained silent at Molly's side.

"One," Molly said.

"This is bullshit!" he said again. Now he sounded genuinely offended. "I'm coming over there, and I'm going to take that thing from you, and I'm going to jam it right up your—"

"Two," Molly said.

He shut up. Molly stared at him. She watched his shoulders. If he was going to jump, she'd see it there first. His legs would move, but he'd have to shift all that bulk and he'd start by leaning forward to charge her.

The moment stretched for what felt like an hour.

Molly was about to open her mouth to say, "Three."

But the blond thug blinked first.

"Fuck this!" he snapped, and turned around and marched toward the door.

His companion followed him, unwilling to turn his back on Molly. Who did not lower the gun.

"You're crazy, you know that?" the blond said at the door, pointing at Molly. "You're out of your goddamn mind."

He slammed the door behind them as they left.

Molly waited another second. She heard Patel let out a massive breath of relief. "Jesus," he said. "I can't believe you did that. They really thought you were going to shoot them."

"I was," Molly said.

Only then did she put the gun back into her holster. "Grab your stuff," she said. "You're not safe here. And we need to talk."

"Wait," Patel said. "You weren't bluffing?"

"Why would I bluff?" Molly asked. "Go on. Get your stuff. Now."

Patel looked at Molly with wide eyes, then rushed to his bedroom to pack.

Molly took a deep breath and let the adrenaline drain out of her.

Maybe she was pretty good at this bantering thing, after all.

THIRTY-SEVEN

Patel sat across from Molly in the diner booth, clutching his duffel bag in his lap. He looked younger than ever, like a kid who didn't want to go to summer camp.

Molly sipped her tea and waited. He was on the edge. She didn't need to push him one way or another.

Something else she'd learned as a mom, not a cop. Sometimes kids just need a minute to sit quietly and think.

"Those guys worked for Devlin, didn't they?" Patel asked.

"That's my guess," Molly said. "They showed up after you called your lawyer about me. I'm willing to bet he called them."

"Yeah, but . . ."

"You thought he was your lawyer? That he was on your side?"

Patel shrugged.

"Lawyers generally work for the people who pay them. Something to remember if you survive this."

Patel took a sip of the Coke in front of him. Without looking at Molly, he said, "They were going to kill me, weren't they?"

"I don't know." Molly believed in being honest at all times. "Maybe they really were just going to take you someplace. You know what you did. I don't."

Patel looked up at her suddenly, glaring. "What's that supposed to mean?"

"Have you done something that would make someone want to kill you?"

Patel turned away, shaking his head.

"Or do you know a secret worth killing over?"

"Jesus. I went to Stanford, for chrissakes."

"You should have told those guys," Molly said. "Maybe that would have impressed them."

"I mean, this isn't my life! I write code! I do financial analysis! I'm not supposed to be running from hired goons! I haven't done anything wrong!"

"I didn't say you did."

Patel curled into himself again, clutching the bag.

"I did what I was supposed to," he mumbled.

He acted like a kid because he was a kid, Molly reminded herself. She reached forward and gently touched his hand. "Why don't you explain it to me. Maybe I can help you make sense of it."

For a moment, the snide look of the know-it-all from back at the apartment returned. "I don't know if you'd even understand it."

Molly shrugged. "Maybe not. But sometimes it helps just to talk it out."

He rubbed his face with both hands. "I doubt it," he said. "Do you even know what Devlin was accused of doing?"

"I thought it was a Ponzi scheme."

Patel smirked. "What, is that what you read on Facebook?"

"Something like that."

"The media always gets the basics wrong," he said. "The Feds accused him of running a Ponzi scheme. But that's just a phrase that everyone knows. They try to make their job easier that way."

"And that's not what happened?"

"Please. You think Devlin could have built a seven-hundred-fifty-million-dollar hedge fund by just moving some money around? This wasn't Bernie Madoff. He didn't funnel money from new investors to pay the old ones. He was smarter than that. He had to put people's investments into something that would show colossal returns so they wouldn't ask too many questions. He had to make it plausible."

"And that's not a Ponzi scheme?"

"No, of course not. A Ponzi scheme is just taking money from new suckers and using it to pay old suckers until you've got enough. Then it's like musical chairs when you stop the music. You take all the cash and everyone else is standing around looking stupid."

"I thought that's what Devlin did here."

"Yeah, but not like that. That's primitive. And it's way too easy to get caught. He had to put the cash into a real asset."

"Okay," Molly said. "Where did he put it?"

"Cryptocurrency."

Molly looked skeptical. "That's what you call a real asset?"

"Wow, you really are a Boomer, aren't you?" Patel said. "Crypto is just as real as any stock or bond."

"Isn't crypto just an electronic entry in some digital ledger?"

Patel looked mildly impressed. "I'm surprised you know that."

"Well. I'm not a Boomer. I read more than Facebook."

"Funny," Patel said. "Yeah. That's what crypto is. You create a digital token—usually we call it a 'coin'—and we let people buy shares of that token. It's just like the stock market. The coin is a security. The more people invest, the more it's worth."

"But it's not a real thing."

Patel shrugged. "What's real these days? You think stocks are worth a thousand times the value of the companies they represent? You think your bank actually keeps your savings in a big pile of cash in a box with your name on it? Hell, no. It's all nothing but ones and zeros. Digital records. Crypto just removes all the pretense. You are investing in an investment. Nothing else. No factories to maintain, no employees to pay, no profits or losses to bring down the value. It's *pure*. As long as people *believe* in the coin, the coin keeps going up."

"Wow," Molly said. "Just like a con job."

"Like I said: Boomer. You think money is real."

"You're not making this sound any less like a Ponzi scheme."

Patel looked pleased with himself. "It was never a Ponzi scheme. It was a rug pull."

"What's a rug pull?"

"It's where you create a new coin, and then you take a

bunch of cash from new investors. That pumps the value of the token way, way up. Then the initial investors dump all their shares of the coin, taking all the profits. The other investors are left with nothing."

Molly got it. "The rug gets pulled out from under them."

"Exactly," Patel said.

"And that's what Devlin did."

Patel suddenly seemed to remember he was talking to a cop, even if Molly was just a cop from a small town in Massachusetts.

"Allegedly," he said, looking cagey again.

"So why didn't he get convicted?"

Patel couldn't help looking proud. "Because if there was a crime, there would have to be profits, right? All that money would have to go somewhere, wouldn't it?"

"Well, yeah," Molly admitted.

"That's where the Feds lost their case," Patel said. "They couldn't find any of the proceeds from the crime. Devlin didn't have them. On paper, he lost just as much as anyone. He was able to say he was a victim like every one of his investors."

"And that's why the jury found him not guilty."

"Yup," Patel said. "The Feds tried to confiscate all his other assets, but they had to give those back. They couldn't prove any of the money he'd made was from the rug pull."

"They clearly never talked to you."

"I pleaded the Fifth, Officer," Patel said. "And anyway, I just wrote code."

Molly shook her head and looked away from Patel.

"What?" he said.

"Maybe I should have let those guys take you."

"Hey. That's not fair."

"Fair?" Molly snorted. "Is it fair to steal millions of dollars from people for some phony currency and run away with all the profits?"

"I just wrote the code," Patel said again.

"Sure. Your parents must be very proud."

"I didn't do anything wrong," Patel said, looking sulky.

"I'm sure that's what you told the prosecutors. And look at that: Devlin got away clean."

"I don't know what I can tell you now. He's been acquitted. That's double jeopardy. He can't be tried twice for the same crime."

"You're right," Molly said. "He can't. Which leads me to wonder why he's still keeping an eye on you."

"I don't know. I don't know anything. I can't tell you or the Feds anything."

"That's not what Devlin's lawyer thinks. Obviously. You called him, he called those guys. Maybe it's time to come clean."

Patel stared at the table for a long moment. Shook his head. And looked up at Molly, his eyes pleading. "I can't. This is my life we're talking about here. I have too much to lose. I just can't."

"Well, that's a shame," Molly said, and signaled for the check. "Good luck."

Patel looked alarmed. "You're leaving?"

She gave him her best smile. "Patel," she said. "You're not an idiot. You're a very smart kid. You must have known you were doing the wrong thing at some point. And being a smart kid, I bet you made sure you'd be protected if it all went bad. Maybe you even thought you got away with it and this was all safely in the rearview mirror. But you think someone who managed to steal a couple hundred million dollars is going to leave any loose ends?"

"Nobody cared until you came around asking questions." Patel looked sulky again.

"Maybe you're right," Molly said. "Maybe you can tell that to those guys when they find you again."

The waitress brought the check. Molly paid with cash. She always left a big tip.

"See ya around," she said.

"Wait. You can't just leave me. I thought you were going to move me to a safe house or something."

Molly laughed. "I'm afraid you've been watching too many movies. Why would I do that?"

"Because those guys will try to kill me!"

"Why?" Molly asked, all innocence. "All you did was write code. Remember?" She began scooting to the edge of the booth, ready to leave.

"Wait!"

Molly stopped. "Why should I?"

"Well, maybe I do know something," he said. "But I don't know what good it would do. He's already gotten off."

Molly scooted back into the booth. She signaled to the waitress for more coffee.

"Why don't you tell me what you know," Molly said. "And then we'll figure out why that makes you so dangerous to Devlin."

THIRTY-EIGHT

One advantage to working with Gary Armistead all these years: Jesse knew his schedule cold by now.

He came to his offices at the Town Hall reliably late every morning, by nine-thirty-five or nine-forty. He made his calls and had his first meetings with department heads. Then he was out the door every day, rain or shine, at ten-forty-five a.m. to get coffee at Daisy's, where he would spend at least an hour gathering constituent opinions on the issues facing the town, or, as Jesse liked to think of it, bullshitting.

Jesse watched Armistead go down the sidewalk toward Daisy's, right on time. The mayor emerged from the parking lot behind the police station and walked up the steps and into the Town Hall building.

Jesse had already been here yesterday, visiting the town planning office. There, it had been easy enough to pull the permits for Ramsey Devlin's monster house. As he suspected, the file was incomplete. The blueprints were copies, rather than the originals that were supposed to be on file, and several items were missing, including the paperwork for the expedited permits to build on the coastline.

Jesse asked Tom Leahy, the clerk in the planning office, where the rest of the file was.

Leahy just said, "Where do you think, Jesse?"

So Jesse made his plan to infiltrate Armistead's office.

It wasn't like he needed to be James Bond. He just had to get past Baylee Rice, the administrative assistant for the Town Council.

Ordinarily that might be a problem. Paradise Town Hall wasn't exactly the Pentagon, but Baylee took her job seriously. She was a twentysomething poli-sci graduate who kept the town running behind the scenes. She managed the town meeting agendas, tracked every budget, and still answered the phones. She was wasted as an assistant, but she loved Paradise, and it was only a matter of time until she was moved up to a position with a real title, instead of just doing all the work.

If Jesse was anyone else trying to get inside the mayor's office without an appointment, Baylee would stop him cold in the hallway.

But that was another advantage to working with Armistead for so long: Pretty much everyone in the town government liked Jesse more than they liked the mayor. Jesse could be curt, he could be brusque, and he could even arrest you on a Friday night if you'd had a few too many.

But with Jesse, you knew where you stood. Everyone who worked for the Town of Paradise had at least one story of a time when Armistead promised them something and then turned them down later. Almost everyone still had at least one scar on their back from when Armistead had stuck in a knife.

That included Baylee, who didn't really love how Armistead treated her as a personal secretary—he regularly told her to make dinner reservations for him, and to buy flowers for his wife, as if he was Don Draper on *Mad Men.* He had also passed her over for a position as chief administrator of the town's Public Works Department.

When Jesse showed up in front of her desk, she smiled at him. That was a good sign. She had to know the whole story behind his suspension. Everyone else did. But she didn't seem to think she was looking at a killer or a kidnapper.

"Jesse, hi," she said. "How are you holding up?"

"Just fine, Baylee. How are you?"

She made a face. "Busy. As always. You would not believe how many times I've had to tell Suit to redo the department's time sheets."

"I probably would," Jesse said.

"I wish you would get back to work. It would make things easier for me, at least."

Jesse saw an opening there. "Well, I'm hoping to do that soon. In fact, if you'll let me into Gary's office, I can probably make that happen sooner."

For the first time, Baylee frowned at him. "You want me to let you into his office? Without him here?"

"Yeah. I do."

She looked troubled. "Why?"

Jesse thought for a moment. Then he figured, *What the hell.* "Baylee, I'm not going to lie to you. It's to find something he doesn't want me to have. And to take it out of there and use it to get my job back."

"Is he going to be angry about that?"

"Yeah," Jesse said. "Probably."

She looked up and down the hallway. "Well, you'd better get in there fast, then." She handed him the keys to the mayor's office.

He took them. "You sure this is okay? He might try to take it out on you."

"Oh, he'll definitely try to take it out on me," Baylee said. "But let's see him manage this place without me. The town would be bankrupt in a week."

Jesse smiled. "Thanks," he said.

She smiled back. "For a minute, I thought you were going to try some line about getting the time sheets back for Suit, or some other lie. I'm glad you didn't treat me like an idiot. I get enough of that around here."

"I'm glad I didn't do that, either," Jesse said. "You deserve better."

"Tell the mayor, will you? God knows he doesn't listen to me."

Jesse opened Armistead's office door and quickly moved to the filing cabinet. There was a ring on the key for the files as well, and he pulled the drawers open.

Armistead appeared to have his own system for putting things away, but Jesse couldn't make much sense of it. There was no pattern he could see. Campaign forms and contributions were at the top, behind another file for the municipal sewer department. Correspondence was stuffed in a middle drawer, with some letters from some people in their own folders and others lumped in by subject.

Jesse knew he had an hour, but he didn't want to waste any more time than he had to. He stopped to think. He knew Armistead pretty well. He should be able to figure this out.

These were Armistead's personal files. Where he kept what he considered important to him. Not to anyone else, and not to the town. He would know where he kept the most crucial information. Things he could use, things that could harm his reputation, and things that mattered most to his ambition.

Devlin fit all three of those categories.

But there was nothing under *D* or in a specially colored file folder or anything obvious. So where would Armistead keep something he considered most important? How would he make it the top priority, even subconsciously?

Jesse opened the top drawer again. At the back, behind everything else, was a bigger accordion file folder marked *A*.

For the most important thing to Gary Armistead—Gary Armistead.

Inside, Jesse found a treasure trove of documents. Gary's personal bank accounts.

He didn't have time to go over all of them, and he had no real desire to violate Armistead's privacy. But he was tempted. There were letters to the State. Probably lots of dirt there. But none of his business.

He found what he was looking for at the back of the file.

The original blueprints to the Devlin house, along with the expedited permits for construction. All signed personally by Armistead.

Jesse looked through the blueprints. He compared them carefully to the copies from the town planning office.

It was exactly what he'd figured.

He was wondering what he would do about it when he heard Baylee say loudly, "Hey, Gary! You're back early!"

Jesse appreciated the heads-up. But he wasn't about to scurry or hide. Not for Armistead.

He turned and waited.

Armistead entered the office, already frowning.

"Hey, Gary," Jesse said. "Looks like your coffee break ended early today."

"Daisy kicked me out," Armistead said. "She doesn't like how I've been treating you. What exactly are you doing in here?"

Once again, Jesse didn't see the point in lying.

"I was looking for the blueprints for the Devlin house," he said. "Turned out you were keeping them in your private, locked file."

Armistead tried for outrage first. "That is my personal property, Jesse! How dare you break into my office! You're not even a cop right now! You have no right to—"

"Gary," Jesse said. "Can we please cut the crap?"

Something in his tone shut Armistead up.

"Look, I don't know what you think you found, but I can tell you: It has nothing to do with the investigation against you."

"I think you know exactly what it has to do with the investigation against me. I think you know this will end it."

"I don't know that," Armistead said quickly. "I don't know what you think it means, either. All I know is that I did a favor for a new resident of Paradise, one who promised to inject new resources and money into our town."

Jesse looked at him, suddenly full of disgust. "I honestly don't get it. Why do you keep doing that? Do you think I'll suddenly suffer a brain hemorrhage and start believing you if you just keep lying long enough?"

Jesse held up the blueprints. "Maybe you actually don't know what this means. But it's only because you're working pretty damn hard not to think about it. This is my life, Gary. Were you really going to let this keep going? Were you going to let them arrest me if I didn't figure it out?"

Armistead stood there, trying to find something else to say.

Jesse got tired of waiting.

"Guess I got my answer," Jesse said.

He pushed past Armistead and left the office.

ARMISTEAD WAITED A moment, to be sure Jesse was gone. This was bad, he knew. This was really bad.

He yelled at Baylee to hold his calls—he'd deal with her later, oh, yes, he would—and locked his door.

Then he called a number he'd had to memorize, since he didn't want anyone to find it written down somewhere.

"He knows," Armistead said as soon as the person on the other end picked up. "Stone has the blueprints and he knows. You need to do something."

"I'll handle it," the voice on the other end said.

Armistead hung up immediately.

He didn't know what was going to happen to Jesse Stone.

But whatever it was, he told himself it wasn't his fault.

THIRTY-NINE

Jesse came back to his condo with the plans for the Devlin house. He wanted Cole to see them so they could talk. Maybe it was important to get Kirkpatrick and Hodges on board first. Maybe Lundquist.

Whatever he did, though, he wanted Cole's opinion. He had to admit that his son had been right in the first place. At the very least, Jesse wanted to avoid another "I told you so."

As he reached the door, his phone buzzed. He juggled his keys to get it out of his pocket. The caller ID said Molly, but she was talking to voicemail by the time he could answer.

He figured he should go inside before calling her back. But Cole had thrown the chain on the door. So he knocked to get into his own place.

It took a long time for Cole to respond, or maybe Jesse was just impatient.

"Who is it?"

"Who do you think? Open up."

"Just a second."

Again, it took far too long for Cole to reach the door. He looked annoyed when it opened, just a crack.

"Get out of here," he said.

"What?"

"I told you, we don't need any. Why don't you go bother someone else?"

"Cole, what the hell are you—"

Then Cole was yanked back from the door like someone was pulling on a rope, and Jesse figured it out, a couple seconds too late.

Two big, dark men reached forward and grabbed him by both arms, hauling him inside the condo before he had a chance to move.

They were not amateurs. They slammed him down hard on the floor while someone else kicked the front door shut. One of them put a fist into Jesse's solar plexus, stealing all the air in his lungs so he couldn't shout or fight back. The other lifted Jesse's gun from his side and roughly searched him for any other weapons.

"Jesse!" Cole yelled.

Then Jesse heard a sound like meat hitting a butcher's counter, and Cole taking in a pained gulp of air.

They hit Jesse once in the back of the head, not bad enough to really disable him, just enough to scramble his brains a little. They dragged him across the room and sat him roughly in a chair. By the time he blinked, they had his arms zip-tied behind him and his ankles bound to the legs of the chair.

Across the room, they were tying up Cole in another kitchen chair the same way.

"Sorry, Jesse," he said.

"My fault," Jesse said.

Cole had tried to warn him by pretending he was just another door-to-door salesman when he knocked. But the thugs sent him to the door to see who it was, and Jesse stood there like an idiot.

He should have known better. He just didn't think they'd get into his house.

Cole was bleeding from his mouth, and his face was bruised. He hadn't made it easy on them, clearly.

But there were six men in the room. Five of the thugs Jesse had seen around. And the one who'd interrupted his lunch. Who'd called himself Suarez.

The man Vinnie called Salazar.

"Jesse," the man said. "Perhaps we can start over again."

One of the thugs dragged another kitchen chair over and placed it in front of Jesse. Salazar took a gun from under his jacket and sat down. He crossed his legs and smiled pleasantly. Again, it never reached his eyes. They were cold and gray.

"You could have avoided this if you'd only called," he said.

"I don't do errands for the cartels," Jesse said. "That's beneath me."

The smile glitched for only a split second. "So. You've been talking to people about me."

"A little. I've had better things to do."

Salazar shook his head. "Jesse. Please. Can we dispense with the melodrama? You will not insult me. Or sway me. Or change my mind. There is only one thing I wish to hear from you. I will do what it takes for you to give me the information. There is nothing else for us to discuss."

Jesse had to admit the man made a strong case. He was completely screwed. He had no escape plan, no last-minute strategy. Salazar had an ego, but he was clearly professional enough to ignore Jesse's insults until he had a chance to torture and kill him. There wouldn't be any way to goad him into making a mistake.

Which meant Jesse didn't have to figure out a plan, either. He settled down into a calm place inside himself. He'd been here before. All he had to do now was wait and endure whatever pain the man would deliver. Then he would try to take advantage of any break or luck he could find.

His father had once told him that Napoleon's battle plan was "First we engage the enemy, then we figure out what to do next."

Jesse hoped it would work for him.

"Now," Salazar said. "I will offer you one last chance to tell me without punishment or torture. I expect you will turn me down, and then we will do the real work. But it's traditional to ask, and you might surprise us all. Where is Ramsey Devlin?"

Jesse shrugged.

"No surprises, then," Salazar said. "Ah, well."

He turned to look at Cole, as if just noticing him. "Who is this man?"

Jesse felt his pulse pick up. "My lawyer. He's here to talk strategy for my case."

"He was willing to die for you. That's more than any of my attorneys would do for me."

"Maybe I'm just a better client."

"That seems difficult to believe."

"I send him a gift basket every Christmas. You should try it."

Salazar smiled but looked a little disappointed as well. So fast that Jesse could barely track it, he whipped his pistol around and cracked Jesse across the mouth. Jesse saw stars and felt the blow in his teeth.

"I told you no melodramatics. We are not here to spar, Jesse. I want to know who this man is to you. Is he your friend? Your partner?"

One of the thugs snickered, but Salazar turned and silenced him with a cold stare. "I am not a bigot, Mr. Stone. I personally do not care about your inclinations. But if you care at all about this man, you should tell me now."

Jesse was not about to give Salazar another bit of leverage. He looked at Cole. Cole, very minutely, shook his head no. He agreed.

"He's my lawyer," Jesse said again.

"Fine," Salazar said. "Lorenzo, shoot him."

One of the thugs lifted a shotgun.

"No!" Jesse screamed, lifting himself and the chair halfway from the floor.

There was an immediate blow to the spot where his neck met his shoulder. The thug behind him. Jesse forgot. He sat down hard, the chair landing with a heavy thud.

"Clearly you care for him," Salazar said. "I'll ask you again, and believe me, it will be the last time. Tell me where Ramsey Devlin is, or I will tell Lorenzo to put the shotgun to this man's head and pull the trigger."

Jesse took a moment to gauge the cartel enforcer. He'd had guns pointed at him and been in hostage situations before.

There was always the question of how far the man with the gun would go, if they were truly willing to take a life, to kill to get what they wanted.

He saw no hesitation in Salazar. He wasn't even sure he saw anything human.

"I don't count to three, if that's what you're waiting for," Salazar said.

"I'll tell you."

Salazar's mouth twitched in what must have been his version of amusement. "Just like that?"

"Yes. I'll tell you where he is. I'll even escort you myself. Just let him go."

Cole apparently couldn't take any more of this. "Jesse, you don't—"

Salazar let out a heavy breath and raised one finger. The thug by Cole's chair raised the shotgun again, reversed it in his hands, and slammed the butt against Cole's skull, knocking him and the chair to the floor.

"Damn it, I said I would tell you," Jesse said.

Salazar stood. "And I told you: We are not negotiating here. You do not get to put conditions on your cooperation. Tell me where Devlin is, or this man dies."

Jesse didn't hesitate. "Inside my jacket pocket. There are copies of blueprints."

"And why should I care about this?"

"Take a look. You'll see it."

Salazar frowned. "This is not hide-and-seek."

"That's exactly what it is," Jesse said. "Look. I promise you. You'll see it."

Salazar nodded, and one of his thugs crossed the room

and frisked Jesse. He found the plans and brought them to Salazar.

Another thug pulled Cole off the floor and set the chair upright again. Cole's head swung around the room as he shook off the blow. He brought his eyes up and found Jesse.

Jesse looked at him. And nodded. As if he could get them both out of this. He wasn't sure he could. No brilliant schemes sprang to mind. But he wanted to offer some kind of reassurance. There was nothing else he could offer at the moment.

Napoleon's plan was not working out so far. Jesse wondered how he ever became emperor of France.

Salazar, in the meantime, looked over the blueprints. He compared one set with another. Then he smiled again.

"Clever," he said. "Actually quite clever."

He looked over the papers at Jesse, eyes narrowed again.

"But how can I be sure you haven't arranged a surprise for me? Is there something else waiting for us?"

Jesse checked the clock on the wall again. It was two-sixteen.

"There's nobody else there now. Just Devlin," he said.

"Convince me."

Jesse shook his head. "I don't lie. Not about the things that really matter."

Salazar watched him. The clock ticked over to two-seventeen.

"I believe you," he said.

He put his gun in the holster under his jacket and dropped the blueprints on the floor. "Vincente, Ricardo, you're with me."

The thug standing by Cole raised his shotgun. "Should I kill them now?"

Jesse tensed. He could leap up from the chair. It wouldn't do a damn thing, he'd get cut down before he took three steps, but it would be better than nothing—

Then Salazar said, "No, Lorenzo. I want you to wait here."

He turned and looked at Jesse again. "In case I'm wrong. It's possible I am not as good a judge of your character as I think, and you are lying. If Devlin isn't there, then I'll come back. Whatever this man means to you, you'll watch as he dies. Slowly and painfully. And then I will start on you, and we will find out where Devlin is hidden. Eventually."

"Sure," Jesse said. "Sounds like a plan."

Salazar laughed. "You are an interesting man, Jesse Stone. I rarely have the chance to enjoy my work anymore. I really ought to thank you."

Then he turned and left the room, two of the thugs right behind him, carrying their shotguns.

Jesse and Cole were left with the three remaining men.

Jesse checked the clock again.

Two-twenty.

He had a little less than an hour to save Devlin and his entire family.

Not to mention Cole and himself.

FORTY

Jesse took stock of the situation. He and Cole were zip-tied at their hands and feet, their feet attached to the chairs; they were both groggy and bleeding from blows to the head; there were three men watching them, two holding combat shotguns that would cut a human being in half with a simple trigger pull; and they were waiting for the inevitable call from Salazar that would mean their deaths.

Jesse had to admit: He'd had better days.

But as professional as the men were, things could have been worse. Zip-ties were cheaper and easier to carry than handcuffs, which is why law enforcement everywhere used them, but that didn't make them the same thing. Zip-ties could be defeated if you knew how. You couldn't stretch them or pull them apart. Most people wasted a lot of time trying to do that.

But you could snap the head that held the strap together. It wasn't made to handle sudden, sharp pressure. With the right leverage, it would pop open and the ties would fall apart.

Then all Jesse had to do was fight three armed men and free his son.

This was going to have to be one hell of a plan.

The men were pros. They'd made only one mistake. They'd zipped his ankles to the chair, thinking it would keep him from moving. That was fine, as far as it went. It would hobble him if he tried to stand.

But it also gave him leverage.

Jesse turned to the nearest cartel enforcer.

"Hey. Any chance I can use the bathroom?"

The man—Lorenzo, Salazar had called him—looked at him with pure contempt.

"Piss yourself," he said.

"Just trying to spare you the mess."

"Gonna get a lot messier in here soon," Lorenzo said.

Dix had told Jesse many times that he carried a lot of anger with him. But when Jesse was in danger, he didn't feel it. Times like this, he felt as calm and clear as he ever did.

He dug around inside himself for a moment. Thought of Cole hitting the floor after this thug hit him. Thought of all the ways in which Ramsey Devlin had wasted his time with this stupid scheme. How many lives he'd put at risk.

"Hey, fuckface," Jesse snarled. "I get out of this chair, I'm going to beat you until you cry for your mother, you know that?"

Lorenzo wasn't as cool as Salazar had been. He bared his teeth, took a step toward Jesse, and aimed the butt of the shotgun at Jesse's head, just like he had before.

Jesse was already pushing himself backward, so the shotgun barely kissed his scalp as he and his chair fell to the floor.

Jesse was ready. He kicked with both legs at the same time he hit. He also made a loud cry of pain as he went down. He hoped it would cover the fact that the thug had barely touched him, and the snapping noise as he broke the zip-ties from his ankles.

Lorenzo made a noise of disgust as he walked over to Jesse. Jesse waited, wanting to time this just right.

"You want some more of that, shithead, you just keep talking," he said, shifting the shotgun from his left to his right to reach for Jesse.

But as Lorenzo leaned over to haul Jesse upright again, Jesse exploded from the floor, his legs now free of the chair.

His hands were still zipped, but he threw his shoulder into Lorenzo's gut. He heard and felt the air leave the cartel thug's body.

He hung on to the shotgun, though.

All Jesse could do was roll to one side, pinning the guy's arm.

Lorenzo recovered fast. He brought up his fist to punch Jesse and get him off his arm.

Jesse raised his knee even faster. His leg went numb as the thug's fist cracked into it, but it definitely hurt Lorenzo worse. He squalled out a curse and yanked away a broken hand.

Jesse yanked at the zip-ties and pulled them close, but they held. He didn't have the leverage, tangled on the floor with the thug.

Lorenzo tried to grab him around the neck, but one hand was securely under Jesse, still hanging on to the shotgun, and the other was useless, with broken fingers. They wriggled around, both looking for an advantage.

But Jesse was out of time. The other thugs were above him now, both aiming their weapons, shouting for him to knock it the fuck off, racking shells into their chambers to make their points.

Jesse was out of options and he knew it.

Then Cole came flying from the other side of the room. He didn't bother to free himself from the chair. He just took the whole thing with him as he launched himself on top of the two other thugs, taking them to the floor in a massive pileup.

Jesse heard wood splintering and more cursing. Cole thrashed and kicked like he was undergoing an exorcism. The chair was a pile of kindling underneath him.

They still weren't going to make it. Jesse could feel it. They were outmanned and outgunned. All it would take is for one of the thugs to finally lose patience with this wrestling match and decide they didn't really need Jesse and Cole alive. All it would take was a finger on the trigger—

Then the front door busted open, sending Jesse's expensive dead bolt flying across the room.

Two men, also dressed in black like the thugs, charged inside, both holding semiautos in their hands.

Somehow Jesse didn't think they were there to rescue him.

FORTY-ONE

For a moment, nobody moved as the thugs all looked at one another in shock.

Then the two new guys aimed their guns. They were both enormous—the truck-sized version of hired bad guys—while Salazar's thugs were sleeker, more like sports cars. The one in the lead was the biggest. He was blond, with a beard.

He smiled, like this was hilarious. "You must be Jesse Stone," he said. "Looks like we got here just in time."

"The fuck are you?" Lorenzo asked.

"Hey," the blond said. "You can fuck all the way off. This guy is going with us. We need him—"

That's as far as he got before Salazar's other thug aimed his own shotgun, pulled the trigger, and put a round right through him.

The other new guy stood there, blood on his face. He was paralyzed for an instant, then turned to run.

The man with the shotgun racked another shell and fired before he got five feet.

The guy dropped to Jesse's floor like a sack of wet concrete.

The echo of the shotgun's boom still reverberated in the condo. There was that pause that even experienced shooters feel, the frozen moment after the sudden violence.

Now or never, Jesse thought.

While the thugs all stared at the bodies, Jesse rolled over and onto his back. He hoped to Christ he was still flexible enough for this trick.

He curled into a ball and brought his zip-tied hands behind his legs and around to his front. He just barely managed it, and he felt a twinge in his back that told him he'd regret stretching himself like this later—provided he lived long enough.

Lorenzo's shotgun was still loose, next to him. Lorenzo realized it. He reached with his left hand and shouted, "He's going for the gun!"

Cole stretched out one leg and kicked Lorenzo in the head. Then he rolled right before another thug put a bullet into the floor where he'd been.

It gave Jesse all the time he needed. He held the shotgun in a pistol grip with both of his bound hands and pulled the trigger.

The thug who'd fired at Cole went down.

Jesse turned to the other, who wheeled with the shotgun, but not fast enough. Jesse fired again. The other thug came apart in the middle.

Jesse was glad the shotgun was semiauto. He couldn't have racked another shell if he'd wanted to, with his hands bound.

He thrust himself to his feet as Lorenzo scrabbled across the floor, trying to get to his companion's fallen weapon.

Cole was already there. He kicked it farther away.

Jesse walked over and poked Lorenzo in the back with the gun.

Lorenzo sighed and turned over, clutching his broken hand.

Jesse rested the barrel of the shotgun on Lorenzo's chin.

Lorenzo looked up at him, mouth turned down in what looked like a pout.

"Do it," he said. "I'm not afraid."

"Then you're dumber than you look," Jesse said, and flipped the shotgun around, taking Lorenzo's move, using the butt to knock the man unconscious.

It took a couple tries.

When Jesse looked up, Cole was on his feet, panting heavily.

"Jesus, Dad," he said. "And you wonder why I never visit."

Jesse couldn't keep himself from grinning. Cole was okay.

He stepped over the thugs and pulled Cole into an awkward, zip-tied embrace.

"He was going to kill you," Cole said. "You told him to let me go. He was going to kill you."

"Yeah," Jesse said. "Thought he might trade."

"He was going to kill you."

"Yeah."

"You did it anyway."

"Cole. You're my son. It wasn't even a question."

Cole sagged into him a little. Jesse held on a little tighter.

Then they both awkwardly began moving, trying to separate even though their hands were still bound.

"Box cutter's in the kitchen drawer," Jesse said.

"Yeah. We have to call Suit. And Lundquist."

"They're never going to make it in time," Jesse said as Cole sliced open the zip-ties. Jesse took the box cutter and did the same for his son. "Take the guns. We've got to go."

"Go where?"

"We've got to save Devlin. Salazar's on his way to kill him."

Cole grabbed a pistol and a shotgun off the floor. Jesse went through Lorenzo's pockets for his phone and his keys.

"What? Where is he?"

"Same place he's been the entire time," Jesse said. "Right at home."

Cole looked confused. "He came back?"

"He never left."

FORTY-TWO

Driving one-handed, Jesse hit the number for Suit on his phone and got voicemail. "Suit, damn it, call me. There are people on the way to Devlin's house, they're going to kill whoever they find there."

Cole had already tried Lundquist and left a similar message.

"Explain it again," Cole said.

"No time," Jesse said.

Jesse skidded around the corner, hitting forty as he came out of the curve. He tried Gabe. Straight to voicemail again.

"Call nine-one-one," he told Cole. "Dispatcher will break through whatever they're doing."

"They're already there by now, Jesse," Cole said.

Jesse knew that. Paradise just wasn't that big a town. The cartel enforcers could have beat them to Devlin's house even if they were walking. Out of time, out of options.

Jesse cursed silently and hit another recent number on his phone.

Kirkpatrick, of course, picked up on the first ring.

"Finally going to confess, Stone?"

"Shut up," Jesse said. "There are armed men on the way to the Devlin house. I can't reach anyone else. You've got to get there before his wife and kid get back from school—"

"Whoa, whoa, whoa," Kirkpatrick said. "Don't you tell me to shut up—"

"They will kill them," Jesse said. "They will kill everyone they find. I'm on my way now, but we need backup and nobody is responding here in Paradise. You have to get there—"

Jesse slammed on his brakes to avoid a slow-moving Bentley backing out of a driveway. He swerved and hit the horn. The Bentley honked back as if offended.

Kirkpatrick heard only one part of what Jesse was saying. "Stone, you listen to me, you do not go anywhere near the Devlin residence," he said.

"Goddamn it, you need to listen—"

"No, you listen," he shouted. "I don't know what the hell you think you're talking about, but you harass Janis Devlin again and I will put you in cuffs, I don't care who you think you are."

Jesse gritted his teeth and braked as he made the hard right turn onto Seaside. The Explorer stayed on all four wheels—just barely.

"Well, too late now," he said into the phone as he skidded to a halt in front of the Devlin house, looming above the ocean. "I'm here. You want to stop me? Come and arrest me."

"Stone—" Kirkpatrick began.

Jesse hung up.

Jesse saw how Salazar had solved the problem of Devlin's

front gate. He'd simply driven one of the BMWs through it at high speed. The ruined car was still leaking steam where it sat in the mangled wreckage of the gate, shoved far to the side of the driveway.

They got out of the Explorer. Jesse went around and opened the back to get to his equipment. He got out a vest and one of the cartel thugs' shotguns.

Cole did the same thing.

"Dispatch says Suit and Gabe are on the way," he said. "Gonna take a couple minutes."

"You wait here for them."

Cole laughed in his face. "Like hell, old man. Someone has to watch your back."

Jesse nodded. Frankly, he was glad Cole hadn't taken him up on the offer.

He wasn't an idiot. And only an idiot would face Salazar and his men alone.

THEY CAME IN through the front door, standard formation. Cole hadn't forgotten the basics of cop work in the time he'd been a lawyer. He covered Jesse as Jesse entered, then advanced as Jesse covered him. There was nothing better than shotguns for a close-up gunfight. A shotgun made accuracy irrelevant: Anyone in range was going down, even if they wore a vest.

The problem was, the other guys had shotguns, too.

They made their way down the front hall. They saw nothing, no one. The house was as quiet and cold as a mausoleum.

They came into the great room, which adjoined the dining area and the kitchen.

To get to the hallway that led deeper into the house, they'd have to cross the wide-open space.

Great place for an ambush.

Jesse looked at Cole, who also stood in place at the entry hall. He was clearly thinking the same thing.

Jesse made a fist: Hold.

They waited, shotguns aimed.

Jesse looked around the entry hall. He saw a kid's tennis shoe, carelessly tossed aside near a console table.

He hoped that didn't mean what he thought it did.

He put the worry aside. One threat at a time.

He leaned over, picked up the shoe, and gently tossed it into the living room, where it made a sound like a light footstep on the carpet.

The two cartel thugs popped up like zombies in a video game, one from behind the couch, one from behind the kitchen island. They had their own shotguns and they brought them up quickly.

But not quickly enough to avoid the spray of shells from Jesse and Cole, who were already firing.

Jesse caught the man in the kitchen twice before he went down. He glanced to the side and saw Cole had put the man in the living room against the wall with three well-aimed shots.

His ears rang.

"Clear?" he asked Cole.

Cole swallowed audibly. Jesse wondered when he'd last fired a gun, let alone shot a human being.

"Clear," Cole said.

They looked around. No sign of Salazar.

Jesse hesitated, wondering if the enforcer was waiting for them, using his men as decoys.

Then Jesse caught it.

The sound of a sob, echoing toward them off the concrete walls.

The sound of a child, trying to hold back tears.

Jesse ran. He knew where Salazar was.

JESSE ENTERED DEVLIN'S man cave at the end of the hall, on the east side of the house.

He had the shotgun out in front of him, but as soon as he was inside, he knew it would do him no good.

Salazar wasn't holding a gun.

He was holding a knife to the throat of Race Devlin, standing on the opposite side of the room, facing what had looked like a blank wall the last time Jesse was in here.

Now it was open, slid back on a hidden track, revealing a thick steel door with a camera and video screen built into the wall beside it.

On the video screen was the face of Ramsey Devlin, who appeared to be in anguish as he watched Salazar and Race.

This was Devlin's panic room. Jesse had seen it on the plans that were hidden from the public, the ones he'd shown to Salazar. He knew from the blueprints that it was steel-walled and embedded deep in the concrete structure of the house. It had its own air supply and food cache and stored water tank. It would take a Hellfire missile to crack it. The door was the thickness of a bank vault, with bolts securely shot into the frame, protected by an encrypted lock that required three passkeys. The only way anyone would get Devlin out is if Devlin opened it.

And it didn't look like he was about to leave anytime soon.

Salazar turned and saw Jesse and Cole. He smiled as brilliantly as ever.

"Jesse," he said cheerfully. "What a surprise. I was just telling Mr. Devlin what I will tell you: If he does not come out in the next minute, his son's blood will be all over this beautiful rug."

FORTY-THREE

Jesse stood frozen in place. So did Cole.

They both turned at the sound of a whimper. Jesse saw Race's nanny cowering on the floor near one of the leather couches. Her lip was badly split and her eye was already swelling.

But she was alive. Good enough for now. Jesse dragged his attention back to Salazar.

"Put your guns down, please," Salazar said. "Or the boy dies."

"You touch him, you lose your only bargaining chip," Jesse said. "And then I will blow your head clean off your shoulders."

Salazar didn't so much as blink. He simply put more pressure on the blade, which dug into Race's throat.

"I believe you already know my position here, Mr. Stone."

Jesse did. He lowered his shotgun, put on the safety, then put it on the floor.

Cole hesitated. "Jesse," he said. "We can't—"

"We are not going to let anything happen to Race," Jesse said, more to the boy than to Cole. He kept his eyes on Race and Salazar. Race was on his tiptoes, trying desperately to escape the edge of the knife.

There was no way in the world Jesse could take a shot without hitting him. Not with the shotgun, anyway.

Neither could Cole, no matter how good his aim.

"Put it down, Cole," Jesse said.

Jesse, without looking, heard Cole safety and lower the weapon.

"Very good," Salazar said.

"Can we check on the girl?" Jesse asked, tilting his head toward the nanny.

"How noble," Salazar said. "No, you may not. You remain where you are. I want your friend to cross over to the glass door and stand in front of it."

Smart, Jesse had to admit. That would block the only entrances and exits from the room. And it would prevent any sniper from getting a clean shot through the glass door.

Cole moved over to the other door. Salazar turned slightly, so he could see them both easily.

Jesse didn't know what to do now.

He checked the clock. It was still not yet three-thirty p.m.

"Guess you stayed home from school today, huh, Race?" Jesse asked, as much to buy time as anything else.

"Got suspended," Race said quietly, miserably.

Your dad's check probably bounced, Jesse thought.

"Shut up," Salazar said. "Both of you."

"What now?" Jesse asked. "You're in charge. What do we do now?"

"It's very simple. I want Devlin to come out of that room."

Jesse turned to the screen in the wall. He could see Devlin watching from his video hookup.

"What do you say, Ramsey?"

"He'll kill me!" Devlin said, his voice coming through a speaker.

"I promise we will both walk out of here together," Salazar said. "Your boy will live. And so will you, for at least a little while. Believe me, Mr. Devlin. That is the best deal I can offer you."

"Stone, can't you do anything?" Devlin said.

"We need to get your son away from him," Jesse said, not quite believing that he had to say this out loud. Thinking to himself, *Maybe this could work*. Maybe in the moment of the switch, he and Cole could rush Salazar. They could get the boy away and take Salazar down. The two of them, together, could make it work.

It might work.

"Just come out," Jesse said. "We'll keep talking from there."

There was a long pause. The speaker was silent. Onscreen, Devlin appeared to be thinking.

Maybe he was even considering it.

Unfortunately, that's when Janis Devlin rushed into the room, screaming.

FORTY-FOUR

Janis pushed past Jesse and shrieked, trying to get to her son.

Hodges and Kirkpatrick shoved into the room a step behind her, in pursuit. Hodges caught her arm and brought her down to the carpet, where she shrieked and cried.

Kirkpatrick, at the same time, saw what was happening and drew his gun. Jesse knocked it down, keeping him from taking a shot at either Salazar or the boy.

He also used the distraction to take a step forward, getting himself a little closer.

But Salazar was not about to be distracted.

"Not another step!" he shouted. "I will kill him!"

"NOBODY MOVE," Jesse bellowed, and Hodges and Kirkpatrick—and even Janis—complied.

The sudden silence was like a living thing, curled up in the room with all of them.

"How the hell did she get inside?" Jesse snapped at Hodges and Kirkpatrick.

"Hey, sue us," Hodges said. "She pulled up just as we did. We couldn't catch her."

Salazar cleared his throat. "If I'm not interrupting," he said. "For those of you who have just joined us now. I will bleed this boy like a pig if his father does not come out."

Janis wailed even louder. Kirkpatrick and Hodges were frozen. Cole, Jesse could tell, was considering going for the pistol he had concealed in the back of his pants.

Jesse could do the same thing: take a shot, too.

But he didn't believe either of them were fast enough or accurate enough to take Salazar before he slashed the boy's throat.

Salazar was quick and deadly. Jesse believed at least that much.

And it didn't take a lot of skill to murder an unarmed child.

"We can talk. We can negotiate," Kirkpatrick said. "Just let the boy go."

Mistake, Jesse knew.

"I do not negotiate," Salazar said. "Ask anyone."

Hodges looked at Jesse. "Any ideas?" she asked.

"Nope," Jesse said. "We're sort of stuck here."

"Well, that's great."

Jesse looked at the screen, where Devlin watched from inside the panic room.

"What do you say, Ramsey? You want to join us out here?"

Devlin looked out of the screen.

"Mr. Devlin," Kirkpatrick said. "He's got your son. This is the only way."

Devlin came a little closer to the camera. Then his hand came up, and he looked away.

A second later, the screen went black.

Janis Devlin wailed again.

Jesse looked at Race, whose face was too young to be that filled with despair. The boy stared at the black screen, as if waiting for his father to reappear.

But nothing happened.

"Well," Salazar said. "I believe he's given his answer."

"Salazar, this doesn't have to be the end of it," Jesse said.

"What could possibly make you believe that, Jesse?" Salazar asked. "Mr. Devlin has abandoned his child. I assume this house is surrounded by police. And there is no way I am leaving this room with the boy. You know that. I know that. What is left?"

Jesse looked around the room, desperate for an idea. He thought he saw one. He just had to get closer.

He put his hands in the air.

"You win," he said.

Salazar looked at him, the blade steady.

"Excuse me?" he asked.

"Don't hurt the boy," Jesse said. "Take me instead. You can walk out of here."

Salazar smirked. "You'll forgive me if I need a little more detail than that."

Jesse looked at Race. The boy's eyes were shut tight now. Tears leaked out of them.

Jesse wanted very badly to hurt Salazar. Very badly.

He put it aside.

"Nobody has a gun on you," Jesse said. "You let the kid

go. I'll be your hostage. I'll walk out with you. We'll drive away together."

"No offense, Jesse, but I am more comfortable with a seven-year-old boy as my hostage than the man who has killed all of my associates."

"Well," Jesse said. "I had help."

"Jesus Christ, Stone," Kirkpatrick muttered from behind them.

"Shut up," Jesse and Salazar both told him, almost in unison.

But Salazar's eyes darted to the Internal Affairs man. Jesse used the distraction to take another quick step forward.

Salazar brought his attention back to Jesse. The knife never wavered. Salazar's hand was as steady as a rock. He did not appear to be the least bit tired.

Jesse could see the muscles jumping under the skin of the man's forearm. He could still slice Race's throat open in a second.

"Salazar, listen to me. You'll have a cop as a hostage. You write your own ticket."

Salazar thought about that, calculating the odds. "You don't think I'd kill you if I got the chance?"

Jesse took another step forward, hands out, pleading.

"I don't care."

Salazar looked almost impressed. "You really don't, do you?"

He relaxed, just a little, at that moment. Like a weight had been lifted from his shoulders.

Jesse allowed himself a moment of hope.

Then Salazar tightened his grip on Race. The boy let out

a whimper as the tip of the knife jabbed the soft flesh under his throat again.

"Tell me," he said. "Have you ever seen anyone successfully walk away from a situation like this? And be honest, Mr. Stone. I have no tolerance for any more bullshit."

There was a long beat as Jesse considered the answer.

"No," he admitted. "No one ever has."

"That's been my experience, too," Salazar said. His face twisted into a pained grin. "That's a shame, isn't it? For both me and the boy—"

But Jesse was finally close enough.

He turned toward the desk, and in one fluid motion picked up the Mark McGwire autographed baseball and hurled it with everything he had.

Salazar never even saw Home Run Number Sixty-Nine coming before it cracked into his forehead.

He dropped to the floor, rag doll limp.

The knife fell from his nerveless fingers and landed on the rug softly.

The ball bounced once and rolled into a corner.

Race Devlin ran to his mother, sobbing.

For a moment, no one else moved.

Jesse had to use his left hand to take out his gun. Something had popped and given way in his bad shoulder.

He hadn't thrown a ball that hard since he was in the minors. He couldn't lift his arm.

Cole got to Salazar before Jesse could, since Jesse was busy fumbling around with his weapon. He kicked away the knife and rolled the man onto his stomach.

Salazar was still out cold, but Kirkpatrick put the cuffs on him anyway.

"Holy crap," Hodges said. To Kirkpatrick, she turned and said, "Did you see that? Did you *see* that? I think he broke his damn skull."

She was trying to get Janis and Race out of the room, but they wouldn't go. Cole, meanwhile, went to check on the nanny, who was still shivering alone by the couch.

Jesse looked at them, then walked—Jesus Christ, his shoulder hurt—toward the door to the panic room.

He knocked, even though he knew Devlin could see everything with his cameras.

"You can come out now, Ramsey," he said.

Everyone waited.

The door slid open smoothly and quietly, a triumph of million-dollar engineering.

Ramsey Devlin stepped out.

For the first time, he did not swagger into the room. He tried to stand up straight, but it seemed like something was pressing him down.

He walked over to his wife and son.

"Hey," he said to them both. "It's okay. I'm safe now."

Race turned away from his father and buried his face in his mother's arms.

Janis leaned forward and slapped Devlin as hard as she could.

Then she half pulled, half carried Race out of the room.

Hodges followed them.

Kirkpatrick stepped over to Devlin.

"Mr. Devlin," Kirkpatrick said in that same annoying monotone he'd used with Jesse. "If you'd please come with me."

"I want a lawyer," Devlin said.

"I'm sure you do, Mr. Devlin," Kirkpatrick said as he took out another set of handcuffs. "I would, too."

KIRKPATRICK PERP-WALKED DEVLIN out of the big house. Devlin was exercising his right to remain silent, for a change.

Cole and Jesse followed, half dragging Salazar between them. He was barely conscious, his feet only intermittently touching the ground as they hauled him along.

When they reached the front, they found half the Paradise PD waiting for them. Suit was in the lead with Gabe, with Jimmy and Barry blocking Seaside with their SUVs. The fire department's EMT truck was parked behind them. Jesse saw the medics looking over Race, with Janis watching him and Hodges watching Janis.

"You know, Jesse, most people would have just taken the vacation," Suit said.

"I'm an innocent bystander," Jesse said. He nodded to Cole. "Just ask my lawyer."

FORTY-FIVE

The conference room at the Paradise Police Station was once again set up for an interrogation, with the video camera aimed and ready. But this time, Jesse and Kirkpatrick were on the same side of the table, along with Hodges and Suit. Ellis Munroe took a seat at the end of the table.

Devlin sat across from them, facing them. He didn't quite have his full attitude, but his smirk was back on his face when he looked at Jesse.

Jesse, his arm in a sling, was a little impressed. It took a special kind of shamelessness to give up your kid for dead and still come out smiling.

They waited. Jesse and Suit were comfortable in the silence; they'd done this many times before. Kirkpatrick and Hodges glared at Devlin as if they wanted to take him out back and serve some personal justice. Ellis did the Wordle puzzle on his phone.

After another eight minutes, Gordon Wilkes, Devlin's

lawyer, showed up. Gabe escorted him into the room and closed the door behind him.

He looked confident. Jesse supposed he earned a lot of his money off that look, but still, he didn't seem like a man whose client was going to jail anytime soon.

"Officers," Wilkes said. "Mr. Munroe. I suppose I should begin by asking: What the hell is this man doing here?"

He pointed at Jesse.

"As far as I know, Mr. Stone is still under suspension. Which makes it frankly incomprehensible to me how you're allowing him to carry out his vendetta against my client—"

"Gordon," Ellis said as he put his phone back into his pocket. "Sit down and shut the hell up."

Wilkes looked like he was about to begin shouting at Ellis. But then he looked around the room again, and at Devlin, who only shrugged. He began to realize there might be facts he didn't know yet.

He sat down.

"Thank you," Ellis said. "As for Jesse, he's still suspended, you're correct. But he's going to be chief again just as soon as the Town Council has a chance to meet. Anyway, it doesn't really matter for our purposes here today. He's a witness, not an arresting officer. We're going to tape this interrogation. You can object all you want for the record."

"My client has nothing to say. I am instructing him to maintain his rights."

"That's fine," Ellis said, standing and turning on the camera. "Then you can both just listen. It might affect how you choose to proceed with your case."

Wilkes's voice rose to courtroom volume again. "I will

not allow you to question my client until I have had a chance to confer with him properly—"

"Your client is under arrest," Suit said. "So either he can sit here and listen or he can go back to the cell. Your choice."

Wilkes harrumphed. Jesse had not actually ever heard someone harrumph before. He looked at Devlin.

Devlin appeared a little more confident. "Sure," he said. "Why not. Let's hear what they've got to say. Might be good for a laugh."

"Jesse, why don't you go ahead and take us through it," Ellis said.

Wilkes looked at Ellis. "You said he's not the arresting officer."

Ellis looked pained. "We can do the whole routine where I pretend to question him for the record, and we lay it all out, but this is going to save time. He knows exactly what your client did. You want to hear it or not?"

Wilkes pointed at Jesse. "Okay. Fine. But I'm not going to let my client sit here and take abuse."

That was too much for Hodges. "Did you know your client was alive, even while we were investigating?"

Wilkes waved her off. "I don't have to answer that."

"Because the bar association might be interested. Just saying."

Wilkes scowled again, but he got the message. He settled into his seat.

Ellis read the boilerplate Miranda warning for the camera, and the time and date into the record. He sat back down again.

Jesse gathered his thoughts for a moment. It had already been a long day.

"First of all, we know you're not dead, Ramsey," he said. "So congratulations on that, I guess."

"It's not a crime to fake your death in Massachusetts," Devlin said.

"Ramsey, be quiet."

"I just wanted Jesse to know," Devlin said. "I checked."

Definitely feeling more confident, Jesse thought.

"I figured you did. That's probably one reason you chose Paradise, isn't it?"

This time Devlin didn't respond.

"See, I never could understand why a guy like you would go out of his way to pick a fight with me," Jesse said. "I even talked to my shrink about it. He gave me some good advice for dealing with someone who's determined to be a pain in the ass, but you just kept coming, didn't you? You drove around drunk and threw a punch at me. I could write that off to bad judgment and booze. I mean, I've seen it before. But then you threw a big party, knowing I'd have to come out and break it up. You tried to provoke me at the museum benefit, and then again at Daisy's. You came looking for me, specifically to poke at me. And you threatened Molly and the department when I wouldn't take the bait. I wouldn't be surprised if you even convinced your son to start bullying my girlfriend's kid, just to see if that would piss me off."

Devlin looked delighted with himself.

"Did it work?"

His lawyer looked like he was suppressing bad gas. "Ramsey, *please*."

"Little bit," Jesse said. "But it mainly made me sad. Kids

don't get a choice when they're stuck with a shitty excuse for a father."

Devlin's smile went away. Jesse suspected he didn't want to think about his son right now.

"Anyway," Jesse said. "None of that made sense for a guy who'd barely escaped a federal conviction on fraud charges. Whatever else you are, you're not an idiot. There's no profit in attracting the attention of the law for a guy like you. I looked at the motto of your firm, the one you've got inked on your chest and carved into your desk. *Cui Bono.* Who benefits? And there wasn't any benefit."

Wilkes faked a yawn. "Well, this has been a fascinating story, Mr. Stone, but if that's all you've got—"

"It's not," Jesse said. "Then it hit me. You already answered the question: You benefit. You *always* do. It just took me a while to see it. I was curious why you came to the station with a whole file about how dangerous I was, Mr. Wilkes. Remember, the very first morning we had Mr. Devlin in custody? That was a thick file. It seemed like a lot for someone to put together the morning that they'd heard their client was in jail for a drunk-driving charge."

Wilkes shifted in his seat. "I am a very thorough lawyer."

"I'm sure you are," Jesse said. "But I don't think you put that information together that morning. I'm pretty sure you did your research on Paradise before you came here. Or Mr. Devlin did. Either way, you were looking for a cop with a bad temper. Someone who might have a reputation for dealing with suspects permanently. Now, I'm not ashamed of anything I've done in my past. But I'll admit: I wouldn't take out life insurance on anyone who might pull a gun or try to harm someone here in Paradise. That's why you thought you could make me into your scapegoat."

Devlin said nothing. Wilkes said, "Do you have any proof? Or is this all just your imagination?"

Suit, who'd been watching the whole exchange so far with undisguised amusement, spoke up. "Tell them about the blood, Jesse. That's my favorite part."

"Oh, right, the blood," Jesse said. "That was pretty clever. That was four or five pints of blood in Devlin's house. More than someone could afford to lose from a small cut, if they were trying to fake a violent struggle. And it was definitely your blood. DNA matched perfectly. There was no way you just cut yourself open and splashed it all over the rug. Not without risking your own life. That was pretty convincing. At least it was to these two."

Jesse nodded toward Kirkpatrick and Hodges, who had the decency to look a little embarrassed.

"But then, my friend the medical examiner, Dev Chada, got a look at a sample under the microscope. And he saw crystallization of the blood cells, which meant the blood had been subject to extreme cold. He figured out that the blood had been stored in a freezer and then thawed."

"We would have seen it eventually," Kirkpatrick muttered.

Jesse ignored that. "How did you do it?" he asked Devlin. "Did you withdraw a pint at a time, then put it away?"

Devlin said nothing. But he looked smug. *Jesus*, Jesse thought. He couldn't help preening when he thought he was clever.

"I think that must have been it," Jesse said. "You couldn't get me to fight you publicly, but you'd created the impression of a feud between us. So you told the mayor to have me come apologize. He did, because he thought it would make you happy, and because it would avoid a lawsuit. You splashed the blood all over the rug, tossed some furniture around, and went into your hiding place. For good measure, you made sure your wife was there to see me, and to call the DA, so I would be placed at the scene of the crime."

"Why would he do all of this?" Wilkes asked. "What possible reason could there be?"

Jesse put a look of surprise on his face. "You don't know? The reason is sitting in the cells back there, nursing an orbital fracture and concussion. He and one of his associates are both waiting to be transferred to the county detention center on six counts of felony murder. Devlin's former business partners sent a hired killer after him."

"I don't know what you mean. What business partners?" Wilkes asked.

"The Colombian drug cartel that invested in his hedge fund," Jesse said. "The ones he ripped off when he tanked his own firm and took all the profits for himself."

Wilkes stole a quick glance at Devlin but recovered quickly.

"I don't know anything about my client's investors. All I can say is he was found not guilty of any fraud. Double jeopardy. He cannot be tried twice for the same crime."

"I don't think Colombian drug lords pay attention to our constitutional rights," Jesse said. "They were already looking for him before he came to Paradise. Which is why he had his house built with a secret panic room. He'd decided he'd fake his own death, frame me for it, and then wait it out until they killed me or I was arrested for his murder. I'm pretty sure he didn't care which. Either way, it would tell the world that he was dead. His wife and child would inherit his estate, and they'd all move on. And he'd have some plastic surgery somewhere and start over."

Nobody spoke. Wilkes and Devlin both avoided looking at the camera or at each other.

"Then I guess you worried I was onto you when I found the actual house plans in the mayor's office," Jesse said. "You probably called your thugs back to Paradise to take the plans away from me. Nick Allen and Kenny Dryden. Former employees of the Devlin Fund's security division. At least I assume that's what you told them. They're dead now. Suit identified them by the fingerprints from the bodies on my living room floor."

Devlin shrugged. "I was in a panic room, just like you said. If those guys were up to something, they didn't run it by me. And they'll never tell you any different."

Wilkes looked distinctly uncomfortable now. "What my client means to say is: It's not illegal to fake your own death in Massachusetts."

"True," Jesse said. "But any related crimes committed in the process of faking your death are fair game. And as Agents Kirkpatrick and Hodges already said to your client, they intend to prosecute for obstruction of justice and filing a false police report."

Wilkes looked like he was back on solid ground again. "Those are basically misdemeanors. Any judge will toss them out once I get this in court," he said. "In fact, we could make a case that my client had no choice. He was on the run from Colombian hit men, and he could not turn to the police, who already had a vendetta against him. With nowhere to turn, he hid in his house, the only place he knew he was safe."

"Like you said, Counselor, that's an entertaining story," Jesse said. "Because, honestly, your client's plan was unbelievably stupid. Only a guy who was used to everyone calling him a genius would think he could get away with it."

Devlin stopped looking smug. He leaned forward a little, as if he wanted to argue. Wilkes placed a hand on his arm. Devlin yanked it away. But he stayed quiet.

"Say whatever you want," Wilkes said. "Ramsey Devlin was protecting his family."

Jesse let that sit, like the lawyer had dropped a bag of garbage on the table.

"Protecting his family?" Jesse said. "Is that why he let a hired killer put a knife to his son's throat? Why he was willing to *let him die* to save his own life?"

Wilkes started a little, and looked at Devlin. Devlin only stared at Jesse.

Wilkes tried to shrug it off. "So he's not a hero. Big deal. You've got nothing serious on him."

"That's the way you want to go?" Jesse asked.

"You've got *nothing*," Wilkes shot back. "You try to charge my client with any of this, and he's going to walk."

"Maybe so," Jesse said. "Good thing that's not all we've got."

He looked up. "Molly," he called. "You want to come in here now?"

Molly Crane entered, with Patel Shirani right behind.

She smiled at Devlin in particular.

"Jesse asked me to be in the room from the start, but I wanted to do it this way," she said. "I was dying to see the look on your face."

FORTY-SIX

What the hell?" Devlin said, struggling to stand up, his cuffed hands still in front of him.

"Ramsey, sit down and calm down," Wilkes said.

"Patel, what the *fuck*—" Devlin turned and stared daggers at Wilkes. "You were supposed to get him away from her! Why didn't you tell me—"

"That's attorney-client privilege!" Wilkes snapped. "You can't use that statement!"

"You really should listen to your attorney," Deputy U.S. Marshal Robert "Bob" Hanrahan said as he entered the conference room right behind Patel. "You've been advised of your rights."

"You tell him, Bob," Molly said.

This was getting to be too much for Ellis, Jesse noticed. He really was a very proper guy. Probably why he loved being a lawyer. So many rules.

"Can everyone please sit down?" Ellis asked.

After a few moments, everyone was at the table and seated.

"Molly, you want to take it from here?" Jesse said.

"Gladly," she said. "Devlin, I believe you know Patel Shirani?"

She pointed at the younger man, who didn't look thrilled to see his former boss.

Devlin looked even less pleased to see his former employee. "Yeah," he said. "I know this guy. And anything he tells you is covered by an NDA."

"Ramsey, for God's sake, stop talking," Wilkes pleaded.

"Patel here was in charge of a special effort at the Devlin Fund. You want to tell us all what it was, Patel?"

Patel wasn't enjoying the show, but Jesse already knew that he didn't have a choice. He'd agreed to a cooperation and plea deal earlier that day with the U.S. Attorney in New York.

"Yeah," he said. "I wrote the code that transferred the proceeds from the investment fund's cryptocurrency into Mr. Devlin's personal accounts overseas. Mostly Panama and the Bahamas, but some in Bermuda and Mauritius, too."

"That's why the fund collapsed and the clients lost all their money, wasn't it? It's what you called a 'rug pull,'" Molly said.

"Yeah," Patel said. "That's right."

"And one more time: Who made all the money from that?"

Patel looked down at the table. "Ramsey Devlin."

Devlin looked proud. Wilkes looked frustrated.

"As we said before," Wilkes said. "This is all covered by

double jeopardy. You cannot try a man for the same crime twice."

"You are correct," Hanrahan said. "Which is why we are not."

He took a sheaf of papers from his inside jacket pocket and handed it to Wilkes.

"Mr. Devlin, you are hereby under arrest for the unlawful concealment of financial transfers to aid in the commission of a crime."

"What?" Wilkes said. Jesse noticed beads of sweat forming at the lawyer's hairline.

"Money laundering," Molly translated. "He transferred all that money into secret accounts to conceal illegal activity. In this case, securities fraud. Which is a *completely separate* federal crime under USC 1956, isn't it, Deputy Hanrahan? Punishable by up to twenty years in prison?"

"Indeed it is, Deputy Chief Crane. That's why I am here, to finally answer your question, Mr. Wilkes," Hanrahan said. "By the authority of the Comprehensive Crime Control Act of 1984, we are seizing all of Mr. Devlin's property on behalf of the U.S. Marshals Service. That will, most likely, include any funds he would use to pay you."

Wilkes looked at Hanrahan, then at the papers.

Then he looked at Devlin one more time.

He dropped the papers on his client's lap.

"Yeah, that's the straw that broke the camel's back. Good luck, Ramsey," he said. He got up and walked out the door.

Devlin, open-mouthed, watched him go.

Devlin looked around the table, now totally alone.

"Jesus Christ," he said. "You can't do this."

"It's already done," Jesse said.

"Chief Stone, with your permission, I would like to take Mr. Devlin into custody," Hanrahan said.

"Ask him," Jesse said, pointing to Suit. "He's the chief."

"Sure, go ahead," Suit said. "We only have him on obstruction of justice and filing a false police report. I'm told those are practically misdemeanors."

"Thank you," Hanrahan said, and got up and took Ramsey by the arm, lifting him from his seat.

Ellis got up as well. "I guess we're done here," he said, and clicked off the camera. "We'll send you a copy of the interrogation, Deputy."

"I'd appreciate that, thank you," Hanrahan said.

Jesse looked at Molly. "Nice work," he said.

"I told you I was Batman," she said.

Suddenly Devlin pulled away from Hanrahan. He practically threw himself across the table toward Jesse.

But he wasn't trying to attack Jesse. He was bent over. Pleading.

"Stone," he said. "You can't let him take me. They will find me in federal prison. They will get to me. I'm a dead man there, Stone!"

"You've been dead before," Jesse said. "I'm sure you can handle it."

Jesse stood. He'd had a long day, and his shoulder still hurt like hell. He wondered if Rachel could give him a cortisone shot if he got over to the ER. Or if he was going to need another surgery.

Devlin managed to get his hands across the table to touch Jesse.

Jesse turned and faced him.

"Please," he said. "If not for me, then for my kid. You want him to grow up without his father?"

Dix would have said to let go of the rope. But that was too much for Jesse.

He leaned down and said, quietly, "He'll be better off."

Hanrahan lifted Devlin firmly from the table and walked him out of the room.

Devlin made some more noises, but Jesse didn't pay attention.

Suit stood up and stretched. "What now, Jesse?" he asked.

"That's up to you, Chief," Jesse said. "Me? I'm going home."

FORTY-SEVEN

Jesse walked out of the station. He really couldn't go home, he realized. It was still a crime scene, with bodies on his carpet. Cole was at the condo with the State Homicide Division's detectives and technicians, watching them gather evidence and making sure they didn't break anything. Lundquist was either overseeing the team or on his way back to his office by now.

It was probably going to be at least a couple days before Jesse could sleep in his own bed again. He wondered if Rachel was ready for him to spend the night at her place or if he'd have to get a hotel room.

He sort of hoped she was ready. He was looking forward to spending some more time with her. And with Jacob.

The air was cold, and it was getting dark earlier now. Summer was long gone.

The streetlights above him came on just as Gary Armistead came out of the Town Hall building.

He waved and smiled. Like nothing had ever happened.

Jesse didn't know how he did it. But Armistead could pivot like an NBA All-Star when he saw the game had changed direction.

Armistead walked over to him.

"Jesse," Armistead said. "I guess I should say I'm sorry. I'm glad this unpleasantness is behind us."

"You heard Devlin has been arrested again?"

"Ellis told me."

"Yeah," Jesse said. "I hope you already cashed his checks."

Armistead gritted his teeth, then swallowed. "Okay," he said. "I deserve that. What can I say? He had me fooled."

Jesse looked at the sky again. He supposed they were going to do this now. Might as well get it over with.

"Did he?" Jesse asked.

Armistead put a quizzical look on his face. "What do you mean? Nobody could have seen that coming. Hiding out in his own house like that? Who would have known?"

"You did," Jesse said.

"What?"

"Cut the crap, Gary. It's been a long day."

"I don't know what you're talking about."

"You knew exactly where he was hiding," Jesse said. "Because you told him when I found the real plans for the house. You warned him."

Armistead's mouth worked for a second before any sound came out. "That is . . . absurd. What makes you think that's even—damn, Jesse. I know you don't think much of me, but that you would accuse me of working to frame you—it's just—"

Jesse cut off his sputtering. "You told him. Because that's

the only way he knew to send his thugs over to my place, looking for me. You called him, he called them."

Armistead stopped talking. He went very still.

"I guess you told him that they had to get the plans or your involvement might become public. They came over with guns instead. I'm sure Devlin didn't tell you they were going to kill me. The only thing I wonder is: Would you have cared?"

Armistead couldn't meet Jesse's eyes. He still didn't say anything.

"I suppose I could even thank you," Jesse said. "If those guys hadn't shown up and distracted the cartel's men, Cole and I might have been killed. But I'm not going to thank you. You put me at risk. You put my son at risk. And a kid could have died because you and Devlin were playing your idiot games. You should be in a cell right next to him."

For a second there, Jesse thought he saw the real Gary Armistead come to the surface. A blank, neutral stare as he calculated the impact of this new information.

Then Armistead said, "You can't prove anything."

"Nope," Jesse said. "I can't. I'm sure you weren't dumb enough to call Devlin from a personal phone or one that can be traced. I've got Suit checking the logs out of the Town Hall offices, but I don't expect he'll find anything."

"Even if he did," Armistead said, "I'm sure I was just calling to comfort Janis. Check on the family."

"See?" Jesse said. "I knew you'd have an answer. You always do."

Armistead looked away. Maybe he felt some shame. Maybe it was another act.

"I would never take part in anything that would have hurt you, Jesse."

Jesse tried not to laugh. "You think taking me out of my job and arresting me for murder wouldn't have hurt me? That's some kind of logic, Gary. What is it like inside that head of yours?"

Armistead glared at him. "I'm not admitting a damn thing. But consider this: I know you think this town can't survive without you. But you cause far more trouble than you prevent. Paradise would be better off without you around."

There it was. Armistead really thought he was the savior of Paradise. And that all that kept the town from being perfect was Jesse.

Jesse didn't know how to argue with that. He didn't really care to try.

"What are you going to do now?" Armistead asked in the sudden silence. He sounded a little nervous.

Jesse couldn't prove anything. But he could make Armistead's life difficult, to say the least.

He finally knew where they stood. It wasn't a cold war anymore. They were fighting for Paradise now.

Jesse smiled at him.

"Right now, I'm going to see a doctor," he said. "And then tomorrow, I'm going back to work."

ACKNOWLEDGMENTS

Many thanks are due, once again, to Alexandra Machinist, and Esther Newberg, and the Estate of Robert B. Parker for giving me this opportunity to walk in the shoes of the man himself. Thanks also to Tarini Sipahimalani, Katie McKee, Tom Colgan, and the entire team at Putnam for making this book better than when I started, and for all the support for me and for Jesse Stone.